Intrigue On a Longship Cruise

Intrigue On a Longship Cruise

Stephanie C. Fox

QueenBeeBooks

Bloomfield, Connecticut, U.S.A.

Library of Congress Cataloging-in-Publication Data
Name: Fox, Stephanie C., author.
Title: Intrigue on a Longship Cruise / Stephanie C. Fox.
Description: Connecticut: QueenBeeEdit Books, [2022].
Identifiers: ISBN 978-1-7343743-1-5 (paperback)
Subjects: 1. Fiction – Mystery & Detective—Historical. 2. Fiction —
Action. 3. Fiction – World Literature – France—21st Century.

www.queenbeeedit.com

Cover design by Stephanie C. Fox
Photographs by Stephanie C. Fox and Carole B.C. Fox
Printed in the United States of America

This book is dedicated to my mother, Carole B.C. Fox,
and to my aunt, Joan A. Fox LaCasse,
who have both instilled in me a love of travel.

Also by Stephanie C. Fox

What the Small Gray Visitor Said

Nae-Née – Birth Control:
Infallible, with Nanites and Convenience for All

Vaccine: The Cull – Nae-Née Wasn't Enough

New World Order Underwater
– The Nae-Née Inventors Strike Back

The Book of Thieves

The Bear Guarding the Beehive

Scheherazade Cat:
The Story of a War Hero

An American Woman in Kuwait

Hawai'i – Stolen Paradise:
A Travelogue

Hawai'i – Stolen Paradise:
A Brief History

The Visitor Experience at the Mark Twain House

The Slamming Door:
Bone Cancer, Asperger's, and Loss

Elephant's Kitchen
– An Aspergirl's Study in Difference

Almost a Meal – A True Tale of Horror

A Timeline of the Longship Cruise

Day One

1. The Longship
2. A Life-Jacket Drill
3. Food and Political Tourism

Day Two

4. Avignon, Smile Candy, and Les Halles
5. A Parfumerie and a Careful Walk
6. Lunch…Not on Rye
7. Footsteps by an Ancient Aqueduct

Day Three

8. Arles, Lavender, and Odd Glances
9. A Cobblestone Tour and Napoleon's Trees
10. Politics and Prose

Day Four

11. Overflowing Cemeteries and a Train Ride
12. Ancient Wheel Tracks and Roses

Day Five

13. Through the Locks, and In Our Wheelhouse
14. Desserts
15. A Provencal Feast
16. Dance-Off
17. Sounds in the Hallway

Day Six

18. Double-Moored by the Presque-Ile
19. Lyon Sites and Sights
20. A Traboule and a Romany Couple

Table of Contents

The Longship

The Longship

After traveling by plane, with two connections – one in Toronto, Canada, and the other in Frankfurt, Germany – and an hour-long car ride during which we had dozed, tired from our long journey, we saw the famous Medieval wall of Avignon, France, ahead on our left.

On our right, we saw a line-up of moored river cruise ships, each from a different company. Ours was about halfway down, with its gangplanks out in welcome. It was the *Longship Sif*, and it was long, white, sleek, and modern with lots of beautiful wood paneling inside.

It was ready for the passengers to come on board.

The murderer arrived at 12:34 p.m.

So did we.

So did a about a third of the ship's passengers, who totaled 182, with a staff of 56 on the Norse company's longship, which was set to travel for the next week up the Rhône River in France, from Avignon to Lyon.

Of course, murderers don't introduce themselves as such, so we just enjoyed our lunch and met people, unaware of anything beyond the pleasant anticipation of a pleasant trip through Provence.

It would be a while before we all settled in, rested up enough to take note of each other, and started to relax and enjoy the trip.

The airports had been crowded. Too crowded.

We felt the stress of it as we made our way from Connecticut to Marseilles via Toronto, Canada and Frankfurt, Germany. There were too many people, too close around us, jostling to fit into elevators, onto escalators, and through check-in lines.

On the bright side, however, I had enjoyed the airport bookstores immensely. They tended to be stocked with the sorts of magazines that bookstores didn't have, and I had gotten a good one: *National Geographic History*.

The pandemic was over, for the most part, contained by a massive, world-wide, scientific effort that had culminated in a vaccine that worked. We had all – all travelers – at last, been inoculated.

But we still wore masks, which I still made.

There was no reason for complacency about further trouble from yet another pandemic, what with the permafrost layer thawing and releasing pathogens that had been dormant for eons.

My aunt and I were looking forward to a relaxing river cruise in France, planning to get some practice with our long-disused French language skills, and to enjoy the food, wine, sights, scents, and tastes of the place.

But first we had had to get here.

"Traveling used to be easier," Aunt Eloise had said in Frankfurt, as we waded through crowds of slowing-moving people, hurrying across the long layout of that airport. "When I was in college, and I went on the SS *France* with my parents, it was a leisurely trip across the Atlantic with nice meals and conversations. Now it's an exhausting rush."

I looked at her. "I've seen the photographs, heard the stories, and since I can't experience that, I'll just tell myself that I won't experience sea-sickness."

We laughed, as did a few people around us in line.

"Arielle, you were born too late to enjoy a slow, calm way of travel," my aunt remarked.

"I know. Welcome to the age of overpopulation."

We had been waiting to board the plane to Germany during this exchange. Lines snaked around the perimeter of the departure gate, crowding into the common walkways. People squeezed past to get to the restrooms.

At times it felt as though we wouldn't make it through all of the required hurdles on time, and we almost panicked that we would not have enough time in between flights to do so. Only in Toronto did we have time to sit and relax. Otherwise, it was one tightly-packed flight after another, punctuated by a frantic race to the next one.

At least there were good movies to watch in-flight.

We had barely made it to our destination, what with two connecting flights, long lines of people and their possessions to be inspected, identities checked, passports stamped, and security scans.

We had had to run, my aunt and I, through the last airport we went through, which had been in Germany. Perhaps it was the precision and efficiency of that culture that enabled us to get through just in time to board our last plane before we got to France.

Lavender fields – industrial ones by the shore of the Mediterranean Sea, right next to dockyards – bloomed in a purple perfusion below on the plane's final approach. As I looked out the window at them, excitedly pointing them out to my aunt, I could almost smell them. Almost.

We had landed at Marseilles after flying on three planes, starting out of New York City. It was a lovely, warm – but not too warm – day. The sun was shining, and it was a beautiful day.

A man from the cruise line met us, put our bags into the trunk of a brand-new, black Mercedes sedan with tinted windows in the back, and drove us to Avignon to meet our ship.

Though we were exhausted, I did my best to make conversation with him in French, as did Aunt Eloise. "Arielle, talk to him!" she urged.

My aunt was a retired art teacher, and I an author who studied whatever topic fascinated me at any given time, though I had some favorites. More on that later. We had in common a love of art and all things French, had both studied the language in high school, and had traveled in France before.

We had also just traveled without much sleep. My mind swam with the movies I had watched on the longest plane ride, *Loving Vincent* and *Mary Shelley*, as I took out my pocket French dictionary, a rubber-covered, red, blue, and yellow *Larousse* one. "I'll try, but I'm really out of it!" I told my aunt.

I had no intention of attempting to simply remember every French vocabulary word I would need in order to have fun on this trip, and travelers likely wouldn't be expected to do that, anyway. People in the South of France were nice, patient people anyway, I had found.

Intrigue On a Longship Cruise

Our driver was no exception. We chatted about his life, career, and family for a while, and looked out the windows at the highway signs and landscape as we went along. Soon we were dozing in our seats, but we were safe. We knew it was only an hour to our ship.

Sure enough, after a short catnap, our driver woke us to say that we were in Avignon, and just in time to see the famous Medieval wall and the half-gone Pont Saint Bénézet. Barely a glance at that, and we were alongside our ship, thanking and tipping our driver. Our bags were taken aboard, and we were ushered into the ship's dining room for lunch. It was just after noon on a Wednesday.

This was a Scandinavian company, with a name that evoked its owners' ancestors: Longship.

The ship's design was beautiful. Its décor was simple, sleek, and Scandinavian, with modern wood paneling and floor-to-ceiling glass windows all around. We had entered from the lobby, which contained a stairwell, a giftshop, a concierge desk, and an excursion director's desk, plus 2 small passenger seating areas, one on each side of the staircase, with deep, cushioned chairs and a small table between each pair, and another with a sofa.

A lattice-work wall of woodwork separated the lobby from the dining area, and a gorgeous floral arrangement graced the corner of the front desk, towering over it.

Intrigue On a Longship Cruise

At last, I thought, we could enjoy a quiet, luxurious cruise with gourmet meals and other amenities, and, most welcome after a grueling journey, a sane number of human beings to interact with. No more crowds! It should be safe, calm, and a great vacation from human-induced aggravations. My aunt and I smiled at each other as we settled in for a comfortable, stress-free week.

Lunch included soup, salad, three entrée options, and two dessert options, all outlined in leather-bound menus. A choice of one red and one white wine were offered with each lunch and dinner. Aunt Eloise chose white. I chose red. She always looked for Pinot Grigio at home; here, it was Chablis and Chardonnay. I was happy with a Cabernet Sauvignon. Either way, I knew that we would have no trouble with headaches, as the French did not use insecticides on the vines, unlike in America.

The waitstaff were well-trained and friendly.

Waitstaff go to school to learn their skills in Europe, whereas in America, they learn on the job. I had been terrible at it, despite a willingness to do my best for people. These people moved with smoothness and efficiency, and they were used to Americans, unruffled by our friendliness and thank-yous whenever they brought anything.

Most of the passengers were Americans, as I had expected after joining a Facebook chat group for travelers who had been on this cruise line many times before, or who were planning to take a trip on one of its ships.

After a year-and-a-half-long worldwide pandemic, we Americans were free at last to travel. We had waited quietly in our homes for as much of that time as possible, only going out to places such as the post office, the fuel pump, and the grocery store, and wearing masks when we did so.

The pandemic had been caused, explained scientists who published a peer-reviewed article in the journal *Nature*, by a wet market in China. A wet market involves filth from wild animals that are normally not close to humans being traded as commodities rather than left alone. One zoonotic leap later, and a pathogen that humans' immune systems were not primed to defend against was infecting us.

I had used the time to make those masks for sale and shipment – out of two layers of cotton, as the Center for Disease Control's physicians recommended – and to write and publish some books. Three books, and a vaccine had been developed, manufactured and distributed.

Aunt Eloise had waited it out in Newport, Rhode Island, at her retirement community of artists. She had planned to go camping at national parks and put off getting a new cat. Then the pandemic had hit. After four months of that, she had adopted a beautiful black-and-white boy cat. He looked like Edward Gorey's cat drawings, and she had named him Meneet, which meant "gift" in Mohican.

Her longtime friend and neighbor, Corrine, was taking care of him while we were away.

My black cat, Bagheera, who kept me company while I worked, was home with my husband, Kavi, who would feed and pet him. He would be well taken care of.

We had made it!

Over 2 million people world-wide hadn't.

During the first half of the pandemic, we had suffered not only from the danger, the horror, and the anxiety of the pandemic, but also from a government that had been heavily drawn from the corporate sector of our economy, and led by a narcissistic television personality.

This personality had not known nor cared how to govern. His agenda had been all about self-aggrandizement, pandering to his base rather than leading all Americans to accept a vaccine as soon as one existed.

Our country was terribly divided between two major groups. There were educated, reasonable people – and by that, I mean people who were educated, people who were reasonable, and people who were a combination of the two, driven by logic, research, and the rule of law.

And then there were people who were driven by emotion, a sense of entitlement, a sense of disenfranchisement whenever they saw anyone else doing okay. Religion was often a factor, and there was serious concern that the crisis of both health and leadership would lead to a breakdown in the firewall between religion and state that our Constitution demanded.

But now we had an empathetic president in his place, one who had a lifetime of experience working with others in government – not just those of his own political party – and the vaccine had been fully distributed.

Not only that, but the police power of the state had been invoked to deal with anti-vaxxers. It was settled law from 1905 that everyone must accept the vaccine, from a U.S. Supreme Court case called *Jacobsen v. Massachusetts.*

Thanks to that, we Americans were once more welcome in Europe. Travel there and elsewhere was something that we had sorely missed, and I had watched the comments in that chat group from time to time about it. People's plans to travel for special occasions had been dashed over and over, and I had been morbidly fascinated to watch as they imagined that it would just be a few more months, and then a few more months, and then again, just a few more before they could travel.

The reality of the path to vaccination was a lot longer.

I was sure that this pandemic, which had come after an interlude of a century between it and the previous one, would soon be followed by another. After all, the permafrost layer at the Arctic Circle was melting, and would soon release more viral pathogens that had been dormant for eons – pathogens that humans had no immunity to.

Thus, I had kept my mask-making materials on hand.

Aunt Eloise and I had packed enough masks for every day of the trip, and we would wear them at all times when were outside of our room, and on tour buses.

It was no longer a requirement, but about half of the people on the ship were also doing it.

The other half were not.

I wondered how those halves swung politically.

But…I was on vacation!

I would simply observe people, not fight.

People were fascinating to watch.

Intrigue On a Longship Cruise

Reading them could be difficult for someone like me, on the autism spectrum with Asperger's, but with the masks, I had been amused to find that it was tough for everyone – neurotypicals and Aspies alike – to read facial expressions. It was a great social equalizer.

Nevertheless, I continued to try to read people.

It was fun to try.

Travel on a Norse longship, with modern luxuries, a small army of gourmet chefs, an expert staff, and few enough passengers to not feel lost in a massive, floating hotel while enjoying the sights, scents, and tastes of the south of France – we could hardly wait.

Well, we could wait long enough to get some sleep.

We badly needed to sleep off the journey to the ship. Having opted to come straight to it nonstop, we were exhausted. We had been up since early the previous morning, and thought that lunch and a few hours' sleep before dinner would help a lot.

We were going to have fun with food tourism, art, history, and cultural tourism, and enjoy the sights, smells, tastes, sounds, and everything and anything else that we possibly could.

It was quite a change from my usual, solitary life.

All of us, Americans, a few Canadians, and an even fewer Australians, were reveling in being released from the confines of our homes. We had had cabin-fever there...and now we were installed in cabins on the ship.

My aunt and I chatted happily with two venerable older ladies from Pennsylvania during lunch. They were Jewish, they were longtime friends, and they had just boarded the ship after a week in Nice at the apartment owned by one of their sons. It was fully furnished, and they had particularly enjoyed the perfumery in Grasse. One had bought an Herbes de Provence fragrance; the other had gone for the region's signature lavender one.

I thought of the lavender fields that I had seen out the window of the plane and planned to find some perfume in that scent.

The cruise's excursion director came by to see how we were enjoying our first meal on board the ship, and she told me to look for a ship called Fragonard in Avignon for that.

After lunch, Aunt Eloise and I retired to our cabin for the afternoon – to sleep.

Our cabin was at the end of the main floor, on the right, with a French balcony. It had a huge bed, all outfitted in white, with an interwoven basket pattern on the duvet cover. The effect was a very chic, Scandinavian décor.

I took the side by the sliding-glass door.

We found towels in the bathroom that were sculpted into swan shapes, and plenty of soaps, lotions, shampoos, and conditioners in tubes, both in the shower and on the sink counter.

The bathroom was a gorgeous, sleek, yet compact facility.

There was a safe for my camera, if I chose to use it.

I unpacked it now: battery charger, camera, and lens, all packed in separate, large, zip-lock bags. The ship had a fascinating array of battery chargers and outlets, each labeled to show that the array accommodated devices from all over the planet. That was because each region of the planet has its electrical grid set up for a different voltage.

We wanted to check everything out before we completely ran out of energy.

I laid out my alarm clock, eyeglass case, cosmetics bag, hairbrush, and whatever else I might want as soon as I woke up from the nap I was about to take.

Aunt Eloise did the same on the other side of the large bed, which was well-appointed in plain white.

We both really, really needed naps…

But first, I couldn't resist checking out the television.

The Longship brochures had promised a detailed system of options, and we weren't disappointed.

The screen lit up with an array of icons to select.

We could watch the news: the *BBC News*, *CNN*, *MSNBC*, and even that travesty of a channel called *Fox News*, were all offered.

We could watch movies: *A Good Year*, a movie about a winery in Provence, France and a stockbroker from London who inherits it, plus a few others, were loaded on another icon.

We were required to watch the Longship company orientation program, and we had the option of viewing the daily menus there as well.

And so on.

We were too tired to do that assignment right now, but would definitely take care of it after dinner.

We checked *MSNBC* and *BBC News* first.

There was a report about a scientist from the French counterpart of the American CDC, which was called P4. P4 was in Lyon. He had fallen ill, and was not coherent. No diagnosis had yet been reached, so the hospital was isolating him.

"I hope that nothing is missing from P4," I remarked to my aunt.

"Yeah, me too," she said. "We'll have to watch that orientation video after dinner, I guess."

With that, we went to sleep.

The murderer wasn't tired.

He settled into a cabin on the level above Arielle and her Aunt Eloise's cabin.

All of the cabins were full, which meant that everyone who had booked this trip had a traveling companion.

When he was alone for a few minutes, he started to unpack his carry-on bag – the one that he had insisted upon carrying personally, refusing the assistance of the *Sif*'s crew.

Quickly, before his colleague was finished in the bathroom, he removed a metal cannister with a tapered top. It was about the size of a water bottle, and not heavy.

He added a box that he had had made just for this purpose, to cover it up.

His companion would recognize the box as something just for him, which he always traveled with, and ignore it.

That was just fine.

Intrigue On a Longship Cruise

A Life-Jacket Drill

A Life-Jacket Drill

A few hours later, a female voice came over the ship's loudspeaker, exhorting us to get up, put on our life jackets, and meet in the upstairs lounge.

"Attention passengers," said a female voice with a pretty French accent. "Please report to the lounge in fifteen minutes with your life-jackets for a mandatory life-jacket drill. You will find your life-jackets under your beds. Thank you, and see you soon."

That was it.

Aunt Eloise and I got out of bed immediately, dazed but rested enough that our headaches and nausea were gone. We would be okay for the rest of the evening, having slept off the worst of the wear and tear of travel.

This was a drill, required as part of the orientation.

We used the bathroom first, brushed and arranged our hair, and got dressed. I put fresh makeup on – fast. (Just me! Aunt Eloise didn't wear makeup. I did. I just like the colors too much to stop!) We got dressed, barely focusing on how we looked, just assuming that we would be sufficiently presentable to appear for this drill.

Now, where were those life jackets?!

Under the bed, fastened to straps.

Aunt Eloise was at a loss to get them.

Her knees bothered her.

"You know, if this were an actual emergency, we wouldn't have done all that personal grooming," my aunt remarked.

I paused from feeling around under my half of the bed to look at her.

"But it's not, and we know it," I said, "so we can."

She nodded and smiled, and I ducked under the bed again, feeling around until I encountered a flat, padded thing. I pulled on it, but it was stuck.

"I found it, but it's stuck. Hang on…"

I felt up toward the top of it, moving up against the bedside table, practically at the wall. A long, flat, seat-belt-like material held the thing just above the floor on the underside of the mattress. I eased it out, it dropped to the floor, and I pulled it out from under the bed and stood up to look at it.

"Huh…it's all flat, with the part that goes over your head flapping over. That was how they anchored it through that strap." Speaking of which, straps hung off of the thing, which I didn't bother to work on. I was already going around to my aunt's side of the bed to get hers out.

I handed it to her and we hurried down the hall, out into the lobby, and upstairs to the lounge, past the huge, attractive, modern painting that featured Norse patterns with a lot of gold and a Norse god staring back at us. It was square-shaped, and it presided over the grand staircase. That, of course was the idea: publicity shots!

I got them loose, dragged them out from under the bed, and handed one of them to her.

We put them on, and went out into the hall.

We had hastily gotten ready to leave the cabin, and decided that we were sufficiently presentable to go out.

We would come back after the orientation to leave these life jackets and worry about more of that later. We wanted to wear something else to dinner. Dress codes were casual, but we had been sleeping, so we had a few doubts about our appearances.

Also, I wanted my camera. I intended to photograph the fabulous gourmet meals to show Kavi and the rest of the family when we got home.

For now, it was time to meet more of the crew and some of our shipmates.

We went down the hall, out to the lobby, and glanced at the front desk. It was a modern, sleek design made of wood, and had a gorgeous, tall, showy flower arrangement in the corner by the office.

Straight ahead was a grand staircase with a painting at the top, and a balcony that ran open all around it, overlooking the lobby. The painting was of the Norse goddess Sif, for whom our ship was named.

The ship had glass entrances on either side of the staircase, and I realized that these were for boarding and disembarking on whichever side we were moored. It was later that we found out that Longships could sometimes be double-moored, which was another reason for the openings on either side. The rule was to pass through the strangers' ship and go directly to one's own.

We climbed the staircase, went past the painting of the Lady Sif, and turned to the left. Actually, we could have turned to the right; it was the same on both sides. We passed a coffee nook where passengers could get pastries and use a coffee/tea machine at random times all day, and a little portrait gallery of the crew. I would have to come back later and look at that.

Into the lounge we went, however, without spending much time browsing, because everyone was heading in there like we were late for an important meeting.

It was an important meeting, and we were pretty much on time.

Inside the lounge were the 182 passengers, including us. Everyone had a life-jacket on, some with the straps in place, some not.

The lounge had a large bar area that extended into the center of the room from the wall by the staircase. Along the windows, which had long curtains and gave floor-to-ceiling views of the river and land outside, were groups of four cushy lounge chairs in pairs that face each other. It looked like eight of these nooks fit on each side of the room, complete with tables that held little trays of nuts. Other chairs filled out the rest of the room, except for the wall of windows that faced out the front of the ship.

We found a spot just past the bar, by the windows, with a view of the rest of the room. I could see the prow of the ship, with its indoor lounge extending almost across this deck, and a small outdoor deck beyond that.

They were mostly older people like my aunt. Was I the only one in my forties? Well, I would find out later, but I looked forward to meeting some of these people. Older people had the best stories.

I looked around the room and noted that a square-shaped bar took up the back center of the room, just as one entered on either side. Glasses hung from the sides, and behind the bartenders were rows of backlit bottles of all kinds.

Intrigue On a Longship Cruise

The staff seemed very friendly as well as efficient. I smiled at them, and they smiled back. Each wore a name plate, too.

A few more people trickled in.

Up by the front windows was where Jonathan, the cruise director, and Clotilde, the, stood as they spoke. Clotilde was the woman whose voice we had just heard over the loudspeaker. She introduced herself and told us that she would be in charge of our daily schedules.

The cruise director was a middle-aged British guy named Jonathan. He had a full head of short hair and a big grin, and as he spoke, it occurred to me that he could have had a side career as a stand-up comedian.

Clotilde was the excursions director. She was an elegant, businesslike woman from Provence, and her outfit was a company uniform with a red vest, a white blouse, a dark blue skirt, and black stockings and solid-looking yet fashionable heels finishing out her uniform.

I looked at Clotilde as she spoke.

She was French, that much was obvious. I would have been disappointed if she hadn't been; I wanted to observe a French person, hear them talk in both English and French, and be able to ask her questions as to where to find particular things – things that only a native of France could be counted upon to know.

Clotilde was very chic, businesslike, and brisk in her manner. Her blond hair was parted on the side and twisted up in a chignon, with her bangs also twisted and pinned to stay out of her eyes. She wore minimal makeup.

The two of them immediately looked at each one of us to make sure that we all had found our life jackets and put them on over our heads. We had. Then they showed us how to fasten them.

Once that was done, it was acknowledged that it was unlikely that we actually need them, but it was the law that we go through this orientation.

The other passengers were listening to Clotilde and starting to take off their life-jackets, so we did that, too. I looked around at them.

Most of them were couples of husbands and wives, and I looked at them, imagining that they had been married for decades to the same person.

Then I laughed inwardly. They could be on second or third marriages, for all I knew. They could be widowed or divorced and traveling with boyfriends and girlfriends.

I noticed some pairs of women traveling together, one older, one younger, and wondered if, like my aunt and myself, they were family members. Probably.

The next item on the orientation agenda was to tell us that passengers were permitted to walk on the upper deck for exercise, which could be done in a long oval pattern for those who really wanted to move around. But…not before 8 a.m., please! Footsteps on the roofs of the upper cabins would prevent sleep for the people in them.

I wondered about Aunt Eloise's thoughts about this.

At home in Rhode Island, she liked to go out walking three times a day, and she was an early person.

I liked to go with her for the late morning and afternoon walks, but never the early ones, and I would stay up late and read after she went to bed at around 9 o'clock at the very latest.

She looked at me, understanding right away, and said, "Don't worry. I know I'll get to do enough walking on this trip. And you likely won't have the energy to stay up as late as you do, getting up a bit earlier for all these excursions."

"You're right. I'll be up for breakfast every day, and off with you."

We nodded and turned to watch the rest of the presentation.

After briefly taking us through the procedure for assembling our life-jackets, she talked about how this ship was now our home for the next week, said that she and the crew were happy to have us aboard, and that we were to meet in this lounge every day at 7 p.m. for a briefing.

These briefings would serve to go over the next day's planned excursions, complete with departure and return times.

Wine was served in the lounge with the nuts every evening, we were told, one red and one white, as it was during lunches and dinners. This was part of the cruise package. We had some white wine as we sat there, listening.

People at the bar were having fancy cocktails, and I realized that they must have paid for the extra alcoholic beverages package on top of the cruise fee. I wondered how they could possibly have room for it all and still enjoy the food, but didn't concern myself with it beyond that. I just knew that we already had a feast, and that that was enough.

We were informed that if, at any time, there were two of the company's longships at a time at any one quai, they would be double-moored. That meant that passengers from another ship would be crossing through ours if we were closest to the shore, and vice versa if ours were to be the outermost longship. No lingering aboard a ship that is not ours! Just get to your own ship and stay on it, was the rule.

That seemed reasonable. One didn't want to get stuck on the wrong ship, heading back the way we had come down the Rhône River!

This briefing was fairly short.

That was where every lecture or presentation would be, and whatever was required for it – a projection screen, a cooking table with heating elements, whatever – would be there as the week's activities continued.

Clotilde explained the equipment we would be using for tours – an earpiece and a receiver that clipped to our waists or went in our pockets, all in our rooms, one for each occupant. It was our responsibility to put them back and recharge them each day, and turn them in to the front desk if they didn't work perfectly. (Spoiler alert: they worked perfectly throughout our trip!)

The only other thing that Clotilde had to tell us was that, when we returned to our rooms from dinner, we would find a printed, 4-page itinerary on our beds. She held one up to show it to us: it had gray artwork in a Norse design at the top, and opened out like a book.

I could hear low voices in conversation, and realized, with no great feeling of surprise, that most of the people traveling with us were

Americans or Canadians. Their accents gave them away. So did their use of the English language; these were educated people.

Well, so were we. I would introduce myself as a lawyer and an author of books on a variety of topics, and my aunt as an art teacher, and hope that that would elicit similar sharing of background information.

I looked forward to it.

Clotilde concluded the briefing, told us to put our life-jackets back under our beds, and to proceed to the dining room, which was below this lounge, right after that.

The meeting then broke up, and we exited the lounge. I made sure to go back out the way we had come, because I wanted to look at the staff portraits on the way.

"Don't you want to go out the other way?" my aunt asked, trying to detour around to the right.

"No, I want to see the portraits, remember?"

"Oh yeah," she said, turning around. "Me too."

We stopped to look. There were four rows of them, with the ship's captain, first officer, and engineer on top, followed by the cruise director, the concierge, the excursion director, and the maître d'. So that was her name: Clotilde Charbonneau. Her hair was down in this picture, but she still looked very remote and businesslike. We saw the chef among the group, and that his name was Ronne Van Rompaey. He was from Belgium.

We then walked out the way we had come, and glanced straight across the balcony.

There was a beautiful wood-paneled library there, with two laptop computers for the passengers' use on one side. Large coffee-table books made up most of the collection. We had been told that we could borrow them in our cabins as well as look at them in the cushy lounge chairs (there were four of them there).

But I had some reading material in our cabin, and I was not really expecting to have a lot of time to look at it. We were supposed to be going out a lot, and expending most of our energy in other ways.

It was just as well; at home, I lived in books and on the computer, constantly reading, editing, writing, publishing…and I was glad that this trip was going to force me to go out and see the things that I read about, and to taste, smell, hear, and maybe even touch them.

Aunt Eloise and I went right back to our cabin, put away the life jackets, and freshened ourselves up for dinner.

Time to meet some of our shipmates!

Food and Political Tourism

Food and Political Tourism

After the drill and welcome in the *Sif*'s upstairs lounge, we were ready to meet more of the passengers and eat dinner. We felt okay, but not fully rested yet. We figured that the coming night's sleep would solve that problem, and for now, were comfortable enough to visit and meet new people.

We looked forward to a whole week of that, plus the food.

Lunch and dinner had some mundane options for those who did not care for food adventures, listed on the right side of the menu. I wondered why people would travel to places where they didn't want to eat the local cuisine. I had wanted France specifically for the cuisine, plus its sights and scents and sounds!

The left side of the menu, contained the food adventures, and I went for them repeatedly. So did my aunt. So did most of the passengers. Most. Not all. Sigh. If I travel, I want delicious food from the region. That's part of the experience!

At the end of the week, I would wonder again who would not want garlic soup, butternut squash soup, pea soup, scallops with soft radishes, asparagus, and potato purée, coq au vin, rack of lamb with herb butter, chocolate lava cake, chocolate mousse, or pears poached in wine, but I didn't ask. I just enjoyed the food.

Upon further reflection, I mused that the adventures of the left side of the menu, with that side's openness to new experiences, and the staid, narrow repertoire of the right side of the menu mirrored the political climate back home in the United States.

Perhaps I like metaphor too much, but so what?

The people we met were from the United States (most of them), Canada, and Australia. That is in order from most to least. There were 182 passengers plus 56 crewmembers. I intended to get know as many of both as possible, because that's the fun of traveling (among other things).

Most passengers were retired, which I had been expecting (older people have the best stories, though!). The age demographic was one aspect to note. Another was race: we were almost all white, except for one Asian-American woman who was traveling with her husband.

I thought of Kavi, my husband, back at home, feeding the cat, going to his lab to work, and playing games on the computer at night. He had work that he couldn't leave, and insisted that I go on a trip with my aunt, whom I had missed visiting with during the long pandemic. I had e-mailed him from my phone to say that we had arrived safely.

Aunt Eloise had e-mailed a friend in Newport, Rhode Island, who was feeding her cat, a large black-and-white male named Meneet, which meant "Gift" in Mohican. My aunt loves all things Native American.

She lived in a large, rambling, Victorian building that had been moved in two parts to merge with the beautiful chapel of a defunct convent. The chapel had red-and-blue stained-glass windows and carved wooden pews. The home was for retired people – all very small apartments. She loved it there.

I went on this trip ready to interact and network, armed with lots of business cards, which list my books on the back. Why not? People took them with interest, and I collected a few, too.

We met political liberals, conservatives, and neutrals. I had no intention of living in a political hidey-hole on this trip, nor of attempting to sell anyone on my viewpoints. This was, after all, a vacation. I just wanted to meet people and learn about their lives and thoughts.

That is what many of them seemed to want, too, though when we encountered liberals, we couldn't help but hit it off and enjoy chatting more.

With the conservatives, we had some rather memorable encounters. For the first evening, we sat with some at dinner. Introductions were made, food was ordered, and wine was served.

Intrigue On a Longship Cruise

They proved to be Trump-supporting, Catholics who had lived in the Chicago area for most of their lives and retired to Naples, Florida. They were part of a group of 26 people from Naples who were traveling with their priest, one Father O'Something.

(If that doesn't tip you off that I didn't seek him out, nothing will! He was pointed out to me, however, and he seemed nice. I just didn't want to chat with a cleric and be interrogated about my views on religion and religiousness.)

Among the people at dinner on our first evening were a retired banker named Max who had probably attained bankster status during his career, his non-career wife, Karen, plus another couple, the wife of which had worked in real estate. She had a flawless manicure with impeccable makeup and highlighted hair, arranged in a ponytail.

It was Karen and the bankster who held our attention.

I settled into my seat and ordered the pea soup and some other items, as did all of us except the bankster, who insisted upon eating the steak and frites (fries) from the left side of the menu. No soup for him, even though it was a wonderful vegetable purée that would have been good for his cold. There's no logic with some eaters! Every lunch and dinner featured a delectable puréed soup, and I had them all.

When asked, I brought out my business cards, and with that, my political leanings and blog were revealed. With a devilish gleam in my eye, I decided to settle in to observe what came next.

When I was asked about my books, I told them what topics they covered, including honeybee colony collapse and human overpopulation.

"Human overpopulation?! Why would you want to touch that hot-button issue?!" said the man across from me. He was a retired banker, traveling with his wife. His name was Max. I got the sense that he had achieved bankster status over the course of his career, which meant that he had risen high in the banking industry.

"Precisely because it is a hot-button, controversial issue," I replied. "If it's bland, it doesn't feel worth working on," I added.

"Humph," he said. Then, after a moment's thought, he asked, "What did you make of *Inferno*?"

"The book or the movie? I read it and watched it."

The bankster looked startled, then said, "I'll bite. I did ask. What was the difference?"

"The book pulled the metaphoric trigger on the population cull and released the virus into the water, thus ensuring that two-thirds of the human species would lose the ability to reproduce – without suffering from any disease. The movie wimped out, stopping the release in time. That virus was different, however; it would have been a horrific disease that killed off half of our species while giving them deaths that look like Medieval horror art, such as we see on public television shows and in some of the cathedrals and Renaissance palaces around Europe."

Faces around the table stared back at me.

Then the bankster's wife, Karen, said, "It sounds as though you disapprove of not pulling that trigger."

I smiled. "In fiction, of course I disapprove. Most likely, Ron Howard thought that pulling it and killing off half of us wouldn't play well at the box office. The book is much better in every way. So is the *Nae-Née* series, because it doesn't shrink from doing that, either. It goes even farther in that it doesn't just say that there will be a population cull. It shows it being done in Book 2."

She looked a bit horrified. "What happens to the people who do this? Do they at least get caught?"

"Of course," I said. "The author ties up that end of it, which gives her a chance to address and deal with as many of the tough questions about human overpopulation as she can. I won't tell you what happens, though, in case you decide to read the books."

"I don't know…it sounds horrifying…" Karen said.

"It's not that horrifying. It's only fiction." I grinned and added, "You can put the book down and go back to a world in which that is only imminent, but not actually happening,"

"What do you mean?" Max wanted to know.

Intrigue On a Longship Cruise

"I mean that we are in overshoot in real life, with only about four decades left of fertile growing soil that can keep up with our growing human population and rate of resource use, and we are busily toxifying our ecosystems. Just watch. I will have a few questions for our guides, too, such as what does the current population do for burial space in finite, completely settled Europe today? There's no room for more cemeteries. The United States has the same problem around big cities."

Sober expressions showed all around the table.

Karen said, "I suppose you are pro-choice on abortion, then."

I stared back, grinned mirthlessly, and said, "Yes, I am."

Was she about to hammer away at me about this? I wouldn't just sit through it, even though I didn't go on this trip to fight about politics.

But no – I was in luck – for now. She just said, "I see."

"So…on that note, what else can we talk about?" I asked.

As we ate, it was mentioned that Max had a cold. Great. I didn't want to get it and miss ANY of the enjoyment of the trip. I imagined not being able to enjoy tasting and smelling the foods and other scents of France. No thank you!

So, when he dropped his menu and I picked it up and handed it back to him, I left briefly to use the bathroom – and wash my hands. The ship's rest rooms were as sleek and beautiful as the rest of that floating mini-hotel, complete with a pile of fresh, rolled, small terrycloth towels, a metal soap pump full of its signature scent, and a sprig of orchids.

I washed my hands thoroughly, wondering how many other passengers would bother? Oh yeah…only 10 percent of us. People are incredibly careless of their own health and that of others. I used a fresh towel, barely touched the door handle, and went back to the dining room to continue the meal.

When I came back, I found a nice surprise: we met Carolyn and Amy, a mother and a daughter who were related to a Spanish teacher at MacDuffie, the private high school I had attended! I had studied French, though, so I only knew who this teacher was. It was one of those things where you simply don't get to know someone because your schedule directs you elsewhere in life.

We had fun comparing notes on the school, though.

It was lovely to meet them and remember life there.

Then Max wanted to know how I marketed my books as an independent author.

"I have a website, with a blog, plus I tweet out links from it every night, and share new blog posts on Facebook. They include memes, photographs, screenshots from videos, plus the links to those videos – anything that is relevant to the topic of the post. I always mention my books in the posts, and tie their topics into them."

"What sorts of videos?" Max asked.

"Well…" I tried to pick just some of them to mention. "…there's a *Saturday Night Live* one of Matt Damon doing Brett Kavanaugh at his Senate confirmation hearings, and Koko the Gorilla's last message to humans. I can't just reel them all off at this point, but that's probably enough for now."

Karen suddenly said, "I am NEVER going to watch ANY of Matt Damon's work again after what he did to Brett Kavanaugh!" thus confirming to all that she was a loyal, unquestioning Republican.

Meryl Streep's remark at the Oscars about how she didn't know what people were going to watch if they took that attitude came back to mind. I was like, "Really?"

Aunt Eloise looked incredulous, and then said, appalled, "Are you kidding me?!"

Karen opened her mouth to say more, but didn't get far.

Max cut Karen off with one word: "Don't."

I just watched. Really, revealing ourselves for what we were was enough for me. This was a vacation, not a fight, and a fight would achieve absolutely nothing. This was very amusing; all I needed was popcorn, I thought, and I could make a show of watching the show…

Meanwhile, my salmon dinner arrived.

I let the waiter pour more red wine into my glass.

Intrigue On a Longship Cruise

I planned not to say anything else until Karen found a new topic. She had done the awkward thing. Let her dig her way out of it!

Karen suddenly looked at the wine and said wistfully, "I can never enjoy wine, because it gives me headaches."

I glanced up from my food, picked up my glass of French red wine, and said, "Actually, you can, because the French don't use insecticides on the vines. That's what causes the headaches. I'm drinking it." With that, I took a sip of wine. "That's why French food tastes better, too," I added. "It's one of the secrets to delectable food: just don't add poison," I said with a mischievous smile.

Karen looked at me thoughtfully, but said nothing.

I went back to eating my dinner.

Whatever she was thinking, it was not obvious to me.

Meanwhile, a woman who had been listening to this exchange between me and Karen, who was sitting at the table closest to Karen, suddenly turned around and spoke to me.

Her name was Helen, and she was from northern California.

"Hi," we said to each other, and then she asked me something, which was preceded by an awful story.

"Are you a scientist?" she wanted to know.

"No. I'm a lawyer and a researcher. I am married to a scientist, though, and I wrote a book about honeybee colony collapse disorder, which focused on beekeeping, just to show what healthy bees are like, and then insecticides and the corporations that manufacture them, plus the lobbyists and politicians who enable them. Why?"

"My son had a job in college spraying insecticides. He only wore a handkerchief over his face. Later, he got cancer in his nasal passages and lungs. Do you think that there was a connection?"

I stared at her, horrified.

"Oh...oh...yeah...that was definitely it. I'm really sorry. There are lawsuits about that, too! Some maintenance guy in California is suing right now over that exact same thing."

Helen nodded, satisfied.

A man at her table who, as far as I could tell was no one that she knew before this trip, but instead had simply needed a place to sit, had been listening to our conversation, I noticed. He wasn't participating in the conversation at his own table. He was just eating and people-watching.

I hoped we had provided adequate entertainment.

Soon, the meal picked up where we had left off.

Max, despite his effort to keep his wife from lighting into me, could not restrain himself from making some remarks of his own. "It doesn't matter. Kavanaugh got in. Still, it wasn't enough to save Trump from having to leave the Oval Office."

"The Supreme Court wasn't even involved in that," I said.

"No. Too bad."

I looked at him.

"Can you remember where you were that day, and what you were doing?" I asked.

"Yes. Can you?" Max asked.

"Yes. I was buying a special edition magazine of the *Los Angeles Times* about our soon-to-be Vice President Kamala Harris. Then I got in the car with my mother – we were out doing errands together – and called a friend, who told me that the crowd had stormed the Capitol."

Aunt Eloise said, "I was watching it on television with a friend."

We looked at Max, and I said, "Your turn."

I really wasn't expecting sorrow or outrage over what happened that day, but I also wasn't expecting what I did hear from him.

"I was there, on the Mall, with the crowd."

We stared at him, momentarily speechless.

I was stopped cold, literally and figuratively.

I recovered pretty quick, though, and asked, "You attended Trump's incitement to the crowd in person?"

"It wasn't an incitement; it was an inspiration." Max looked at me like someone across a barricade.

I looked back him, then asked, "And were you inspired to do as he exhorted the crowd to do?"

"Yes, I was."

"Did you follow through on that, or just feel the emotion?"

"I just felt the emotion. Then I decided not to get myself arrested."

"Oh." I nodded. "So…you left the area?"

"Yes. I met my wife at our hotel and we ate lunch there, in the bar, and watched what happened on television. That was no way to deal with things."

Karen nodded. "Much better than getting swept up in an unruly crowd," she said. "Safer."

I wondered, though, what Max had meant by "no way to deal with things". Was he suggesting that it was the mob, or himself, that had not dealt with things properly? I decided not to pursue the topic.

"So…what are you most interested to do and see on this trip?" Aunt Eloise asked, since it was blatantly clear that we could find no common political ground.

We could feel the state of de facto civil war that America was in. I was embarrassed and worried to travel out of our country with this going on, and wondered what the wait staff must be thinking about us as they moved around our table.

As it was, China and Russia were sick and tired of American hegemony. Actually, our nation's dominance on the world stage was pretty much over, and that simply left us as a major player on it. The state of empires was fluctuating. That was part of the reason for the rise of MAGA moronism.

Again, I wanted the burden of a change of subject to fall on these people. They, after all, were the ones who had introduced discomfort to the interaction.

Karen said, "I love to see the historic sites. But…as I have traveled over the years, I realize that I have accumulated so many things. Now I think I need to figure out something to do with them all – someone to give them to who would want them."

Aunt Eloise said, "I can relate. I downsized dramatically when I retired from teaching and moved. I gave Arielle some things, and I gave my son, Dylan, the dish cabinet and the dishes that had belonged to my grandmother."

Karen nodded. "We collect so much as we go through life."

At least that much felt like common ground. We were all people, and wherever we were from, whatever we believed, there were always basic things that we would have in common. I would bet that we all loved to watch the 4th of July fireworks shows on television each year, complete with the celebrity performances.

Max had surprised me, though, by coming across as more extreme than his wife. Perhaps he wasn't telling us – or her – everything.

And I didn't expect that he would, either.

I was still a bit curious about him.

"Max, tell me about your career." I smiled as I said this, inviting him to talk about himself. I hoped he would.

I was not disappointed.

"I worked on Wall Street at the beginning of my career, worked my way up through the ranks of Blackstone Inc., and then got a seat on the Federal Reserve Board, also in New York City."

Definitely a bankster, I thought. "How many years did you spend doing all that? Did you like it?"

"Yes, very much. It was about thirty-five years."

"Was that your entire career?"

"No. After that, I worked for the U.S. State Department, liaising between the American CDC and the French P4."

"Really?! How interesting – Pathogen 4. Did you get to meet the married couple at the Center for Disease Control who helped set up P4, a British woman and an American man?"

Max did a double-take. "How do you know so much about that?"

"I read a lot, and I need to in order to write. Also, my husband, Kavi, has Ph.D.s in virology and genetics. He works on stem cells, mostly, but it helps him to know all about those fields."

Max said, "Kavi? Is he Indian?"

Sigh. Max was likely racist. "Yes, he's Indian – Indian-American, born and raised in the U.S.A."

"Kavi Ravendra?" Max asked.

"Yes. Have you heard of him before?"

"Yes. His journal articles have been cited to me."

"Oh," I said, pleased that his work had spread far and wide.

"Max," Karen said, "What a nice coincidence to meet his wife!" She looked at my business card again and read my name. "Arielle N. Desrosiers, J.D. – you have a law degree. You use your own last name, don't you? That's why we had no idea." She smiled politely.

I grinned. "Yes. This is quite a coincidence. Have you ever met my husband?"

"No," Max said. "I did a lot of traveling for the Trump administration. He was considering reducing funding for the CDC, and he cut the pandemic response unit, but then the pandemic started, and I had to join the scientists in telling him that we needed them."

Incredible. I kept my facial expression as deadpan as I could, and said, "Yes, I remember reading about that. Obama created that team, so it had to go." What did it matter how my face looked, though? He had already caught on that I was a liberal – and he no doubt heard the sarcasm in my voice.

Max nodded. "Pretty much. It was a fire sale."

Dessert arrived: the chocolate lava cake.

I paused to admire it, complete with its raspberry and raspberry coulis sauce. But just for a moment. I had more questions for people.

"So," I said, picking up a different thread, "you traveled to P4."

"Yes, before the pandemic. I visited with a scientist I knew before the pandemic, before Karen and I boarded this ship."

"Really? Who? Would I recognize the name?"

"I don't know. It was Jean-Claude Babineaux. He gave me a tour of his lab. Have you heard of him?"

"Yes, Kavi has corresponded with him, and I have edited scientific journal articles that they have co-authored. Of course, there is always a string of co-authors with those articles, but it's cool to work on them, and interesting to read them as I do it."

Max studied me.

"So…how was Dr. Babineaux when you saw him?"

"Okay. He was coming down with a cold, though. I'm sure I caught this from him. But don't worry; it's not a dangerous pathogen."

"I'm not worried," I said. "But I won't shake hands with you and invite it in."

We all laughed at that.

"So, other than that, you just had a nice visit with him and then met Karen to board the *Sif*?"

"Yes," Max said. We had a delicious lunch in Lyon, and then Karen and I took a chartered flight to Avignon. Well, to Marseilles. We stayed overnight there and were driven here the next morning."

"Julia Child had a place near Marseilles," I said.

"We stayed in the city," Karen said.

"That makes sense. You had a boat to catch." I grinned, and then focused on the lovely French food we were eating, and enjoyed it.

"What did you eat in Lyon at that lunch?" I wanted to know.

Karen laughed and said, "Max always gets steak and fries!"

Max grinned. 'That's true. But Jean-Claude is a foodie. He had frog's legs and a salad. He always gets the most unusual thing on the menu – the special."

I grinned back. "He sounds interesting."

Karen and Max looked at each other and exchanged a slight smile.

The rest of the meal continued quietly enough.

Meanwhile, I had no idea that I had made any impression on Karen about anything at that moment, but she took a liking to me. She became very cheerful, smiled at me, and tried some wine.

When we took our leave of them after dessert, she was friendly, and we felt that we had spent an interesting time with them.

On the way back to our room, Aunt Eloise said to me, "I saw them trying to shut you down, and it didn't surprise me that they would do that. Don't let them stop you from doing what you do. You're fine."

She had noticed me thinking quietly, and deduced that I was analyzing the interaction, wondering, as usual, whether or not I had navigated it well enough.

"Thank you!" I said, as we walked down the hall.

She was quiet for a moment, and then added, "Actually, I don't need to tell you that. You know it."

We reached our stateroom at that point, smiling.

Aunt Eloise had another thought. "I'm not going to tell them about Dylan, beyond the fact that he's a photographer."

Dylan, my cousin, was transgender.

He could also fix anything – carpentry, computers, you name it, he could fix it if it had a problem.

So could my Uncle Louis, my mother's younger brother, for that matter.

"Neither am I," I said.

We pretty much wrote off Max and Karen as anti-gay rights, religious people who buried themselves in prayer and ritual, but who could not be counted upon as friends in a crisis that didn't fit into their parochial world and mindset.

"We won't just meet open-minded, secular people wherever we go," I added.

"No, we won't!" my aunt agreed.

When we were ready for bed, we weren't tired, so we watched the orientation movie. It lasted about 15 minutes. We scrolled through the other options and found that each day's itinerary and menu could be viewed. It was changed daily. Printed packets for the day with the tours that we had booked, along with more details about them, would also be provided, we had been told by Clotilde.

After looking through all that, we went to sleep, looking forward to seeing more of France the next day.

Odd though parts of this vacation were, it was fun.

Intrigue On a Longship Cruise

Avignon, Smile Candy, and Les Halles

Avignon, Smile Candy, and Les Halles

The next morning, I woke up at what would be an unheard-of hour at home: half past six. It was just for a week that I would not be a night owl. I would be able to fall asleep at 10 p.m. this way. Already, I felt fine, not too tired, not like I couldn't wake up. This was unusual for me, but it suited the schedule of this trip.

Aunt Eloise would also be making an adjustment for the week. She would not go for a walk at half past five in the morning, because we were on a river cruise ship, and the roof was off limits at that hour. "But," she insisted again, "that's fine." We would be taking walking tours.

At breakfast, we found a feast that was to be repeated daily.

"I'm going to gain weight if I eat like this too often," Aunt Eloise said.

I laughed. "It's only for a week, and we're going to be walking and thinking it off. We should enjoy every last wonderful taste and scent and sight and even sound that comes our way all week. Next week, we can go back to eating small breakfasts and light lunches, and walking around our neighborhoods."

She was going to stay overnight with me and Kavi in Connecticut and walk with me for one more day, just to get over jet lag, too, before returning to her cat in Newport. That would get us both back on track.

Aunt Eloise grinned. "You're right. I'll eat for fun now."

And that was what we did.

A delectable feast of options awaited us in the dining room.

There was an omelet bar with an array of fillings: cheddar cheese, bacon, spinach, mushrooms, scallions, tomato, and shrimp. There were croissants, bagels, and pastries. There were all sorts of fruits, including melons and berries, and smoked salmon on toast.

An interesting item, new to us, was a Norwegian one: a cup of yoghurt in a small glass, topped with a little granola and some berries. Lingonberries were a theme throughout the tour, as a garnish on many plates.

As if all that weren't enough, menus were presented. Pancakes and crepes were an option every morning, if we wanted them.

I looked it all over and decided to plan on a week of trying some of everything, though not all at once. It was a feast in more ways than one – of options, and of delectability. As it was, I loved breakfast foods, though of course I didn't eat this much at home.

"I have to look at this and remind myself that I will use the energy I take in when I go out on the tours," I said to Aunt Eloise. "We're thoroughly booked on tours that will keep us out and about on every day but one – the one when the ship will travel upriver through locks."

She nodded and smiled. "That will be interesting. I want to go on the captains' wheelhouse tour."

"Me too! We can ask them questions, too. There are two of them." We each got omelets, smoked salmon, and berries.

Nickolai, a young Romanian man with dark hair and a cheerful smile, make the omelets. He seemed very happy. He did this job for weeks at a time, and went home to a town outside of Bucharest when the ship wasn't running. It paused operations during the winter holidays, though not for long.

People were trickling in to the dining room.

It was slowly filling up, and it felt odd to me to be up while it was still not really light out. Everyone was rather quiet, as if just waking up.

Orange juice and coffee helped, though.

Gradually, conversation picked up, I noticed, as the room filled up some more and people had to sit with strangers and get to know them.

We didn't have that experience until halfway through our meal, though. At that point, Carolyn and Amy joined us at the small table we were at, sharing our view of Nickolai at the omelet bar. It was fun to watch him cook.

"Are you going on the tour of the Papal Palace?" Amy asked.

"Yes," I replied. "Are you?"

"Yes. We wouldn't miss it."

Aunt Eloise nodded. "I don't know how anyone can come so close to this famous walled city and not go in and see it!"

"We have wanted to do this for years," Carolyn said.

"When I was in college, I learned about the schism and the century during which there were two popes, one here and the usual one in Rome, and I've been curious to see it since then. This is going to be great! And Les Halles – it makes me think of Peter Mayle's books and chef Julia Child, shopping to prepare some gourmet French recipes. I know it was Marseilles, not here, but it's not that far to drive. She probably checked this place out."

Anticipatory smiles all around. This was going to be great.

"No doubt there will be a few other things that we aren't thinking about that will make it all even better," Amy added.

Yes, this was going to be a great morning.

This, I thought to myself, for someone who didn't usually like mornings!

But we were on a fabulous vacation. This was different.

After breakfast, we returned to our cabin, used the facilities, and collected our gear. I made sure that my Nikon camera was ready to use. My father had gone to a lot of trouble to equip me with a battery charger, two batteries, and two memory chips with a couple of terabytes' worth of capacity for all the images I could possibly record.

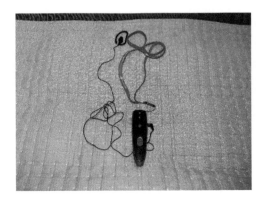

Intrigue On a Longship Cruise

We grabbed our earpieces, put our money-belts on with our passports and Euros inside under our shirts, and headed out.

Our key cards were to be turned in at the front desk when leaving the ship, and picked up when we returned. In exchange, the ship's concierge had given us each a cardboard ID that matched the plastic key cards in size. It was made of thick white paper with perforated edges, and it was kept in a fancy drawer with wooden slots – one slot for each cabin, with one for each passenger. When off the ship, it was with us. Upon returning, it was to be turned in. This was a security measure; it was how the ship's crew accounted for whether we were on or off of the *Sif*.

The other card that we were given was a plastic one with a large letter and number indicating our tour group. To meet up with our guide, we looked for the one who was carrying a huge, round, double-sided, cardboard sign with those same characters on it. It was called a lollypop sign.

It was time to disembark from our longship for our first tour.

We walked down the gangplank and onto the sidewalk, and there it was: the city of Avignon, with its Medieval wall. The wall is one of the few that still exist intact, which makes the city a UNESCO World Heritage Site.

Our guide was an elegant, smiling, youthful-looking woman with gray-and black-streaked hair. (My hair was starting to go gray, so I was interested to see this juxtaposition.) She looked elegant yet casual, with her hair loosely pinned in a high bun. Her name was Cerise, which means "cherry" in French.

The first thing she did when she greeted each one of us was to have us point our electronic touring devices at her lollypop sign. These devices lived in chargers in our cabins when we weren't using them. I felt the device vibrate and saw a small plastic outline on its +/- button glow briefly purple.

We wore these things hanging from our necks on lanyards, with thin cords connecting from one side up to our earpieces. I wore mine on my left ear. Once activated, we could hear Cerise talking as if she were right next to each one of us.

Once satisfied that each device was in working order and on, Cerise took off, leading us across the zebra stripes, as she called the crosswalk (she was interested to know what Americans called it) and over to the city wall.

A parking lot stretched out to the road in front of it, and as we got close to it, we noticed that cobblestone paving had replaced its moat, along with small gardens here and there. Cerise told us that they were herbs, and sure enough, we saw lavender, sage, rosemary, tarragon, and other edible plants.

She paused to ask us if we knew what used to be in the moat. "Sewage," several of us said. It had been filled in, of course, since a defensive moat was no longer necessary. Cars were parked here and there in the huge parking lot outside the wall, and there were places for bicycles, too.

Cerise smiled and led us through the small gate, pointing out the fact that the metal drawbridge was no longer in use.

We found ourselves on a narrow street. It was wide enough for cars to drive through it, and it had sidewalks on either side. Cerise told us that she would come back with us or tell us the way and leave us to find our own way back if we chose to look around and shop later.

Aunt Eloise and I decided to shop later on.

Cerise walked us past a parfumerie called Fragonard, and told us that it was a family-owned business with branches in several cities and towns. We took one look in the windows and decided to visit it later. I also took a few photographs of it.

Next, Cerise led us to a building with a mural where a window once was, and explained that the window had been removed and its space covered over to save money on taxes a few centuries ago.

Now that windows weren't taxed, it was more expensive than it was worth to have that spot reopened and a new window installed. A few decades ago, when a movie was made in Avignon, a mural of the lead actor and actress in costume was painted on that spot instead.

After that, Cerise took us to the city center to see the hôtel de ville (city hall), the opera house, and a clock tower. This was called the Place de l'Horloge, meaning the Clock Place, because of the clock, which has a pair of figures in it that lean together to kiss each other whenever the clock chimes. Their names are Jacques and Jacotte.

49

There was a beautiful carousel in front of the hôtel de ville, which we walked all around. The tops of each section had beautiful paintings.

Restaurants surrounded the place, complete with outdoor seating. We found ourselves envying the residents of this beautiful city, including Cerise, who said she lived here.

When we had seen that, Cerise said it was time for us to see the Palais des Papes – the Papal Palace. This was what had made the city famous before its wall was a big deal. Back in the 14th century, having a wall around a city was a standard feature, after all.

The schism between Avignon and Rome was a different thing. There were seven popes in France before Rome decided it wanted the seat of Catholic government to be back there, at which point Avignon chose two more of them. These were the disputed popes – the ones who were declared to be invalid by Rome. After that, there were only popes in Rome again, not in Avignon.

But, for 68 years (1309-1377), the seat of Catholic government was in the city of Avignon, in Provence, France. During that time, a huge palace was built, with wing after wing, a couple of courtyards, lots of beautiful frescos that we weren't allowed to photograph, and a fabulous banquet hall with a cedar ceiling.

Cerise led us through a narrow alley, out into an open space where Renaissance fairs were held, up a wooden staircase, and into the palace.

We saw black-and-white frescos in the first room, which Cerise told us had been painted after the popes had left. It was okay to photograph those, but not the ones with blue, farther on, because it could fade.

Those frescos had lost their faces to vandals a few centuries later, who pried those chunks of the images off to sell. Some have been found and reaffixed to their original spots, but most haven't.

We went into the first courtyard and were shown around it, with Cerise pointing out a window high up in one corner that had the pope's bedchamber inside. The oldest part of the courtyard was being excavated by archaeologists.

We saw the pope's throne in one room:

The banquet hall was an elaborate room once upon a time, with a high platform at one end for the pope to eat from, a slightly high spot for visiting kings and queens, and none for the other guests. The other end had a dressoir – a place for the waitstaff to plate the food after bringing it out of the kitchen.

Cerise took us into the kitchen and showed us the open flue that looked straight up at the blue sky. This was where the huge fires had burned to cook the banquets:

But it was the ceiling that was most interesting. It was made of cedar, and was an exact restoration of the original one, with one notable exception: it was not painted like a sky with stars. There were no plans to do that, even though that was how the ceiling had been when the popes were in residence.

As for other aspects of life in residence here, we were shown images on a huge touch-screen television in room after room. Some of these images were photographs that had been staged in the grande cuisine, or big kitchen, some were of the pope's chambers, which have their original wall and ceiling art, and still others, like that blue and starry banquet hall ceiling, were done with computer graphic imaging.

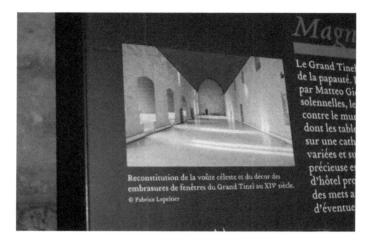

Reconstitution de la voûte céleste et du décor des embrasures de fenêtres du Grand Tinel au XIV siècle.
© Fabrice Lepeltier

We lingered over these computer screens because the images took us back in time to show how the banquets were presented, in still shots. It was fun to be a virtual time traveler for a few minutes!

The pope's bedchamber was also in blue, with designs on every beam of wood across its ceiling. Even though it was ancient and peeling, it was still beautiful.

We looked out the windows and saw the bell that was rung whenever the cardinals chose a new pope (no black or white smoke back then!):

Looking up in the other direction, we saw a golden statue of the Virgin Mary presiding over the palace:

Cerise led us through courtyards, halls, up and down ancient stone staircases, and even to an area with a model of the entire palace, which enabled us to appreciate the scope of it:

There was one huge room near the end of our tour that had been the cathedral, but was now an exhibit hall. We spent a long time looking at everything.

During that time, Cerise paused in the center (at least, it felt like the center of that space, even though we were in a maze of displays!). She told us that the room had been designed with music in mind, and that the acoustics in that spot were excellent. And then...she demonstrated it, surprising us with a beautiful soprano rendition of *Ave Maria*! We all stopped looking around us and just listened to her.

Yes, great acoustics – and a wonderful voice.

When we had seen it all, Cerise announced that we would have about twenty minutes to see the gift shop, and then we could meet her outside before moving on.

The shop proved to be in two sections, first down one steep staircase to a room full of lavender, Herbes de Provence, wine, and olive oils, and then down another. I found some Medieval party music on a CD in that room, bought it for my father, and walked out into the sunshine with my aunt to find Cerise.

We walked through a few narrow streets when she resumed the tour. Around one corner, we encountered a man with a barrel organ. His pet cat was stretched out on top, luxuriating in the sunshine and its human's company. What a life!

Next, our guide stopped in front of a confectionerie, or candy shop, and told us a lovely story along the way: There was a queen during the Medieval times who was always sad. She never smiled. Why, we do not know. Perhaps she was homesick for wherever she was politically traded from. Maybe the king wasn't nice to her. Whatever the reason, she never smiled.

The chef at Avignon decided that he would try to make her smile, so he created a delicious candy to tempt her with. It was made of a mixture of honey, ground almonds, and orange zest, and coated with marzipan. He brought it out on a platter and presented it to her, explaining that he had made it especially for her.

The queen tasted it, and…she smiled! Ever after, this candy was cut in the shape of a smile. Cerise paused outside the shop in case any of us wanted to buy some, which we did.

The ladies in the shop gave us some to try, and, cliché though this may be, we couldn't help but smile, too. It was delicious, so I bought some because of the story, and because it was too good to taste only once!

Our next stop was a church, the Basilique Saint-Pierre d'Avignon, which we were walked through at a brisk pace after being warned to keep our conversations low and to a minimum so as not to disturb the people who were in there praying.

It was a beautiful one, with detailed carvings over the door to the nave, oil paintings and tapestries inside, and people sitting with their eyes closed in some of the pews. I kept walking, saying nothing. I may be an atheist, but I'm not interested in blocking other people from what they want to do if it doesn't bother anyone else.

Intrigue On a Longship Cruise

As we headed out the side door, however, I noticed the priest standing by the altar next to the incense candles. He was wearing a long white alb with gold embroidery, and glasses, and he had an irate glare.

I glanced at him, confused and annoyed, and followed Cerise out. "That priest was about to scold you for having a camera," she said, "so I spoke to him for you."

"Huh. Thanks!" I said, still puzzled. "I don't see what his problem was; I didn't photograph people praying and set off the flash in anyone's face." I had no choice but to wear the heavy thing on its strap, resting out in the open against my chest, for all to see.

"Well, he saw that you had a camera. That's why I stopped him from saying anything to you. I saved you."

Wow. Religion was important here, even today.

I noticed that phrase: she had "saved" me. From what? Probably an outraged barrage of bullying. I had spent elementary school among nuns and priests, because my mother thought that the academics in public school weren't rigorous enough for me, and found that some clerics reveled in bullying people – not all, just some.

But that meant that there was occasional religious zealotry, which could devolve into bullying. I felt lucky that my family wasn't religious, and that we emphasized culture, logic, and knowledge instead. "Saved" – I wouldn't have been cowed by an irate priest!

As we walked with our guide, I wondered when I would spot the Catholic priest from Florida, but he was likely in another group, and I didn't see him that morning. Avignon was a popular destination, and rightly so, for our ship, and there had been at least six groups of us at the pier.

I avoided religion except as a cultural experience, so whenever I encountered someone who really cared about it, it was a surprise, and I liked it that way. Art, Catholic churches, and ancient Roman sites were standard tourist fare for this trip, however, so I expected to see lots and lots of them.

Our next stop, was about a kind of worship that I shared – that of delectable food made from fresh, organic ingredients not tainted by insecticides.

We were going to visit Les Halles of Avignon!

Les Halles is what the French call their food markets, and this was a thing I had learned long ago from reading about the life and career of Julia Child. The one in Avignon takes up a city block, but just the ground floor. The upper stories are a parking garage. You wouldn't know it to look at the place, however, because the top of the building is camouflaged in greenery.

We went in and found ourselves in gastronomic heaven. White tile flooring, overhead lighting, and stall after stall of food stretched before us. We saw towers of every variety of edible mushroom, cascades of fresh herbs, mountains of breads, arrays of poultry and cheeses, sausages, fruits, honey, spices, and fish. We couldn't look at it enough.

The chef from our ship was likely a regular customer here, I found myself thinking as I looked forward to lunch back on our ship.

We were invited to taste some pickled garlic and olives, complete with wooden toothpicks and cups to throw used ones into. It was mild, and left no aftertaste. The French are food geniuses, I thought to myself! I didn't say that aloud. No point in stating the obvious.

At this point, Cerise invited us to wander around a bit, see everything, and circle back to her in twenty minutes at the front door. We would have a chance to buy postcards, look around, and get directions back to the ship if we weren't going to walk around with her any further.

Aunt Eloise and I quickly bought several postcards that variously showed lavender, the wall of Avignon, and the market. We weren't deltiologists – probably none of us on the tour were – but it was fun to have them as compact souvenirs. We would write to Kavi and Dylan later, and the *Sif*'s staff would post them for us. I wrote one to my friend Sylvia, too, on a lavender card.

After that, some of us wanted to take off and shop a little.

Cerise reviewed the route out of the city for us, and off we went, on our own.

A Parfumerie and a Careful Walk

A Parfumerie and a Careful Walk

Aunt Eloise and I headed straight for the Fragonard parfumerie.

It was halfway along the walk back out, which made it seem easy enough to find, visit and then return to the *Sif* in plenty of time for lunch.

Fragonard Parfumeur
20 Rue Saint-Agricol
84000 Avignon
France
+33 4 90 82 07 07
https://www.fragonard.com/fr/boutique/avignon

We found it, and I remembered that photography was not allowed inside of the stores, so I took a photograph from outside, on the sidewalk, before going in. It was easy; the shop's walls were all glass.

A moment later, we went in, smiled, and said "Bonjour!" We were immediately greeted by the most wonderful scents, which were not only in the air but plied upon us by two calm, patient women. They showed us many different ones, all in prettily decorated bottles, vials, tubes, sachets, and boxes.

I felt like a kid in a candy shop as I went inside.

"Bonjour!" said the women who were in there, one behind the counter and the other near the back of the shop.

"Bonjour!" my aunt and I said back.

We turned and stared, smiling, at the displays. Everything had a gorgeous floral pattern on it, and there were little strips of paper on a table in the front and toward the back, meant for sampling the scents.

The women spoke fluent English, and told us what notes of enticing fragrances were in each scent.

We were the only customers.

Perfume wasn't the only product offered, but it was what I wanted to buy.

The women picked up the long, white strips of thick paper and sprayed fragrance after fragrance onto them, letting us whiff several. Some appealed to me, some didn't, and some were just nice, but not my favorite.

Aunt Eloise watched me, clearly not intending to buy anything, but she enjoyed the show.

I chose a scent called "Emilie", which was described as "a bewitching floral composition that blends sumptuous fragrances of rose and jasmine with a more delicate violet note, then wraps them in sandalwood and amber."

Marketing! Well, it was suitably seductive. I sprayed some on in the shop, said "Merci beaucoup!" and paid.

"Kavi will love that on you," Aunt Eloise remarked.

The women bagged my purchase, tossed in the long, thin white paper testers that were still redolent of the other scents we had sampled, and we paid for our perfumes. We thanked them and went out into the sunshine, turning right.

I smiled and looked carefully down the narrow streets ahead of us.

Time to get back without getting lost!

There was one slight deviation in the route where the street wasn't a straight line back to the city's famous wall, but that was about it.

As we headed back the way we had come, back to the opening in Avignon's UNESCO World Heritage Site of a Medieval wall through which we had entered the city, I saw that we were in a narrow and deserted alley.

We walked down it, and Aunt Eloise paused to point out a stone wall in front of a courtyard. An elegant house with pretty shutters stood behind it.

The wall was adorned with signs.

Yes — adorned! Each one was a plate of transparent glass with neatly tapered edges on all sides, held in place by sweeping curves and swirls of iron. On the plates were names of people, and the word "Avocat" was below each one.

"It's a law office!" I said, delighted.

Aunt Eloise stared at it some more.

"It must be an old and exclusive law practice," I commented. "In Europe, it is almost impossible to join the legal profession without family connections. You need those plus the resources to work for free for several years. The L.L.M. students explained it to me when I was in law school, and the international law professor also talked about it."

Aunt Eloise nodded, interested to hear about it.

My aunt, meanwhile, was slowing down to look at something. "Arielle," she said excitedly, "don't you want a photograph of this?"

I looked around us warily.

We were completely alone on a narrow street.

"Let's go," I said. "We should walk straight out of this lonely area immediately and out into the open. We don't want to be an easy target, loudly conversing in American English without watching our surroundings."

My aunt seemed amazed, and, given the fact that I was a shutterbug who usually wanted to document everything and then write about it in full detail later, I could hardly blame her.

"That would be nice," I said, "but look around. No one is around, that we can see. We are Americans, and we are speaking our native language, accent and all. We have bought stuff. We should walk quickly and quietly until we are out of the city wall and into the light, where we can be seen from a distance. Then we can relax."

My aunt gave me a startled look, then followed me.

Aunt Eloise agreed, and we moved along.

Down a few more blocks, we came to the long street that encircles the city of Avignon from just inside its wall. Bicycles and cars were parked along it.

A tunnel was straight ahead, and we had to walk under a section of the wall to leave. It had once been a putrid waterway that had been filled in. Now it was a gorgeous walkway.

We kept moving until we were in the tunnel that led out of there, almost into the sunshine, where the herb gardens of rosemary and lavender plants bloomed.

Only then did I take the lens cap off of my camera to photograph the papal seal, which depicted the key to the city, that was embedded in the stone walkway:

A few more steps and we were out in the sunshine.

When we exited, we could see the half-bridge in the near distance to our right: Pont Saint-Bénézet. It was built from 1177 to 1185, and destroyed by flooding, so it was abandoned after that.

No one was around, but we could see parked cars here and there, the ships moored at the quai in the distance, and the Pont Saint-Bénézet off to the right. All that remained was to safely cross the Boulevard de la Ligne, which we did with no trouble. The cars were not being driven by impatient road-rage cases, apparently.

"Nothing happened to us," my aunt said to me, with a gleam in her eye. "You were extremely cautious, and no one appeared."

"That's just the way I like it," I said.

"I'm teasing you!" she said. "I agree with you for being careful."

"Oh!" I said, "Well then…I'll keep it up."

We headed back to the *Sif* for lunch, happy.

This was going to be a fun trip.

In fact, it already was!

Lunch...Not on Rye

Lunch…Not on Rye

At the suggestion of the concierge, a pretty, petite woman with a short, dark ponytail and dark-rimmed, round glasses, we headed into the dining hall for lunch.

It was August, the ideal time to tour Provence, and we looked forward to going up the Rhône River. We happily anticipated touring Arles, some small towns upriver, and finally the city of Lyon. We would also visit the famous Pont du Gard.

After we sat down at one of the longer tables with some of our new shipmates, a.k.a. fellow travelers, we settled in to enjoy a delectable lunch. There was pea soup with fresh herbs, which we all decided to try. The menu offered several items, including a salmon entrée and a chocolate mousse, which we both ordered.

Our order for the entire meal was expected to be done at the beginning of the meal – so we had to make up our minds and leave the kitchen time to prepare it all.

As we were sitting there, we exchanged names, business cards, and pleasantries. I introduced myself. It was fun to meet new people and find out about their lives and careers and interests.

Aunt Eloise sat there quietly as I started off the conversation, so I smiled and introduced her, too: "This is my aunt, Eloise Desrosiers. She is a retired art teacher and not-retired artist who graduated from the Rhode Island School of Design. We're looking forward to seeing Arles, of course."

The woman next to us, a retired sommelier named Alice, from upstate New York, commented, "You pronounce 'aunt' like a European."

I laughed. "No, I just really, really don't like to pronounce it as if she has six legs and goes around collecting crumbs."

Everyone else laughed at that.

Then Alice piled on: "You talk like a book," she said, but her tone was friendly.

"Well, she does write them," my aunt said, "and she always makes me hungry when I read them."

"Hungry? Why? What are they about?"

I replied, "As a lawyer, author, and researcher of many topics, I like to build stories around my favorite ones, including human overpopulation." That caused heads to turn, which I always found fun.

"But I include details of the recipes that the characters cook and bake and eat in restaurants and cafés, just to fill out their lives for the reader. It adds some human interest to it all."

"And then I get hungry," Aunt Eloise said, laughing.

There was more laughter around the table.

"No danger of that here," said Declan, who was retired from a chemical corporation, where he had been an engineer. He and his wife – Alice – had been on eleven Longship cruises already. "This garlic soup is delicious."

"It's delectable," I agreed. "I'm looking forward to the salmon. The gourmet French food is about half of why I wanted to go on this trip."

"We're not overpopulated, are we?" Alice said, like she didn't believe it. Then, of course, she added, "I don't believe it."

I warmed up to the challenge. "I hear that all the time, usually when someone doesn't like the data, even though science is just science, and the data is correct. We are at 8 billion humans planet-wide. The U.S. is third, with 335 million people, behind China with 1.5 billion and India with 1.4 billion."

Stares all around.

"How many can the planet support?"

"Under 2 billion humans."

"But the planet can just grow more food, right?"

"We're using up fertile growing soil, water, sand, and space, polluting the oceans with nuclear waste and plastic – oh, and we're even polluting outer space with orbital debris."

"Okay, I guess I believe it."

Laughter from the others…it sounded a bit nervous.

"So, I said, "what else can we talk about? With that out of the way, we might as well get back to the business of having fun. That's what we're all here for, anyway." I grinned.

Everyone relaxed and our thoughts returned to the next excursion.

The man sitting next to me looked like he could have conducted an art program on public television, and surprise! He was a retired art professor from St. Louis. He had curly salt-and-pepper hair and a beard, and was very nice. His name was Michael.

I insisted upon switching seats with my aunt so that she would be next to him. This man was going on the all-day Vincent van Gogh tour, and would paint a picture in the style of the Dutch artist, per the specialized tour.

"Are you going on that one?" he asked.

"No," my aunt replied. "I do black ink point drawings, and colored pencil ones. I really just want to walk around and see the city without being gone for the whole day. That tour sounds nice but tiring."

Michael grinned wryly, and then said, "My wife insisted that I do this. Painting in oils like the impressionists is what I do to relax, but I'm not a great artist. I taught a course on the French Impressionists for thirty-five years. I'll have fun."

We smiled. His wife, Selena, was chatting with Pearl, a retired emergency room nurse, and hadn't noticed this exchange. Selena turned out to be a retired elementary school teacher who had published one children's book.

"What is your book about?" I asked.

"It's about a girl who wants to be a teacher," she replied with a smile.

"So, you wrote what you know. I do that, too."

Selena smiled and asked what I knew and wrote. I told her that I wrote a short story about a girl with Asperger's for my first story, but had moved on to longer projects, including novels and social, political, economic, and scientific allegory about banksters and honeybees. "Those were separate books," I added.

"Interesting!" she said, and took my card to look at the list of titles.

Her card was very colorful, with a little crayon drawing of a girl.

Mine was periwinkle blue, with a bee logo and a lot of words.

I loved collecting other authors' cards and seeing how they were set up to emphasize different things.

Everyone here but myself was retired, I noticed, but I had been expecting that. Older people made the best conversation, I thought!

The salmon lunch arrived.

Several of us had ordered it, and there was a pause in conversation while we admired it and then tasted it. It was delicious, of course.

Then it was back to conversation!

The nurse's husband, George, was a professor of zoology from Washington State. "Really?" I said, interested. "What did you specialize in?"

"Predators," he said with a friendly but deadpan facial expression.

I wanted to hear more. "Which ones?"

He seemed a bit surprised by my interest, but answered, "Bengal tigers, leopards, cheetahs, lions – you know, big cats."

"So, no house cats," I said, just to see what he would say to that, and waited.

"Well, I would compare them in my lectures."

We were at a large table, one that seated eight, however, and now we noticed another person. The eighth seat was empty, as the ship wasn't yet fully boarded.

This man was sitting at the next table, listening to us quietly, until he suddenly said, "Did you ever rank all of the predator species of the Earth?"

The professor looked at him, and then said, "No, but we did rank the cats. However, there are studies – outside my field, of course – that say that the dragonfly is the top predator of the animal world."

"But that's an insect," the retired nurse said. "You mean to say that entomologists and zoologists agree on this?"

The professor smiled. "I don't know about agree..."

I broke in with this: "The top predator on the planet Earth is us. It's humans. We fly higher, dive deeper, move faster, and kill more and kill every species. We use technology to do it, but we're definitely part of the Earth's ecosystems, however much we manipulate them."

Everyone looked at me, startled, except my aunt.

My aunt nodded. "She's right. We're monsters."

People looked at her, then back at me, and then considered this. A moment later they all seemed to relax and accept the idea. Liking an idea and accepting it as fact were not the same thing, after all.

George had another question for me: "Which sort of law do you like best? National? International? What else?"

I grinned. "What a loaded question. I like so many kinds – I read the entire international news section of the paper – we get *The Hartford Courant* in Connecticut, which is the nation's older newspaper – plus any major developments in national U.S. law. I also follow anything about pollution, such as plastic, chemical, nuclear, or other waste, and bioweapons, all of which have United Nations treaties, but outer space law is my favorite. I did my law thesis on orbital debris."

I turned to the man who had asked the predator question and asked him one. "So – what about you? Tell us about yourself." I did so with what I hoped was a polite smile.

He gave me a closed sort of smile back and said, "I'm retired."

I wanted to ask him more, but the next course of our lunch arrived, and our attention was diverted by it.

While it was being served, this man took out some food from a black messenger bag that he had slung over his chair. It was a package of crackers.

Just then, the man I had seen with him on our tour of the Papal Palace joined him, taking the empty seat.

Now was the time to chat with them.

"Hello," I said with a smile. "I'm Arielle. What's your name?"

This man had slightly graying hair, and a pleasant expression on his face. His traveling companion reminded me of a graying version of the actor Peter Stormare, but somehow, I doubted that he was Swedish. I got a distinctly Eastern European vibe from them both. Perhaps it was the effect of having interacted with Ivan, the nice Romanian waiter. I would find out if I could, and as unobtrusively as I could.

The man I had spoken to smiled back, took his seat, and said, "I am Vasily Legasov. I am a retired scientist, as is my friend, Boris Volkov."

Vasily had a very pleasant, guileless smile. Actually, it was a big, silly grin. He was a nice guy, I thought, and I continued to think so as lunch continued. He was affable, and easygoing. When he smiled, his eyes were upturned into slits, and that grin took over his entire face.

His traveling companion was like a foil to his personality, though; he looked annoyed by the openness and friendliness.

Nevertheless, the conversation continued without a pause.

"Oh, how interesting," Pearl, George, and Declan chorused.

I wanted to hear more, even though I could have sworn that Boris kicked Vasily under the table.

Alice said, "It's unusual to see anyone besides Americans, some Canadians, and perhaps some Australians on these tours, and I've been on three other cruises. Where are you two from?"

Boris sighed, and settled back into his seat as Vasily said, "We're from Russia. We wanted to travel around and see some countries that we never had time to visit and learn about while we were working."

Nods all around.

"Tell us about your work," I asked. "What branch of science did you work in? Do you each have a Ph.D.? If so, what are they in?"

Boris looked rather annoyed, but not Vasily. Why would anyone with a Ph.D. not be proud of it and willing to tell what it was in, I wondered?

Vasily replied, "We both have Ph.D.s, and they are in biomedical science and virology."

"Very interesting," I said. "Are you saying that you each have one in each of those areas?"

They both now smiled modestly and nodded "yes" to that.

Everyone looked suitably impressed. I was leaning over my soup, eating the last drops of it, hanging on every word.

Aunt Eloise was listening with a polite but interested smile.

"My husband has two Ph.D.s," I said. "Where did you work? At the same place? At a university?" I was curious to hear more about them.

Boris looked a bit frustrated. He picked up his crackers and offered me some. "Try some of my rye crackers. I make them as a hobby."

"Oh, no thank you. I don't like rye. I'm fussy," I said.

Aunt Eloise laughed. "Yes, she's very particular. But she loves all things French."

"Well, except for sweetbreads and foie gras," I said with a grin. "No brains, liver, or other organs for me!"

The other Americans all laughed and agreed with that.

"We're going to get full eating the work of the gourmet chefs here anyway," I said to the Russians. "Aren't you excited about eating it for a whole week?"

"Oh yes," Boris said, "but I always eat some of these with my medications."

"Oh…" We all nodded and left it at that.

"So, where did you two spend your careers, and doing what sort of work? I'll bet that will be fascinating to hear." I picked up the previous topic, not willing to be deterred.

Boris looked rather frustrated, but not Vasily.

Vasily seemed a lot friendlier and more approachable…and likeable.

"We were colleagues at the ISTC – the International Science and Technology Center in Moscow, and later in Astana. We worked in biopreparat."

"Fascinating," I said. "How was it living in Kazakhstan after being at home in Moscow?"

Boris looked at Vasily, who didn't notice, and said to me, "Are you sure you don't want to try a rye cracker?"

I looked at him, nonplussed. I noticed that he was opening a different package of them, and that these crackers looked slightly different – speckled.

"No thank you. It's just a flavor that I have never liked. Especially the seeds. That batch looks like it has seeds. I really just want to eat the French food."

Boris withdrew the crackers. I didn't care if I was offending him. I would not eat something I didn't want – not even a bite – just to avoid offending someone. I was actually annoyed that he hadn't taken my first refusal as my final answer.

I turned back to Vasily, hoping for an answer about Astana.

He smiled and said, "It is called Nur-Sultan now. It was nice there. The city has a beautiful, modern, new area, a showcase, in fact, and the people there are very nice to be around."

We all nodded and smiled, satisfied at last with that information, and began to talk amongst ourselves about other topics.

It turned out that both of the professors and I had something in common: we loved to watch *The Late Show with Stephen Colbert.*

"He's great at miming, and he loves to perform," I said. "And, of course, his political commentary and 'Meanwhile' segment is great. 'Quarantinewhile' won him an Emmy Award – that, and the rest of his show-via-Zoom. He did better with that than the other late-night hosts, I thought."

"Yes!" George said with enthusiasm. "He really did, and it was fun to see his wife helping him. We got to see his dog, one of his sons...I switched around to see the other late-night hosts' families, too. It was fun, and made them seem even more relatable."

"I did that, too," I said. "But Aunt Eloise is an early bird. She doesn't know these comedians like we night owls do."

She and I both smiled at that.

"When Arielle visits me, she gets up around 9:30 a.m., and stays up reading for a while after I go to sleep. But it's okay; we have the whole day to spend together."

Alice asked, "What do you do together?"

"We visit the historic house museums of Newport, then take a drive to Westport, Massachusetts, and tour the farms there."

"My aunt loves to draw certain places in that town. Her favorite restaurant is there, too: The Bayside Restaurant."

"They have eggplant fries with peppercorn and chipotle dips. She likes the chipotle one. And the most wonderful cornbread!"

"Aunt Eloise loves that cornbread. It's made with orange zest and a particular brand of cornmeal – Gold's."

Alice was already looking it up on her phone. "Found it! I'm going to go there at some point. It sounds great. Thank you for telling me about it."

Dessert arrived: berries and soft cream with a cookie stick in it.

We smiled, enjoyed the rest of our meal, and listened to the others talk about their families and their interests. Alice would be taking the excursions that involved a lot of walking to vineyards, of course, and those lasted all day.

If we did that, we would miss out on the art, archaeology, and historic sites, we told her when she asked why we hadn't chosen the all-day excursions.

"Plus, a break in the middle of the day is nice," Aunt Eloise added.

All excursions had had to be booked online, in advance, with fees paid for some, while others were included in the basic cost. Lucky us; we just happened to want the included ones.

Back in our room, Aunt Eloise had a question for me.

'Arielle, what is biopreparat?"

I looked at her.

"It's preparation against the possibility of a bioweapons attack. Virologists do that in Fort Detrick, Maryland, and they keep a stockpile of microbes to study, plus a small number of vaccines. If we actually got attacked, we would have the raw materials with which to make lots of vaccines against whatever microbe – smallpox, bubonic plague, anthrax – but we don't keep vast quantities ready. People would still die before the response was fully mobilized."

"So we have to worry about nuclear weapons attacks, chemical weapons attacks, and this."

"Yes, and you just listed all three in decreasing order of cost. Bioweapons are the cheapest to produce, which actually makes them the scariest ones out there. They can be made at home if a scientist knows what they're doing, including personal protective equipment, depending on the microbe."

"Why not keep enough vaccines available all the time?"

"There is a U.N. bioweapons treaty, which was signed in 1972, saying that no country shall create stockpiles of a microbe as weapon, and to do so would look like a violation of it. It's called the Convention on the Prohibition of the Development, Production and Stockpiling of Bacteriological (Biological) and Toxin Weapons and on their Destruction. Yet, for defensive purposes, the United States, Russia, and other nations maintain institutes with laboratories and at least some supplies of many really nasty microbes to study all this – just in case."

"No wonder Boris didn't want Vasily to talk about it." Aunt Eloise thought a moment, then added, "He seemed to know that you understood what he was saying."

"Definitely," I said. "It took a while to understand what was wrong, since reading people is not my forte, but he was a bit obvious by being unfriendly."

"Well, we won't bother him with any more questions about it, so he ought to be able to relax."

"I didn't think he was relaxing at all. He kept trying to give me those rye crackers. It was really annoying!"

Aunt Eloise laughed. "You are no pushover, though, so he couldn't distract you. You were smart not to take any, even if you had liked rye. I wouldn't take something out of a package that someone else had been carrying around, much less eating from."

Indeed.

We got ready to go out again.

We were going to see the ancient Roman aqueduct, Pont du Gard.

It was on our bucket lists, and we were excited to see it.

Vasily and Boris headed back to their cabin after lunch.

They were going to see Pont du Gard, too.

I could hear them talking as they headed up the staircase, presumably to go get their gear for the afternoon's tour.

It sounded as if Boris was displeased with Vasily, who was arguing back. He sounded defensive, like he was a bit annoyed at being bothered about something.

Somehow, I was sure that it was over telling me what they had done for a career.

Footsteps by an Ancient Aqueduct

Footsteps by an Ancient Aqueduct

It was a beautiful, bright sunny day, and a bit hot.

We were on our way to see the famous Roman aqueduct, Pont du Gard. Jérèmie was our guide to this UNESCO World Heritage site. He was perhaps in his early thirties, with dark brown hair and brown eyes, tall, and thin. He wore a plain white shirt that buttoned up the front and long pants.

He introduced us to Gaston, our driver, a middle-aged man with a huge, friendly smile who wore his sunglasses perched on top of his stubble-haired head. Somehow, he managed to look cool. It seemed to be all about attitude.

Or maybe it was the French mystique, combined with all of the walks that they build into their daily lives. When I was a teenager, I had participated in a summer exchange program with a French boy from Toulouse, and learned about the regimen of daily walks. Portion sizes of everything were small yet satisfying, and I never saw anyone who was overweight.

But back to the tour…

We were driven to the Gardon River, and then were directed again by a lollypop sign made of cardboard, boarded the appointed bus, and found ourselves with perhaps twenty other people on the tour. The drive took under an hour.

Jérèmie led us from the bus to the visitor center, which was a bit of a walk from the famous site. The visitor center had been built over and around some fascinating ruins, complete with detailed exhibits of archaeological artefacts in the lower level. He paused outside to talk for a while.

The area where we stood was partially shaded from the direct, intense sunlight by a trellis. One side had a café and gift shop. The other side led down into the museum and theater.

On the walls of that side was a map of the entirety of the area:

After we had listened to Jérèmie outline our tour's agenda, he led us down into the air-conditioned building. We were then treated to a lecture about thermal baths and how they were engineered, complete with cutaway looks at the remains of some.

Lead pipes were used, which is really the only drawback to Roman water delivery infrastructure. A sewage draining system was part of their ancient cities, and the bathhouses had everything that a modern health club offers, including exercise classes, baths, toilets (with no privacy other than sex segregation), and mosaic murals of women in outfits that resembled bikinis as they played an athletic game.

Photography inside that gallery was not permitted, so I did my best to remember everything that I saw. I'm pretty good at that, though I would have liked to be able to show my family those mosaic tiles.

When Jérèmie was satisfied that his lecture had included enough data, he led us up into the afternoon daylight, through the mulberry trees that lined the outdoor atrium, and off toward the aqueduct itself.

As we walked, he pointed out an olive tree that has been alive since A.D. 908. It was given to the site when it was declared a UNESCO World Heritage Site in 1989.

This tree looked great for its professed age. Its trunk swept around, spiraling upward in graceful curves, and it had lots of leaves. I should have asked about its olives!

Just around the corner was the famed Pont itself.

A pont is a bridge, and the Gard, also known as the Gardon, is a river. Pont du Gard is an ancient Roman aqueduct, built between 40 and 60 A.D., with no mortar. The water ran through the top level. In the 19th century, a train passageway was added on one side. It's still there, but is open only to foot traffic today (and that's a good thing).

We stood on the side with the walkway and listened to our guide for a few minutes. At this point, he announced that, after he spoke, he would show us one more spot, and then leave us to walk around for an hour. After that, we had to be back on the bus by 4:45 p.m.

For a moment, however, he made a mistake and said 5:45, but in French time – meaning that he told us to be back at 17:45 hours. The French use military time. I double-checked this with him for the group, and he jumped, horrified, and practically shouted, "Oh no, I mean FOUR forty-five – sorry! Be back at 4:45!"

I laughed and joked that it would have seemed odd if he and Gaston drove back later with almost none of us.

He nodded, having calmed down, assured that we had the right time and would be going back with him and Gaston.

Jérèmie led us right up to the aqueduct and told us about the train, and that the water flowed all through the mountains around us. We all looked every which way for a moment at those mountains, and then at the aqueduct again.

He paused to show us a few more things, including a sign that warned visitors not to climb onto the monument. Clearly, lawyers had thought of stupid tourists taking lethal selfies. I guess that is a problem all over the planet now. I was glad I was an old-fashioned tourist, with my heavy Nikon camera. No such stupid risks for me!

We all stared up at the ancient aqueduct, and listened as we were told that it still worked. Of course, today the French relied on other water delivery systems, but it was, nevertheless, amazing to consider that an almost two-thousand-year-old piece of infrastructure still functioned. How was that for posterity?

Jérèmie told us that 44 million gallons of water passed over a distance of 31 miles through a narrow space of 25 inches in this ancient piece of technology. The stones weighed 6 tons each, and were hoisted as high at 160 feet to build it. 800 to 1,000 workers built it, and that data was something I checked later. I had wanted to know – were they workers or slaves? They were workers.

Next, he brought us around to the right and down a short path. And then we looked up and saw it, presiding in its glory over the Gard (or Gardon) River. It was a spectacular sight.

We could smell the river below, and even glimpse some fish swimming in it. It gave off a distinctly salty scent. A flat riverbank of small gray rocks ran up to the water, the level of which seemed very low.

Some people were sunning themselves on a blanket. Others were swimming, and we even saw a canoe. Maybe it wasn't that shallow after all. But I did wonder how anyone could be comfortable lying on only a towel over rocks.

Jérèmie announced that, if we wanted to walk the 80 steps down, we could go and take a closer look. There was plenty of time for that, and to go back to the visitor center and see the movie about Pont du Gard, he said. It played over and over again, continuously.

Good to know; we definitely wanted to see it.

We looked through the trees as he left us.

The path down to the river looked steep, and I knew that it would take me a while to go down it, balancing carefully, panicking over the height, and so on.

Also, I was not about to drag my aunt down 80 steps, nor have her wait for me at the top. Her knees certainly didn't need those narrow steps. So, we went back up the short hill to watch the 15-minute movie about the aqueduct.

We found ourselves alone for a few minutes as I took my photographs. Aunt Eloise took some with her phone to show Dylan, my cousin, but she didn't bother with very many. I would be sharing all of mine with her anyway, when we got home.

I hoped Dylan would find my efforts adequate – he was a professional photographer!

Well, I was satisfied with the images I shot.

And then there was my father...enough of that! This was my vacation, and neither of them could do anything about choosing the angles at which I shot from.

I laughed at myself, and then paused, listening.

"What is it?" Aunt Eloise asked.

I listened some more.

"I thought I heard people talking very quietly, in English and in Russian, and walking near us. Then no talking; I only heard footsteps after that."

Aunt Eloise said, "Well, I don't hear anything now."

"No, neither do I. But I'm not going near the edge of anything – as usual! And it would take too much time to go down and up those steps. Let's go back now. Have you seen enough?"

She nodded and smiled. "Yes, I have. Let's go."

My aunt did seem ready to go back.

The movie was interesting, and we would have regretted it if we had skipped it. After that, we checked out the gift shop, and bought a few postcards, and then went back to the bus.

A few older couples were already on it.

I noticed that Max and Karen came back about ten minutes later, chatting about missing a mass. Karen was hoping that Father O'Something wouldn't mind.

Somehow, I thought he would get over it even if he did.

Not far behind them were Vasily and Boris. Vasily had a camera, too, and he was smiling.

"Did you go down the steps to the river for a photograph?" Aunt Eloise asked him. "We decided not to."

"Oh yes, I did," he said happily. "And some nice local people who were sitting down there took a photograph of me and Boris in front of the aqueduct." He showed us on the camera's back viewscreen.

"Nice!" I said, smiling.

Boris looked like he was enduring it, but Vasily didn't notice. He packed up his camera with a satisfied smile.

I just had the lens cap on mine; no sense dragging a camera bag everywhere I went!

I wondered about those two. They didn't seem to be a couple – just retired colleagues. But they didn't seem to be friends, either. Perhaps they were just two people who knew each other and both wanted to travel here. I wasn't about to inquire further.

A half-hour later, everyone else was back and the bus took off to rejoin the *Sif*.

It was well worth the trip to see Pont du Gard.

But what about those footsteps?

Later that evening, I put such thoughts behind me because it was time to enjoy another delectable meal.

Part of the fun of telling the tale of this adventure, with its excursions, interactions with many different people, and feasts of art, history, archaeology, and culture, is the feast of gourmet French food.

Aunt Eloise and I were having a wonderful time with it!

There were crab cakes with a delicious rémoulade sauce to start off the evening's meal.

We enjoyed every bite.

Meanwhile, we chatted with some nice people from Philadelphia, Dionne and Isaac. They were retired (this entire set of passengers, except for me, was retired!). Dionne had been a librarian at the Wharton School of Finance there, and Isaac was a professor emeritus economics from that school.

Dinner was scallops over a potato purée with asparagus and garlic cloves – soft, sweet, pink, roasted garlic cloves.

Crepes with Sauce à l'Orange and vanilla bean ice cream.

It was worth ingesting every last delectable calorie.
We would walk it all off tomorrow!

Arles, Lavender, and Odd Glances

Intrigue On a Longship Cruise

Arles, Lavender, and Odd Glances

Arles (don't pronounce that "s"!) is where the Dutch impressionist Vincent van Gogh spent his most prolific period (over 200 paintings). The yellow house where he stayed with post-impressionist Paul Gaugin is gone now, but the hospital where he stayed remains. It's not a hospital now, however. That site has a garden for the public, and a museum, and a shop, and there is a little café.

Any point of interest in the city of Arles that has something to do with Vincent van Gogh is marked in the paving stones with a metal plate and an outline of him carrying his work materials.

Our guide, Cécile, talked to us a bit about the artist. She said that he likely had a combination of bipolar disorder and epilepsy, hence the fits, rages, and hospitalizations. She didn't mention Asperger's, but I know it when I see it in a historical figure. He had it.

The Cafe de Nuit, where he created one of his most famous paintings, has changed ownership many times over the past couple of centuries. She disclosed that he never ate there, as the food wasn't very good! A new owner has it now, and has chosen a name that is as similar to the painting as possible. The menu was outside on a chalkboard.

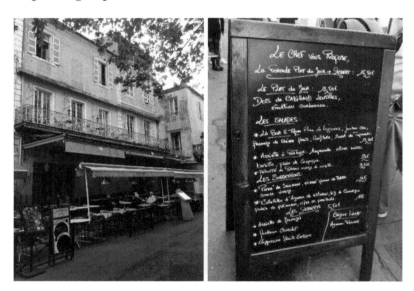

Cécile showed us the hospital where Van Gogh stayed. It has a beautiful garden now, and is called the Espace van Gogh.

We walked around the courtyard of the place, took photographs, used the restrooms, and visited the gift shop, which was full of products that reproduced Van Gogh's paintings. I found an eyeglass case with a cleaning cloth in it with a Café de Nuit theme on both.

Van Gogh was most prolific during his time in Arles, 1889-1890. Outside, the place looked like a walled fortress:

Cécile also showed us the city's ancient Roman sites, including an arena which is called the Arles Amphitheatre. It was built in 90 A.D./C.E. (Anno Domini/Common Era).

We climbed up the massive white marble blocks, which were half as tall as an average-height human, and sat on the massive, hard stones to listen to her. Each one was a huge cube of white rock, probably marble, and as high as my waist. Les Arenes, it was called en français. It had seating for 20,000.

Cécile told us to sit on the stones.

Max appeared at my left and gestured to me to go up first.

"No thank you!" I said, "I don't like heights. And my aunt's knees don't like climbing."

Max glanced at my aunt, looking a bit annoyed.

Aunt Eloise just nodded at him agreeing with me.

Granted, as an Aspie, I am terrible at reading facial expressions, but I was annoyed back, whatever his reason for not liking my refusal to climb any higher. No one should pressure people to do that.

Max went up to the next level of stones, and I turned to concentrate on the level right in front of our guide, which overlooked the arena floor. We were the equivalent of one story up from it.

I hauled myself up onto one of the huge white blocks, and Aunt Eloise did the same right next to me. I was sticking to my plan of staying with my aunt and avoiding any areas that seemed high up; I don't like to be high up unless there is something to hang on to, and even then, I don't go near edges. Avoiding vertigo so that I could focus on memorizing everything I learned while photographing it occupied most of my attention.

Cécile told us that, when the Roman Empire fell, so did centralized government. That plunged Europe into the Dark Ages and the Medieval time, I knew. My hope for specifics was not to be disappointed; our guide was full of vivid details of life in that time here.

After the Roman Empire fell, Cécile said, the interior floor of the Amphitheatre was completely filled with about 200 houses, as the city walls did not yet exist. The people were using the arena itself as walls for security.

I imagined what that was like: a tiny city-full of people residing in the small space (for a city – of course, I was judging it by present estimations of what constitutes a "city"), all to keep themselves safe from marauders.

Still, inside the Amphitheatre itself was safest. Others took the risk of living outside and farming to feed the lot of them.

This was during the Dark Ages – the 5th to the 10th centuries.

But even after people spread out beyond the Amphitheatre, deeming it safe to live around it as well as inside it, there were still many houses inside until the late 18th century.

Finally, in the 19th century, those houses were removed, and events of various sorts began to be held inside it once more. Bullfights replaced gladiator games, trading the wholesale slaughter of one species for another.

In addition to the security afforded by the Amphitheatre, there were also more walls built around a larger area (which today seems small), complete with gates. Walls, which are now in ruins with only their gates still standing, delineated the city limits of Arles in Medieval times. The gates are now all open, and their decorative effects are preserved.

She walked us out through what had been the concessions areas, and showed us some ancient plumbing systems in the passageways around the arena. The exits have what we today find to be a hilarious name, if a bit gross: vomitoria. The exits vomited people at the end of each show.

The site had restrooms, which we used, and while we were in there, I saw Karen. She was washing her hand off carefully.

"What happened?" I asked, looking at the blood washing away.

"Oh, it's not a big deal," she said. "I scraped it on those stones as I climbed up to listen to the guide. It doesn't hurt."

She had scraped the heel of her hand, but it wasn't a deep cut.

I imagined the ancient Romans – Gaulish Romans – attending events here, and realized that this must have happened a lot. The seating area certainly hadn't been comfortable. I wondered what sorts of concessions had been prepared in those little ovens that we were shown on the way out of there, too.

We came out of the arena and saw shops that sold sweet-smelling sachets of lavender – "lavande" in French – and then came to a wall with a fence after walking a bit farther.

Cécile told us about French bureaucracy. She said that it takes many months to arrange a visa to travel to certain countries, such as India, and that her son was a high school teacher who missed out on a trip there with his class because he waited too long to apply for one.

Sigh. (I learned that exclamation from Aunt Eloise.)

She walked us past the building where one applies for visas:

The problem, she said, it that it isn't open very often, nor for long. How infuriating, I thought – not enough chances to take care of business!

Our guide continued on through the city, showing us the ruins of a Roman theatre, which was built to hold performances outdoors. It is now behind wrought-iron fences, with a carefully curated museum entrance, but plays are still performed in it. And why not?! It makes sense to use the premises for their intended purpose.

We looked in at the ruins of the outdoor theater. Actors and actresses were killed after the performances as part of the entertainment, unlike in Greek performances, she informed us.

Intrigue On a Longship Cruise

We listened to her as we walked along, mostly keeping our eyes on the historic and archaeological sites, but at this point, we all glanced at one another, appalled.

One glance, from Boris, however, was different. He was staring at me! I looked back at him as if to say, "What do you want?!" Seriously…was he expecting me to look dramatically horrified and surprised by this? None of us were. We knew what an empire was, and the United States is one. All empires have odd entertainments. We have football, with horrific, crippling injuries to limbs, and concussive damage. Attendance is optional, not required.

Boris looked away.

It occurred to me that he and Max had been on this tour, as had their respective traveling companions, Vasily and Karen. Vasily and Karen were enjoying the tour. Max and Boris, however, each seemed to be gauging everyone's reactions to the lecture. Boris seemed to check on my reaction often.

It annoyed me, but I didn't let it ruin my good time.

As she walked along, Cécile would pause now and then to show us photographs in a book of images in plastic pages. It contained the sites as rendered by artists, showing how they looked in Roman times, plus people today in the city, attending various events. They would dress as ancient Roman citizens for plays:

She also had some images of Arlésienne girls in traditional gowns and ribbons. They compete to represent their city, she told us, and the most beautiful and most intelligent is chosen. A brain is required, of course, to talk about the history and culture of Arles. I found some postcards with that artist's work later and bought them.

The best lavender store in Arles is called Le Chateau du Bois, Cécile told us. It smelled wonderful in there, and we shopped in it.

Le Château du Bois
42 Rue de le République
13200 ARLES
France
0033 (0)4 9052 01 35
http://www.lechateaudubois.com/en/home

I noticed our excursions director, Clotilde, in the street by this shop while we were there. She was dressed in blue jeans, sneakers, and a jacket with the Longship logo and red color – comfortable for walking around cities and towns. She was checking on our tour.

Aunt Eloise loved lavender. When she was a kid visiting her maternal grandparents in the Bronx, the bathroom smelled like lavender, thanks to the products that Great-Grandma Rénard used.

She made sure to buy some lavender soap and lotion, as did I. It felt really special somehow, even though there were plenty of places to get lavender back home. I guess it was because we were buying French lavender, produced locally, and we were close to the source. And, as an added dividend, it just smelled wonderful.

We were shown the city hall and a few other sites, too, plus some shopping areas. The buildings were beautifully appointed, imposing structures with a copper fountain in the courtyard that warned us that the water was not potable.

As if anyone would actually drink it! It wasn't running anyway.

We looked around the square – the Place de la République – at the buildings, and noticed that one of them had been turned into a museum.

It was at this point that Cécile announced that we would have some free time, and then be led back to the bus. Accordingly, as we did at the official end of each tour, we all plied her with coins, worth one or two Euros – tips.

When it was time to go back, I ended up walking with another guide, Lisanne. We went ahead, just a few paces faster than the others. Aunt Eloise hung back, chatting with Pearl.

As I walked with Lisanne, I talked about Van Gogh, telling her what I had learned about him before coming on the trip.

Several years ago, the CBS magazine show *60 Minutes* did a story on him, one which I mention from time to time, in which it told the story of his death. This is it:

The life and death of Vincent van Gogh | **New revelations about Vincent van Gogh's death suggest that the troubled Dutch painter may not have killed himself after all.**

He did not commit suicide, and he likely had Asperger's. He was shot by a stupid, wealthy, irresponsible young man who was fooling around with a pistol as he walked back at the end of the day from a wheat field where he had spent the day painting.

He had hung around with a group of these kids out of loneliness and a lack of a group of his own, so they were people who knew him. When they found him stumbling back from the wheat field, the ones who knew the shooter took him in to lie down and called a doctor.

The doctor called the police.

Van Gogh lied to the police to save the boys from getting into trouble, and knew he would be easily believed due to his reputation for depression and difficulty earning a living. The lie worked, and when one of their friends (not the shooter, but perhaps a witness) was an old man, he talked.

As an Aspie myself, I won't let this go. The evidence does make it a plausible story. And just because Van Gogh had problems, that didn't necessarily make him suicidal.

There is a wonderful movie called *Loving Vincent* that analyzes the circumstances of his death. It is beautifully done entirely in the style of a van Gogh painting. My aunt and I had seen it on the plane as we traveled to our ship.

Lisanne listened, but would not accept that story of the artist's death, because it was not an official one accepted by the authorities. It was depressing to hear this, but I didn't bother hammering away about it. It wasn't a surprise anyway. I was mostly just satisfied to have shared it and attempted to sow doubt in her mind about the official story about Van Gogh, libel though it was.

Arles is south of Avignon, where we started. Overnight, the boat had gone south to the vicinity of Arles, and then headed back to Avignon while we toured Arles, so the bus drove us back there.

Once we were settled aboard again, we had another lovely lunch on board the *Sif*, which was followed by our afternoon tour.

Naturally, I shall not omit that lunch from this tale!

We got back in less than an hour, got comfortable, and headed without delay to the dining room.

I made a point of finding Selene and Michael, so that we could find out about his painting excursion. Aunt Eloise had fallen into a pattern of letting me lead the way to choosing our table at each meal, happy to see who I would introduce us to next. She, too, wanted to hear about this activity.

Michael had spent all day with a painting instructor, as had the rest of the people on that tour. It was a small group that we had noticed boarding a separate, small van – perhaps nine people.

"The instructor talked for a very long time," he said. "So long, in fact, that there wasn't as much time as any of us had hoped to work on a painting. I have it wrapped up in our cabin, but it's not finished."

"Will you finish it another time?" Aunt Eloise asked.

"Oh, definitely!" Michael replied. "I'll take it home with me and do it. It'll be fun. I'll remember what he talked about and just continue from there."

Lunch arrived – salads and more white wine.

We had the soup at every opportunity. The chef kept up a steady repertoire of smooth, velvety concoctions with fresh herbs, a few chunks of vegetables, and a wonderful taste. Today it was lentil soup.

"What did you paint? I mean, was it a scene, a still life, what?" I wanted to know. Clearly, we were never going to see what was a work-in-progress.

"It's a still life of flowers," Michael said. "I took a photograph of it for later, and I'll just have to do my best with that."

Selene took his phone from him, scrolled through the images, and showed us one of lavender, sunflowers, and greens.

"Definitely worthy of a Van Gogh-inspired painting session!" I said. "That looks beautiful without being exactly the same as his work."

Aunt Eloise looked at it and agreed.

"Aunt Eloise," I said, "I'm a bit surprised that you didn't want to go on that excursion."

She laughed. "I'm happier doing my black-ink and colored pencil drawings now, and I really just wanted to see Arles and spend time with you," she replied.

I smiled happily. I was glad; going along through Arles wouldn't have been the same without her.

Selene said, "You and I are artists, too, Arielle – with words. Don't you think so?"

I smiled. "Definitely! Writing it word art. I think of writing a novel like a painting. It slowly takes shape, with little touches here and there, embellishments, changes, and additions. Then I review it to see if I've has put too much of a thing here, there, and in other places – or not – and after spinning and weaving all of the details I want into it, it feels as though I've painted an elaborate picture in words."

"And she makes me hungry when she does that," my aunt said. "If she writes about this trip, at least I will have already eaten everything that she describes, because we keep ordering the same things."

Michael was listening, and he cracked up at that. "Of course you do. This is a food adventure as well as a tour of other pleasures. I can't imagine ordering steak and frites all week. There are people who are doing that. Have you seen that movie that's available in our cabins yet, *A Good Year?*"

"Oh yeah, and I'm sure we'll watch it again this week. Why not? I take it you are remembering that scene in which Russell Crowe's character plays waiter-for-a-day and tells those crass Texans who were seeking Ranch dressing in Provence that MAC-Donald's was in the next town, and to get lost."

He shook with laughter. "Yes, I am."

We all laughed.

"Well, none of us will do that!" Aunt Eloise said.

We all nodded, and ate our caramel sauce and bananas with gourmet cookie sticks.

It was warm, soft, and intensely flavored with vanilla bean. Definitely worth eating – and appreciating.

How one could travel and not want to eat something special, something that you don't find at home, was incomprehensible to us.

A Cobblestone Tour and Napoleon's Trees

A Cobblestone Tour and Napoleon's Trees

Our next stop was in the town of Viviers.

It is a small Medieval city on a hill, enclosed by a wall.

The boundaries of that wall had long since been outgrown, and the town stretched all around it.

Our guide, Josseline, met us at the pier and led us down the main street from the quai, which was lined with a variety of sycamore tree that was planted by Napoleon's troops all over the South of France to provide shade. These trees have a beautiful tri-colored bark. When the river floods, their trunks get submerged, but they recover and live on.

Josseline was 70 years old. She was a retired high school teacher of German, and she lived in a town nearby. The rest of her family, she said, had moved to the United States, but she loved this old town, and had no intention of leaving it.

I got the distinct impression that she wished that she lived inside the walls of Viviers, but it was fully occupied. I didn't blame her; she was a historic interpreter here, it was beautiful, and she obviously loved this place.

We followed her up the street, listening to her through our earpieces. Josseline told us that she would show us a few sites in the lower part of the old city, and then bring us up to the top to see the view. It was a very rainy day, with some mist, but I took photographs anyway. You can't always have perfect sunny days when you travel.

111

Once inside the walls, we paused in a narrow street to listen to Josseline. Almost immediately, we were distracted by a cat. It had gotten itself locked out of its house for the day, while its humans were off at work, and it was unhappy in the rain.

"I'm sorry!" Josseline said to it, as it meowed plaintively on its doorstep at her, looking up at the knob and back at her. "I cannot open…"

She took us down another street, found what she was looking for, and stopped in front of what seemed like a random doorstep. It was anything but random.

It had waist-high ledges on either side of it, made centuries ago. They were meant to hold a countertop that could be put out in the morning and taken in at the day's end, so that a shopkeeper could display whatever wares were offered for sale: baked goods, etc.

Josseline stood in the middle and demonstrated this ingenious set-up and we all imagined it in use week after week. "There were so many details to an old city," Aunt Eloise remarked, "details that one would miss without you!"

Our guide smiled, happy to be appreciated.

Viviers was full of lovely, hand-lain, cobblestone streets and hills. At some point during the 20th century, they were torn up so that the infrastructure below — drainpipes for sewers, etc. — could be rebuilt. The stones were then painstakingly re-lain. They go in multiple directions, which provides traction during the rain. It was raining, so we experienced this with our guide instructing us as to how to take advantage of it.

We walked all around Viviers in the rain, and on the Rue de la Roubine, we saw a Renaissance house that the city's tax collector built. It had beautiful carved faces on its facade. It was called the Maison des

Chevaliers. Josseline talked about the condition of this building, which had been falling to ruin. Historic preservationists had gotten involved, determined to take care of the carvings left by stonemasons. It would be terrible to let the details of the city fall to ruin from neglect, and volunteers who lived in Viviers were making good progress in raising funds for this in their spare time.

Josseline told us how it was paid for: with the tax money that the owner collected but didn't forward to the crown. Eventually, the king's officials got him and executed him. Some people are just idiots!

She showed us a bridge that was built to connect houses. Its purpose was to give the owners of the house more space without increasing the total of taxes that had to be paid. The less of the house that touched the ground, the lower the tax bill. I was reminded of the window tax problem that we learned about in Avignon.

Everything we saw was as beautifully constructed as it was functional. It was either that, or I just loved the aesthetics of it all. It was probably both.

At the top was the oldest section of Viviers, inhabited by only 23 people, Josseline told us. About those 23 people who live at the top of the hill in Viviers: they are not priests, even though they live in the cathedral quarter of the city. They are descendants of the homes' original owners, and many live alone.

The rest of the people in Viviers crowd into the other buildings.

She took us to the very top of the little Medieval city to look out at the view of the valley around us, and, off to the northeast, I saw nuclear reactor silos in the distance. "Yes," Josseline told me, "We rely on nuclear power."

I was disturbed to find this out. France, the most beautiful European nation with the best food (well, supposedly Belgium's was even better, but that wasn't the point!), produced that food due to a sweet spot of an ecosystem. I wished that nuclear fusion energy could be figured out and harnessed in time to replace it before anything went wrong!

We looked around at the view some more, and at the Cathédrale Saint-Vincent de Viviers. It was oddly familiar-looking, standing across the open, grassy space atop that hill. Josseline paused to tell us that it looked like a miniature version of Notre Dame de Paris. So that was what it was!

We turned to look around some more. All around us, there was a different view, and it was worth it. To the west, we could see the city falling away from our vantage point. It was all much closer, so the rain didn't impede efforts at photography. The images came out pretty well when I checked them.

While we were up there, Josseline brought us away from the cathedral, which she was saving for after the visit to the hilltop, to see the ruins of a tower: It had been a lookout point for the city's guards several hundred years ago.

After waiting for fifteen minutes or so to give us a chance to walk around, take some more photographs, and to just look out and admire the view from the top of that hill, she led us inside the cathedral, through the massive, carved, wooden front doors.

We all stared in every direction, admiring the carved, wood-paneled pipe organ, which was over the front door, and the huge, colorful, stained-glass rosette window.

Then she led us over to the right, and pointed out a plaque made of white marble. "These are the names of the men from Viviers who were killed in World War I," she began. I sensed what was coming next, and was glad that she would include it.

"In 1914, it was decided by the government that the population of Viviers was growing too large, so the young men of Viviers were conscripted to fight in the infantry on the front lines, to make sure that they died." Josseline stopped to let that sink in.

As someone who studied population growth in a finite world, my mind had already raced through the implications of all that, moved on to considerations of the emotional outrage that the entirety of the historical data added up to, and stopped at that.

I had a few silent thoughts about all this:

All those weddings planned and not had, and the dreams of brides cancelled. No lives spent with their guys beyond being boyfriends, or perhaps fiancés…well, maybe some became husbands before they got killed, but then…nothing else. Maybe some of those girls lived out their lives as widows raising kids alone, but not many, and if they had the chance to get married again, that would have been rare.

Better to just have access to as much birth control as one wants than to be stuck with a resource war, but humans are too stupid for that. Funny…academic conclusions never put it that way, but I think that they should!

My flat, deadpan demeanor betrayed none of this, however.

I left that to my spoken words, flat though their delivery was.

"So the powers-that-be – or were – rigged the system to ensure that these guys…135 of them…would not come home, get married, mate, reproduce, and thus add to the human population of Viviers," I said, summing up and underscoring her rendition of the facts.

"Oui, exactement," she said, then corrected herself, switching to English to say, "Yes, exactly." People lapse into their native languages when they get emotional, I have noticed.

"Overpopulation is an inflammatory topic," I said, "and one that I have studied with a mixture of fascination and outrage."

People turned to look at me.

A slight smile spread over my face – but only slight. It was borne from disgust at the human species. "It makes one angry at the previous generation for not having planned carefully – for having carelessly allowed one to come into existence, grow to full awareness of what one wants from life, such as good food, interesting work, and the enjoyment of a family, and then to be denied access to the resources necessary for all that."

I went on, "Access to birth control and the knowledge of when to apply it would have prevented such misery on the part of the women who lost these guys, knowing that they had lost their chance at all that. Plus, the guys knew that it was denied before they got killed. That's the cold reality, and it's important to notice the unhappiness caused by doing anything about the problem of human overpopulation. I'm not into acceptance and resignation."

Josseline smiled. "That's good."

"Yes. But, thanks to 20th century medical technology, Viviers obviously ended up overshooting its walls anyway. I mean, look at it; and you don't live inside its walls."

"No, and I would prefer to do so. It's beautiful, and historic. Outside, it's convenient and all new, but it loses all that."

"Do you shop for groceries at a Carrefour store?"

Josseline glanced back at me and smiled. "Yes. So, you know about French businesses."

"A little bit." I smiled politely.

The Catholics on the tour, however, looked displeased.

"But that would have denied their parents the chance to have them, which would have left those parents forever sorrowful at not having had children," said one of the Catholic ladies on our trip. She was now retired, no doubt with adult children and grandchildren. "Plus, Catholics don't believe in birth control."

I was smashing their comfort zone a bit, to say the least.

"Yes, I know," I said with a smile. "All that is quite selfish to the offspring. The parents get what they want, and the kids get misery. To then expect and require the kids to respond to that misery with acceptance and resignation is the ultimate act of selfishness. People have no such duty of obedience and acquiescence to authority on that count."

The Catholics gave up.

Our guide looked both pleased and amused.

I was thoroughly enjoying myself.

I looked at my aunt. She was trying to hide a smile.

We all headed down the steep city streets in the rain, but not far; Josseline wanted to show us a small, enclosed courtyard in the section of the city where that elite 23 lived. We were in luck! She was elated to find that her friend, who lived inside the city limits, and had a key to its gate, had left it unlocked for her.

We were pleased, too.

That friend was leading another tour group from our ship.

In we went, and Josseline happily showed us a well.

It was no longer used as a water source, thanks to the advent of water-delivery infrastructure throughout the city, all underground – under those intricately-laid cobblestone streets.

Down the steep streets we went, and I noticed that there were many metal, red-painted posts on the sidewalks. I asked Josseline about these, and she told us that they were there to keep cars from parking up on the sidewalks, thus making them unavailable for pedestrians. As for the red, that was just here, she told us. The color varied depending on the place in France, or the posts could just be left unpainted, showing the metal.

When we got close to the quai, I paused by one of those sycamore trees to look at their tri-colored bark more closely. It was peeling. Josseline said that that was due to the floods that happened from time to time, but that the trees were holding up. People in the South of France were worried about their continued survival, however.

Intrigue On a Longship Cruise

We had had a wonderful, fascinating time, we told Josseline, and thanked her as we gave her some Euro coins for a tip.

When we boarded the Sif, a nice surprise awaited us on the gangplank: Chef Ronne was waiting for us with trays of cocktails, served in little shot glasses that were shaped like cylinders with a heavy base. The maître d', Guy, was with him, and so was Jonathan, the cruise director, to help serve the drinks and relieve us of our tall, red, cane umbrellas.

These drinks were delicious – warm apricot brandy with a twist of orange. It was a small dose of alcohol, just enough for a lovely taste and a quick warm-up on a dank, rainy day; nothing that would intoxicate an adult.

It was perfect.

Later that evening, before dinner, I visited the laptop computers on the upper deck of the ship, in the library, and looked up Viviers on Wikipedia.

Its current human population was a mere 3,689, and yet it had exceeded the walls that bordered it. I wondered how many people those walls could actually house in reasonable comfort and space.

There was no population data for 1914, which was disappointing.

I thought about current world population. The total, according to worldometers.info, the world population clock, was now 8 billion – far too many for our food production systems to accommodate, no matter how much they were finessed by science and economics.

After that, I remembered our conversation with Boris and Vasily.

If I was going to look them up, I didn't want to be caught in the act; their cabin was on this level.

I glanced around at the library. It was an open room that anyone could walk through at any time. My back was to the cozy niche that overlooked the lobby and atrium area. The niche contained walls of coffee-table books and other recreational reading, plus four low, cushy chairs. I faced a wood-paneled wall.

Deciding that they weren't about to teleport into spots at my shoulders and stare at the screen at that exact moment, I proceeded to look up the International Science and Technology Center. It was a very short article. As Vasily had said, until 2015, the Center had been located in Moscow, Russia. After that, it was relocated to Kazakhstan.

Had these guys worked on vaccines, bioweapons, or both? And, what made it possible for scientists from a nation that notoriously paid them low salaries, to travel on a Longship cruise, a vacation that was completely unrelated to their work?

Deciding that I probably would not get any straight answers if I were to inquire further, I deleted my search from the computer's history and decided not to ask them anything about it again.

Boris had been much less than congenial.

Anyway, he was annoying, pushing with his rye crackers.

Next, I looked up Max.

After trying a Google search and the Blackstone website, I paused, frustrated. It made sense that I couldn't look up the people who worked there and read all about them. It was an exclusive, insular entity, after all.

But Wikipedia had a file on him.

It was all there: Blackstone, and Federal Reserve Board, and more. Max had been Trump's ambassador of sorts, coordinating pandemic response efforts between the CDC and P4. His responsibilities had been limiting costs (not a surprise!), and checking to see how soon travel restrictions could be lifted for business and tourism.

Good grief…making money ahead of health and public safety.

Intrigue On a Longship Cruise

I read through it all quickly and then closed that out, looking around to make sure that no one was observing what I was looking up.

The coast was clear; one woman sat alone in a cushy lounge chair, poring over a coffee-table tome about lavender. She was thoroughly absorbed in it. Good!

As I sat there, Aunt Eloise appeared next to me and asked me to look up our route, so we spent some time checking out places we were going to see on Google Maps. She wanted me to zoom in on the historic district of Lyon, because we were both interested in the marionette museum and shop there.

The ship had large screens here and there for passengers to look at with a version of Google Maps – the cartoon version. It showed icons for the *Sif* along the Rhône River and dots for the cities and towns.

What we wanted was the satellite version, so we looked at that.

Aunt Eloise used to make the most amazing papier-mâché puppets. She still had several, and brought them into elementary schools sometimes, just to amuse the students.

I had some, too: a green witch with detailed eye shadow and mascara, and red-painted pumpkin-seed fingernails was my favorite. There was also an old man with a white beard, scraggly hair, blue eyes, and a black, sparkly shirt. And a red-headed woman with her hair in a bun who reminded me of a drag queen. Her eye makeup was quite impressive, of course.

We found it: the Guignol Marionette Museum. There was a shop, which we hoped to visit, but it didn't look as though we would have enough time to go into the museum. Oh well...the website showed that the shop alone looked like the current section of a museum!

As we perused it all, Karen suddenly appeared, startling us out of our focus.

We didn't mind.

She was in quite a good mood!

"Arielle," she said, "I just wanted to tell you that I have been having a lovely time drinking the wine on this trip, with no headaches, thanks to what you told me about insecticides not being used in France. Thank you!"

I was amazed, but recovered quickly and said, "That's great!"

It was rather amazing; research and science had broken through.

The power of dispassionate data is unquestionable.

"What are you looking at?" Karen asked.

"A puppet shop and museum in Lyon," I replied. "I want to go there, and so does my aunt. She used to make some elaborate puppets, and we still have them."

"Oh, how interesting! Are you going to buy one?"

"I think so. Maybe more than one. We'll see," I said.

"Well, show me, if you get a chance," Karen said.

"I will." I smiled.

Good thing I had finished my other research before she showed up! The last thing I needed was for her to tell Max that I was looking him up on the internet.

Politics and Prose

Politics and Prose

At dinner that evening, we sat with Selene and Michael again, and we met a nice couple from Cambridge, Massachusetts. Their names were Dionne and Isaac. It turned out that the husband was a professor of physics at MIT, and the wife worked at the Isabella Stewart Gardner Museum.

"And what do you do?" she asked us, smiling sweetly.

My aunt introduced herself as the retired art teacher that she was, adding that she now does colored pencil and ink-point drawings. "I like Native American art, and have traveled as a camper all over U.S. National Parks. I saw many sites along the Lewis and Clarke Trail."

"Interesting!" Dionne said. She looked at me.

I added, not moving on from my aunt yet, "Aunt Louise graduated from the Rhode Island School of Design – bachelor's and master's degrees." I liked to brag about her, and she certainly wasn't going to do it.

Impressed glances were sent her way.

"She wants to hear about your career," my aunt prompted me.

I grinned. "I know. I just wasn't ready to move on from you yet." But now I was. "I graduated from the University of Connecticut School of Law, did my thesis on outer space law, which is a mix of international and environmental law, and moved on to editing academic journal articles of various kinds – not just law – for hire, publishing books on my own, as I am self-taught, and I am an author of 14 books. My imprint is called *PhantomCatBooks*, and it has a black cat logo."

"What are your books about?" the professor asked.

"Honeybee colony collapse disorder, banksters, hedge fundsters, corporatists, law, politics, dystopian science fiction, Asperger's, cats, and – my favorite topic – human overpopulation and the ecosystems collapse that results from it. My most recent book is a novel about a stranded female alien botanist. She was stuck here for the summer of 2020, when the pandemic was just starting."

Isaac looked impressed.

His wife looked at him. "What did you expect her books to be about, romance novels?"

He cracked up. "No, not really." He looked back at me. "You said you edit academic articles?"

"Yes – the kind that get published in high-impact, peer-reviewed journals. Everything is interesting."

There was a pause while our orders were taken. My aunt and I chose the crab cakes, coq au vin, and an almond tart.

At the next table, I could hear what Max the bankster ordered: steak and frites. He could get that in America, I thought, disgusted. Travel was wasted on him. It was like he was here for the luxuriousness of the experience more than anything else.

I turned back to our current dining companions.

They had ordered what we had ordered.

"But how can you follow what they are about without a background in science?"

"I can understand enough of it to follow them. Being interested in many things and curious about the world helps. The rest of it is about editing for the usual things, like grammar, spelling, punctuation, and, most importantly, flow. A lot of scientists are terrible writers. That leaves their work locked into a small audience – too small to reach enough people to change the world without someone like me helping them. And…my husband is a virologist who works in stem cell research. He's my human science encyclopedia."

"I see," he said, with a laugh…though I wasn't yet sure that he did. I waited.

"Could you follow a paper on the Higgs-Boson particle?"

"I don't see why not. When it was first understood, I read about it in *The New York Times* and watched the video on that site. It was fascinating – more like the "celebrity" particle than a "god" particle – with most other particles drawn to it, while the remaining ones moved around on the periphery, having a much easier time getting wherever they were going by not trying to move with the majority."

"Sounds like you were on to something there," he said.

I grinned. "Yeah…I ended up seeing it with my own metaphor. It was more like neurotypical people as most of those particles, being attracted to a star, while the particles that moved around the periphery, independently, were the ones with Asperger's – because we Aspies do that. That was how I understood it. I thought it was the coolest thing."

I paused and let that sink in.

The professor suddenly smiled. "Let's trade business cards. I may just hire you to edit my next paper!"

I smiled back, took out a card, and took his.

"He's working on a paper about the Higgs-Boson particle," Dionne told me, smiling at us.

"Wow – that sounds terrific!" I said, laughing. "So that was what you were up to: checking to make sure that I would be able to follow what you're writing about!"

Dionne and Isaac both laughed it up.

Aunt Louise looked thrilled, too, and happily picked up her spoon as the cakes with remoulade sauce arrived.

It was delicious.

So was the coq au vin that followed. We all enjoyed it.

Selene and Michael told us that they had been on Longship Cruises before.

"On one of them, a young honeymooning couple were among the passengers. Usually, the people who travel on those cruises are all older and mostly retired, but not them. The cruise was a wedding gift, and the couple left in the middle, because it was not their kind of fun. They wanted to meet lots of people their age and party, not tour historic and archaeological sites," Selene said with a sigh.

We all stared at her as she told us this, and then shook our heads.

"Yeah," Michael said, sounding disgusted. "They probably wanted a loud, party cruise. They probably went night-clubbing when they jumped ship. We were near San Remo, Italy, so I'm sure they found what they were looking for."

Selene suddenly grinned. "They were seeking a Higgs-Boson kind of vacation experience, I think.

We all burst out laughing.

"Ugh. No thank you," I said. "Older people are much more fun to chat with, and there's a lot less noise with a lot more interesting stories of careers, interests, whatever. I'd take this sort of cruise over that."

"Hooray for cultural tourism," Dionne agreed.

"Dionne," I said, "right after I graduated from college, my best friend from there, who lives near Boston, took me to your museum. It was right after the Vermeer painting and the others were stolen. That is a beautiful, fascinating building, with great gardens. Our visit was in the summer," I added. "And the café was a real treat."

"Yes, it is," she replied. I feel very lucky to work there."

"A huge part of the travel experience – at least, to me – is great food. I don't understand the idea of not going on a food adventure and trying the most delectable recipes, even at home in the United States. But...I don't want processed junk, or organs."

"Me neither," echoed both my aunt and the professor.

"I'm with you there," Dionne said. "The people who travel and want to eat the same sorts of things that they can get at home might as well just stay home," she added with a rueful, wry smile.

Isaac added, "I notice that a lot of the people on this tour are doing that." He glanced at Max as he said this.

Max, fortunately, was facing the other way and oblivious, chatting with a friend from his church group. So was Karen. Good!

Dionne asked about my novel. "So you had a pandemic book," she said, "about an alien. And a female alien. How did you come up with that?"

"Well, I read for fun about aliens before going to law school, then tried to write this same novel the day after I graduated, but it came out as the novel that went halfway to nowhere. Later, I realized that authors do that when they're starting out. Jane Austen did that with *Pride and Prejudice*; she wrote it, put it in a drawer for several years, and then rewrote and liked it. I figured that, if she could do that, so could I…twenty years later. I liked it when I rewrote it, and it had a point at last."

"What was the novel's point?" Dionne asked.

"It was that we humans are wrecking our planet's ecosystem with human overpopulation and pollution, and that our politicians aren't doing enough to stop it. They're more interested in power – at least, when the GOP gets in – and I spent a good chunk of the dialogue on that, chatting with the alien about it. Her species had been there and done that, which helped drive my point home."

"That's terrific," Isaac said. "I take it you talked about Trumpism, fascism, and a few other perniciously poisonous 'isms'?"

"She certainly did," Aunt Eloise said, as she polished off her coq au vin. "And she made me hungry, with all of the recipes she prepared in that novel – smoothies for the alien, and Indian food, and her own fruit tarts."

Isaac shook with appreciative laughter. "I want to read it just for the food, I think, but also for the politics. And you chose a female alien?"

"Of course. I'm female. Why not?" I replied with a grin.

"Why not indeed," he agreed. "Did you hear about the Harvard astronomer who wrote about an alien probe?"

"Oh yes – after my alien went home, of course, or I could have talked about that in the story, too," I said. "It was on *60 Minutes*, so I got the book and read all about 'Oumuamua. It was fascinating – and exciting. It was particularly exciting to read about how he dared to go ahead with his theory that it is at least a piece of a probe from another planet, rather than let his colleagues deter him. I loved that."

I looked at my plate as the almond tart arrived. It was a work of art. Every slice of almond seemed to have landed in the most attractive position on it, and the crust was flawless. It even had raspberry and apricot sauce, and a dusting of pistachios next to it. When I cut into it, it was soft, too.

Dionne stopped me there. "Wait – 'Oumuamua – what's that?"

"It's the name that was given to that object. It means "Scout" in Hawaiian. It got a Hawaiian name because it was observed from a telescope on Mau'i."

"That is cool!" Dionne said.

"Yeah...I love stuff like that."

"She does," Aunt Eloise said. "When she went to Hawai'i, she made a detailed study of the history, culture, art, volcanoes, and language. Then she wrote a travelogue about it all."

Isaac pulled out my card and studied the back of it some more, looking at the books on Hawai'i. I had two of them, because one was just the history bits from the travelogue.

Dionne turned to my aunt. "What about you? Did you write about your Lewis and Clarke tour?"

She laughed. "No. I drew things from it, though."

"We should make a website with your work on it, Aunt Eloise. You have lots of great pictures to show. You could have the photographs from your trip on it and your art. It would be great."

She rolled her eyes. "No...too much work."

"But it would be a great way to share it all."

"I'll think about it." She grinned, and ate the last bite of her tart.

We didn't feel like leaving the table just yet, so we all ordered decaf café au laits and hung around for another half-hour.

Isaac had another question for me.

"What about all those U.F.O. reports that came out last year?"

"You mean the ones in which the U.S. government admitted that alien spacecraft really do visit us, and that Air Force pilots have seen them and reported them, and that they're not going to conceal them anymore?"

"Yes, those reports."

"I was sorry that they came out several months after I published my novel. It was so much about the pandemic and masks and wearing masks that I didn't want to seem to dwell on the fact that I was writing about hosting an alien almost out in the open. As it was, I built in plenty of near-misses of discovery."

"You mean, discovery by outsiders that you had an alien in your house?"

"Yes."

"Can you give me a teaser/preview? I don't mind spoilers."

I thought for a moment, then agreed. "There was an incident with the in-laws in which the eight-year-old nephew left his mask on the kitchen counter and disappeared. My alien was trying so hard during the visit to seem polite without just taking off her mask and showing her whole face, and then it seemed to be all for nothing when he reappeared, having put on the alien's environmental suit. He messed it up. I tried to make it a distraction – an example of why I just don't want kids, but that suit had to be repaired. I was really worried that it was ruined...and that my brother-in-law, an aerospace engineer, would catch on."

Aunt Eloise look at me, nonplussed.

I suddenly felt the old worry that I had felt when that incident actually occurred. If that book is a work of fiction, why, then was I talking as though I were still so agitated about the incident? My anxiety was crossing over, and I hoped that I just seemed like an author who had built a good story.

Evidently, my aunt was the only one who was on to me, because the conversation moved on.

"What are the names of some of your characters? How do you choose them?" Selene asked.

"I have some preferences. I like all things French, and I use the Behind the Name website. I like to know what names mean. Roselle was the narrator. But for the alien, I made up a name. I used 'Canna', for a flower that Georgia O'Keeffe painted, because I was pretty sure that no one on Earth goes by that name. Plus, the alien is a botanist."

"I love it," said Michael.

"Well, you are an artist," Selene said, nudging him playfully.

"How did you focus on Georgia O'Keeffe?" he asked.

"I love her flower paintings, and I did my senior forum paper on her in college," I said.

"Aha." He nodded, understanding.

"We've been to Ghost Ranch," Selene said.

"Really?!" Dionne said. "So have we!"

And with that, the conversation turned away from my alien.

Good. I was afraid that I would give myself and her away if it hadn't done that!

A little while later, we were in the upper lounge.

Denis, the ship's piano man, was playing us some songs.

Okay...I just had to phrase it that way. And he did play some of Billy Joel's songs.

Denis knew a lot of them, and despite being French, he sung many American pop songs in perfect English, with an American accent.

It was too bad that there was no chance to ask him how he learned it all, if he had traveled to the United States at all, or whatever else we might have liked, because the idea was to let him entertain us continuously with the songs.

We enjoyed it, though, and many people sang along.

Then a beautiful sight came into view out the port windows.

It was the round Medieval tower over the old city of Tournon-sur-Rhône, lit up. Everyone moved over to get a good look, and I put my camera lens up against the glass for a photograph. It came out well:

"Kavi and your father and uncle will have a great time with your photographs when you get back," Aunt Eloise said.

"My mother will be interested, too. I'll write a blog post detailing this trip and put some of these images in it, and she'll have fun showing it to her friends and chatting about the post as they talk on the phone. I wonder what Dylan will make of my images, though," I added.

"I'm sure he'll think that they're very good," my aunt replied. "He's not here taking them, so he'll be pleased with what you do."

I laughed. "I mean, he's a professional photographer, trained in the latest digital techniques plus using them on social media. I'm self-taught, and not as tuned in to social media as he is. Plus, I have to climb over chairs and shoot the images as the ship moves."

She laughed. "Don't worry. The results look good to me!"

I looked at my camera's digital viewscreen and decided they were.

"Yeah…I can always crop the edges of lots of them anyway."

Later, in our cabin, Aunt Eloise waited until we were settled in for the night, and she asked me about it.

"Arielle, I know that you keep a sane grip on reality, and that you have never had any trouble separating fact from fiction, including your own."

I had been starting to get sleepy, but I jerked awake at this point.

I looked at her. "Yes…I do that." I waited.

"So…" Aunt Louise asked, "just how did you come up with the idea for that story? It seemed, from the way you referred to that incident and the damage to that suit, as if it were real."

I sighed. "Okay, you got me: it was real."

"I knew it!" she said, sounding vindicated.

I looked at her. "Don't tell anyone. I was afraid to tell you over the phone, the internet, anything that could be tracked by the Men in Black, whom you now know about from reading that story. Plus, I couldn't be sure that you wouldn't just think I had lost it."

"I don't think that you've lost it. And I won't tell."

"Thank you." I breathed a sigh of relief.

She gave me a very big grin.

A moment later, I said, "Actually, I'm glad you're on to me. I hated that everyone else in the family knew but you. The only way that Kavi's family could know was from a face-to-face visit, and only Sunil seemed to figure it out at the time, but my parents and Uncle Louis knew, so I hated it that you weren't in on it all along."

"Well," Aunt Louise said, "now I am. I know it's only because I live in another state. It's okay."

We settled into bed, and I picked up the *National Geographic History* magazine I had bought in the airport.

Aunt Eloise picked up a novel that she had brought. It was about Sacajawea, the guide who had led Lewis and Clarke on their expedition.

I read one morbidly fascinating article about ergot poisoning in Medieval Europe, flipped through the rest of the magazine, couldn't stay awake for more, and gave up.

So did my aunt at that point.

"I'll borrow your novel when you're done…most likely when we're back home," I said.

"Okay."

We were too tired to read at the end of each day that we went out on a tour. All that walking, listening to our guides, learning history, art history, French culture, and archaeology, plus visiting with people while being spoiled with gourmet French cuisine wore us out. But it was a good tired, and we could read when we were at home.

"Can't we, Aunt Eloise," I said, referring to the reading we would postpone. It wasn't really a question. In fact, even saying it was purely rhetorical.

"Yes, we can!" she said, settling into her pillow for the night.

She turned to smile at me before we fell asleep.

Sometimes, it's just fun to state the obvious.

I fell asleep soon after that, not feeling one bit guilty about not having done any reading. The book I had brought from Bradley International Airport could wait until I got home. It was *Hidden Figures*, about the African-American women math geniuses at NASA who calculated everything without a computer during the Mercury and Apollo programs. I could hardly wait to read it, but it would just have to wait, however cool it was, and it was obviously very cool. Oh well!

The bed on the *Sif* just felt too good not to fall asleep in immediately. It was just right, and I was just tired out enough to enjoy a good sleep every night.

Overflowing Cemeteries and a Train Ride

Overflowing Cemeteries and a Train Ride

Breakfast the next morning felt like a luxurious routine.

That meant that we were getting used to this.

"We're getting spoiled," I said to my aunt.

She just laughed and said, "Order something that you really want to go with the buffet food and enjoy it while it lasts."

I did.

Blueberry pancakes, maple syrup, and fresh berries dusted with confectioner's sugar seemed a bit unlike French food, but I also had a croissant with raspberry jam and a café au lait, plus several other delicious breakfast goodies, so who cared?!

We saw Max and Karen at breakfast, sitting with someone who had to be their parish priest and a few other people from their church at the next table, and waved as we came back from the buffet.

Dionne and Isaac sat with us.

Conversation was minimal, because we were all focused on getting ready to go out on our next tour.

It reminded me a little bit of college, all this steady keeping to a schedule of fascinating, intellectually-oriented activities. But it was better; no homework!

I shouldn't say that. I have a habit of assigning myself homework.

I was committing it all to memory so that I could label all photographs once I got home with them, and write up a detailed account of the trip for my blog.

After all, what was the point of traveling on such a wonderful tour if I didn't document it for other people to enjoy later?

"I agree with you on that point," Dionne commented. "We're going to do the same thing with our photographs!"

Good; I wasn't so peculiar then. Well...at least not among this group of people.

I knew damned well that I was peculiar among most people.

Most people did not go on such tours, if previous conversations had taught me anything. They opted for party cruises. How exhausting...

Speaking of exhausting, we were in for a day of lots of walking and moving around, which was actually good considering the extra calories that we kept taking in.

We were escorted to the pier, where we met Sybille, our next guide.

She stood waiting for us with the customary red lollypop sign and her microphone ready. Her hair was curly and shoulder-length; she wore minimal makeup and comfortable shoes.

I noticed that about the French women who brought us on tours: they were each beautiful in their own way, some elegant, some utilitarian, but all with just enough cosmetics as to enhance their features without looking shellacked. Their clothes looked comfortable and attractive at the same time. But, of course they did: walking was part of the job.

It contrasted with some of the American women on our tour, though. Not us; my aunt and I would never sacrifice comfort. I wore minimal makeup, and had pockets in every pair of pants and every skirt and dress that I owned.

Our shoes, as required by the tour company in the information that we had been given before departing, were all closed-toe ones. Mine were black Mary-Janes with thick rubber soles for walking. The point of that was to not have to worry about style whether we were walking or attending some event. (For a formal dinner, I had slipper-like dress shoes, also with comfortable rubber soles.)

The first things we noticed were more of those beautiful sycamore trees that Napoleon had had his troops plant. They were just everywhere. It was a gray, overcast day, which actually made them easier to look at in detail.

Sybille took us around the city, showing us a school, a church built into rock, a bridge, lecturing about it all as we went along.

We all took photographs and listened.

As it turned out, the tower we had all been so impressed and fascinated by the evening before was built into a cliff that overlooked the city. It was a château – the Château de Tournon – a museum.

We didn't go in, but instead, kept walking. Sybille had a lot of places to take us, on a whirlwind, fast-tracked tour of the area. That was okay, though; we wanted to see more than one thing.

We definitely did that; our next stop was outside a high school that had been founded in 1536 by Cardinal François of Tournon. It had a pretty yard behind an iron fence, and a statue to its founder.

From there, Sybille took us to the riverfront. She wanted to show us the bridge, which was fairly new for France. It wasn't for motor vehicles; it had wooden planks and was too narrow for anything other than pedestrians and bicycles.

In fact, as we stood at the end of it, listening to her explain that it was built to accommodate shipping traffic, higher above the river than its predecessor and with locks, a bicyclist came across it and almost crashed into me. Aunt Eloise dragged me out of the way, and the bicyclist, who was having trouble balancing, fell over. But it was okay; he wasn't going all that fast, and he wasn't hurt.

Next, she took us for a train ride. That was a short bus ride away. As we rode along, I asked about cemeteries, because we passed a large one during the ride.

"Sybille," I said, "I study overpopulation and ecosystems collapse, and I am wondering: Like every other nation, France has an ever-growing population on finite land. Cemeteries are not getting any bigger. Where do they put the corpses? Do they bury them, cremate them, what?"

Sybille seemed not to mind this question at all. But, she did not know the full answer to this. She told me what she did know: "Most people choose a burial in a cemetery, but it is for a period of only 30 years. An additional 30-year term may be rented if there are relatives to visit and tend the grave. I will find out more and tell you the answer before your afternoon tour."

"Great! Thank you very much. I am very curious to hear it," I said.

The bus drove on through the countryside and pulled into a parking lot. We all got out and looked.

We were to ride through the Doux Valley to see its beautiful views on the Train de L'Ardèche.

Sybille informed us the train had been used by farmers to move their goods down a mountain. We were to ride in the 10th car and see the engine turned around at either end.

We paused outside the trains to look around and photograph them.

We also had an opportunity to see some signs that showed us the historic site details and the lay of the land:

Then we boarded our train. It was, as far as we could see, an antique one, and very pretty, with ironwork in graceful curves and wood paneling and seating. It had a sign up in one corner, and I looked at it: regulations!

We settled into our seats and looked out the windows for the few minutes that preceded the ride. There was a turnaround apparatus right outside our car:

We got in, settled into the seats, and the train chugged slowly out of the station. The views were nice. We saw an old mill on a dam, and a bridge.

Suddenly, the train came to a halt. Something was blocking the tracks. How would we get back if the train's engine couldn't detach and move to the back car as planned?

No problem. It pushed us backwards. We hadn't gone very far. It turned out that a huge rock had fallen onto the tracks during the night, and would have to be removed later.

We got back on the bus, unperturbed, and rode off to collect four hikers and their guide, with Sybille lecturing about wines and rare vintages. Along the way, we saw a Valrhona chocolate factory.

It was only now that I realized that that wonderful, delectable chocolate was named for the Rhône River valley. I laughed at myself for never having thought that through until now.

Valrhona is some of the best chocolate in the world. When I worked at Williams-Sonoma, we sold it. If a bar fell to the floor and broke inside its wrapper, it was gleefully marked out of stock and "sacrificed to the tasting goddesses," as our supervisor phrased it. Sybille appreciated that sentiment.

Just before we boarded the bus for our afternoon tour, Sybille came and found me with the answer to my question about overflowing cemeteries.

The answer turned out to be that bodies were kept in their own graves only temporarily, as long as their relatives were still around and willing to pay the 30-year rental fee for the plot. After that, it was relocation to a mass grave, thus unmarked. "Only the famous can lie in place, undisturbed."

I would rather just be cremated and get it over with, I thought to myself! Cheaper, easier, and space-saving…

I thanked her for her research and promised to write her a great review, which I did later on in the day. The guides were impressive with their knowledge and with their determination to fill in any gaps, and no question seemed wrong or silly to them.

Intrigue On a Longship Cruise

Ancient Wheel Tracks and Roses

Ancient Wheel Tracks and Roses

Lunch had been a brisk but enjoyable treat.

Then we were off to see the city of Vienne.

(Yes, that's Vienne, France, with one letter different from the city in eastern Austria!)

The *Sif* had moved up to the north during lunch.

We were led to the gangplank, supplied with red cane umbrellas, and off the ship. It wasn't raining, but it looked like it could.

The city of Vienne had (you guessed it!) a cathedral and more ancient Roman ruins.

Each guide we met, and each site we toured, yielded some new and fascinating information. I was in my element. So was my aunt.

Our guide was a tall, thin, older man named Alain who had a short beard, white hair, a baseball cap, and wore jeans and a red jacket. He warned us to stay with him, as he was a fast walker. He looked it!

By now, I had told several of the guides, including Cerise and Sybille, that I had worked as a historic interpreter in the Mark Twain and Harriet Beecher Stowe Houses in Hartford, Connecticut. The major difference was that it was far more difficult for me to actually lose a tourist! A minor difference was that I had had to make sure that no one touched anything. Not here; these guides could allow us to sit on, lean on, and touch many things.

Alain took us through a park first, where he showed us a section of an unearthed, ancient Roman road.

The road had a foot-stone for pedestrian traffic – just one was left – and wheel tracks.

I took some photographs of it and stared at it as our guide talked about it, fascinated, losing myself in imagining what that road was like in ancient Gaul, which was what the Romans called France.

This was just a piece of what was once a busy road, full of carts and carriages drawn by horses and a few litters for aristocratic ladies being carried. It would have had some manure in it, perhaps a bit of mud, and plenty of rain coursing along it.

Pedestrians would have worn leather-strapped sandals and boots, and they would have definitely wanted to balance and hop their way across that muck on those foot-stones.

The park also had some beautiful stone statues:

When we had all looked at that, we moved on to see the Cathédrale de Saint Maurice.

As we walked through the city, I glanced around at our group. Both Vasily and Boris were on this tour, with Vasily enjoying himself immensely. So were several of the people from Naples, Florida, including their priest, though I had not learned their names as yet. We probably wouldn't have time to get to know them all, anyway. It was hit or miss meeting people at meals, and during the tours, we were busy studying and walking.

However, we did hear one name, which was that of the priest from whom I had been thinking of as Father O'Something. He was Father O'Shaughnessy. He had a jolly face with a steadily, happy mood to it, thin white hair, pale gray-green eyes, and a pot-belly that seemed incongruous on his thin body. He wore sneakers, jeans and a windbreaker, and no collar that we could see.

He wasn't wearing any sort of habit at any time on the trip. In fact, if Karen and Max had not been calling him Father O'Shaughnessy, we would not have realized that he was their priest, let alone a priest.

We did realize that he had been absent from the piano song fun of the evening before, but that was our only other clue.

Many statues on this cathedral and others in France were decapitated in October of 1793, at the height of the French Revolution. The reason was that they were mistaken for kings, and all royalty was being guillotined, so that meant symbolically doing it everywhere and anywhere that there was an image that even seemed like it fit that category. Thus, lots of saints lost their heads by mistake.

158

Or not...religiousness and religious worship was under attack at that time, too. The interim government outlawed it.

We went inside and looked around, listening to Alain.

Alain pointed out that some of the stained-glass windows had modern patterns, and said that they dated from the 1950s. They were replacements due to damage during World War II. The windows that hadn't been ruined, which were a little more than half of them, had their original figures of stained glass. I liked the original better, but what can you do?

Damn all wars... The new windows had beautiful hues of blue, but they weren't of the same quality. At least the windows were completed, and the weather was kept out. The technique used by Medieval glassmakers that gave the colored panes a satiny appearance had been lost over time.

We walked around on our own for about five minutes, looking at the beautiful tapestries that were hung along either side of the altar, and at the huge pipe organ.

Next, Alain led us to the left of the altar, to go down one of the side aisles of the cathedral, and out. It was definitely worth photographing, but the lights were off, and I wasn't going to break the rules by turning on the flash of my camera.

When I commented to my aunt about this problem, the priest turned on the lights! I thanked him and took the photograph.

I was amused to think of what might happen if the resident priest were to appear. Surely, another member of the same organization couldn't be faulted for showing off the premises in what was literally and figuratively a better light. But, no challenger appeared, so we just enjoyed the better-lit view.

Next on the itinerary was a Roman temple from the time of Augustus, the 1st emperor. It was named for him and his 3rd wife, Livia Drusilla, who was a ruthless and clever politician in her own right: the Temple d'Auguste et de Livie.

It wasn't a particularly large structure, but it was somehow impressive to look at. I noticed the plaque that had been added, almost a millennium and three-quarters later, when the city of Vienne decided that historic preservation was a worthwhile idea.

Meanwhile, the temple had been used as a church, until 1792, and then it was a commercial court, followed by a library and a museum. In the mid-19th century, it was restored and left as a historic site. Half of it was gone; this was only the rear part of the original structure.

As an amusing side detail, Alain pointed out a large sculpture to the right of the temple, in the square. It was made of thin sheets of metal, and it was of a cow, courtesy of the Yoplait corporation.

We glanced around at the buildings that were close around the temple. A bookstore faced the front of it, and something caught my eye: a copy, en français, of a Where's Waldo book.

Next: we were shown a Roman park called the Archaeological Garden of Cybèle, complete with the remains of an excavated sewer system, exposed by archaeologists.

We all listened to Alain describe what was once a thriving city meeting area, looking around as he spoke, trying to imagine it.

After that, we went up the hill to see a mural of people from many points in time participating in the same theatrical production, then walked back down again through a rose garden.

The roses were still in bloom, and I smelled and photographed some of the blossoms. Their scents were sweet, even in late October. There were pinks, of course, and white, red, and a peachy-pink. One of them was a unique beauty of red-and-white streaks:

Next, we headed for the city hall, passing a 900+-year-old building along the way. It was shorter than the others, and on the end of its block, with a lattice-work of wooden beams. Since the U.S. doesn't have any structures that are that old, I had to photograph it:

The city hall – hôtel de ville – was set into a car-filled courtyard:

At the hôtel de ville, we boarded a trolley that took us to the top of the city, to Mont Pipet. It was odd to think of a conveyance that didn't operate on tracks as a trolley. It was more like a series of modern passenger cars, all linked together.

We passed a cemetery as we rode through narrow streets of houses.

Once up on Mount Pipet, Phillipe pointed out the Roman amphitheater, which we could see by looking straight down.

It was called the Théâtre Antique to Vienne, and performances were held there. We could see the stage, with modern sound and lighting equipment under a covered, triangular structure behind it.

There was also an old church. We went inside to look around and hear a tale of some children seeing a vision of the Virgin Mary. Its door had beautiful ironwork.

I must admit that I zoned out during this lecture. The church contained some dimly lit statues that commemorated the incident, which were the main focus of the place. There wasn't much art to learn about, compared with what the cathedral had, but it was, after all, a small church. It was really all about one event, it seemed.

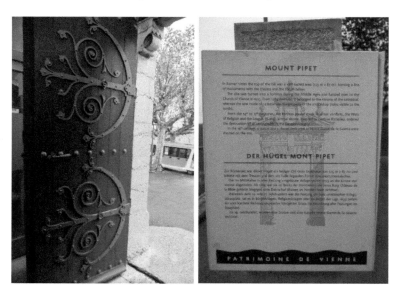

Intrigue On a Longship Cruise

It was still raining, and getting dark out. That was the end of our tour of Vienne, so we piled back into the trolley and headed back to the pier.

When we boarded the *Sif*, Chef Ronne and Guy were waiting for us with more cocktail glasses.

We all tromped up the gangplank, surrendering our cane umbrellas to Jonathan as we came in, and accepted a tiny cylindrical shot glass as we passed into the lobby.

I put the glass up to my mouth and gagged. Rye! It was rye whiskey.

"Ugh." I touched the liquid with the tip of my tongue. "I can't drink this. I just don't like rye." I went over to the front desk, gave back my tour card, got the room key-card in exchange, and looked around for a place to put the rejected drink.

Ana, the Portuguese woman who ran the desk during the day, smiled and told me I could just put it on the end of the desk.

I thanked her and did.

A moment later, so did my aunt. She had had just one tiny sip.

"You really don't like rye, do you?" said a person at my left shoulder.

I turned around and found Vasily there, smiling.

I wondered if he would be insulted on behalf of Russians and Eastern Europeans everywhere, and worried about that for a moment, but that wouldn't make me like rye, so I gave up on worrying and said, "No, I just don't. But, there are plenty of other flavors in the world."

He grinned at me. "Not to worry. We love rye, but it is the food we are used to, and this is a vacation, not a punishment."

He took one more shot glass, knocked it back like someone who needed a lot more alcohol to get drunk, and seemed stone-cold sober.

I shook with laughter just observing this.

Boris was knocking back a second shot, too. I think it was mine!

My aunt and I watched as the two of them had a couple more shots of the stuff, then walked off, grinning to myself.

Apparently, the rye whiskey wasn't a bit hit with most of the passengers, so Chef Ronne wasn't at all perturbed by this.

Vasily waved at us as we went.

In our room, we paused to relax before going out to the dining room. We used the bathroom, cleaned up and got comfortable, and turned on the news. I put the camera battery I had been using in the charger and installed the other, fully charged one.

The BBC was reporting a story about P4, the French version of the CDC.

Some scientist from there was sick, cause unknown.

I perked up at that and listened.

"Although the scientist worked with rare and highly infectious diseases, we can confirm that his illness is not due to one of those. The hospital staff is puzzled by his case, and are working to determine what is ailing him."

With that, the news moved on to efforts to move away from fossil fuels without resorting to more nuclear fission power, with a brief mention of the work being done to develop nuclear fusion energy.

Then it was time to leave for dinner.

We headed out into the hallway.

People were steadily coming out of their cabins, and we joined them. We were right on time, too: the doors to the dining room were open. Arriving early, we had quickly learned, meant wasting time hanging out in the ship's lobby, staring at the array of items for sale.

This evening's dinner companions turned out to be Joe and Stacey. They were from Florida, but they were not part of the Catholic contingent from Naples. This couple was from Orlando.

Joe was a large, burly guy with a thick head of graying hair who worked for a large food distribution corporation. He looked like someone who would fit into that world well, including any event that involved sports. I waited to see if that assessment would bear out.

Stacey had curly blonde hair and glasses, and a very serious demeanor. She was a molecular cell biologist, and she worked in a hospital.

"Really?" I said, interested right away. "What do you do there?" She obviously wasn't a physician or a nurse who cared directly for patients.

"I study the tissue samples taken from patients, and blood and urine samples, and anything else, to see what they are so that the doctors can make diagnoses and decide on a course of treatment."

"That's great," Aunt Eloise said. "Her husband," she nodded at me, "is a virologist. But he works in a university laboratory."

Stacey looked at us with interest.

I added, "He also studied stem cells, and that's what he works on."

Stacey nodded, and we let that line of conversation drop.

"Are you enjoying the tours?" Aunt Eloise asked her.

Stacey thought for a moment, then said, "Yes, in the afternoons." She smiled.

"She likes to sleep late in the mornings. That's what feels like a vacation to her," Joe said.

His wife nodded. "The tours are nice, just not the early ones."

Our order was taken next. Tonight, we met Malena, a waitress from Mykonos, Greece. She was a young woman with dark hair pulled back in a ponytail, high up on the crown of her head. I imagined that it was likely a lovely place to live, but not every resident could be a guide in some gorgeous scenic spot all year. No time to ask, though...

Dinner offerings included the usual steak and frites and salmon on the right side of the menu, and some interesting items on the left side.

Aunt Eloise and I immediately turned our attention to the left: We ordered the mushroom soup with red bell peppers and herbs, lamb with herbed Dijonnaise sauce, carrots, haricots verts, and potatoes, and, for dessert, gateau chocolate (that's French for chocolate cake!) with lingonberries, chocolate ganache, and a truffle candy.

Joe got the steak and frites.

Sigh...

He chatted with us a bit about his adult daughter, who was married to a guy with a Hispanic name. They had a couple of kids. I asked what Joe liked to do when he visited them.

"We see the grandkids, that's about it," he replied.

"Do you and your son-in-law have any interests in common?"

"Let me put it to you this way: he's the guy who sleeps with my daughter," Joe said.

Stacey looked less than pleased with his answer, but said nothing.

Rather than let an awkward silence drag out, I said, "It sounds as though you don't like him."

Joe didn't have anything to say to that.

I wasn't about to tell him about Kavi, my Indian-American husband. The hell with it; I suspected that he might say something nasty about him. Kavi and my father liked each other well enough, and would enjoy eating family meals and watching movies for hours amiably enough.

We managed to continue our conversation well enough, asking about what tours Joe and Stacey had chosen. I got the distinct impression that what he liked about this trip was being constantly on the move more than anything else.

When we went back to our cabin, however, my aunt surprised me by saying, "I think that Joe was playing with you, that he liked you, and so was showing off for you."

"Showing off?! How – by acting like a jerk? Stacey looked displeased, to say the least."

"Well, I don't think he realized that he was not having the playful effect that he hoped for with you. And I'll bet Stacey doesn't like him that much. She said she's not going on every tour that he is."

"I could see that, though she must like some of the tours...as long as they're in the afternoon."

Aunt Eloise laughed. "Yes, that's it!"

"Even I want to go on morning tours, and I'm a night owl at home!"

Aunt Eloise grinned now. "But you're a historian and you love this stuff. She's here partly to rest."

"Right."

We watched *A Good Year* on the ship's video system and went to sleep after that. That Provence movie never seemed to get old.

Through the Locks, and In Our Wheelhouse

Through the Locks, and In Our Wheelhouse

We got a break from touring as the *Sif* moved up the Rhône River, and a tour of the wheelhouse. There were some more locks to go into, rise up through, and come out of.

We could have sat around and read our books, but we could do that at home, anytime, when there were no new sights to take in.

"We'll enjoy those books later," Aunt Eloise said. "You spend so much of your life reading that a break will do you some good. Let's go roam around the ship and look out the windows and meet more people. Maybe we'll make some new friends."

"Yes! Maybe we'll meet people we can keep in touch with after we get home. Who knows?" I agreed. Would I actually find people who wanted to do that? It was worth a try.

I was so much on my own in life, because I am a book editor, writer, and publisher. People who do that work alone and spend the majority of their time alone. It was just as well, considering that I am on the autism spectrum, but enough is enough. I could always enjoy having more friends – even distant ones, who would mostly interact with me online. At least they would count as face-to-face ones after connecting with them in person.

We enjoyed a nice breakfast to start with, of course.

I had eggs with smoked salmon, Hollandaise sauce, and tomatoes.

It was delicious.

I wondered, as I enjoyed meal after gourmet meal, just how French each meal actually was, but there was definitely a significant amount of the experience that was, and it was all absolutely delectable, so I didn't waste time worrying about that.

Kavi would have laughed at me if I had mentioned this, and told me to just relax and enjoy it, so I did.

After breakfast, we went upstairs to the lounge and walked around, looking out the windows. The scenery kept changing as the ship moved purposefully up the Rhône River. I had fun photographing it.

I even photographed the inside of a lock as we passed through it. It was just a concrete wall, but it fascinated me to see a wall that was routinely filled up with water to raise ships and drained of it to lower them:

It looked uniformly gray, with no green algae. That was probably because it wasn't constantly submerged.

Rhea, a woman I had met during the tour of Arles, was there, and I chatted with her. She was from Cape Cod, and worked for a travel agency. Now she was traveling, and she had brought a camera that looked similar to mine, at least from a distance. Hers was a Canon, though, and mine was a Nikon.

She was tall, with her brown hair up in a small, high ponytail, and she wore roundish glasses with a serious expression on her face. She quietly observed everything that went on, sitting in a chair by the window, watching the view outside and in.

I didn't want to stay in one place for very long, though, because we were moving through the locks and there were more chances for close-up views of them. Rhea didn't mind.

I took another photograph, and then we met Melissa and Matthew Callahan, and Matthew's sister Ellen. There were all in their sixties and seventies, I guessed. Ellen seemed a little older, but not by much. She had glasses and short, wispy white hair.

She smiled at us politely, but didn't talk much.

Melissa and Matthew were retired wine dealers from Maine.

"We live in Camden, and we used to supply restaurants along the coast," Melissa told us. "Now we're enjoying touring the French wineries, seeing where our products came from."

Melissa had a short, impish coiffure. It was a sandy color, streaked with auburn highlights. Her smile was very friendly and sincere. She had brown eyes.

Matthew gave us a big grin. "It's been a lot of fun."

He had an equally pleasant smile, and a thick Boston accent. His hair was white, short, and it stuck out a bit in upswept curls. He was slightly bald, but not much, and he had green eyes.

"So that's why we haven't met you yet," Aunt Eloise said. "Those tours have you gone all day!"

They laughed and nodded.

"You're here for the historic sites tours, then," Melissa replied.

"Yes," I acknowledged. "We love those."

Ellen had recently been widowed after over 54 years of marriage, and her brother and sister-in-law had insisted that she come along on this trip with them. They wanted to get her out of her house, out with people, and to have a change of scenery.

This was certainly an extreme change of scenery, and about as lovely a change as it got without being at all uncomfortable. She was spending the majority of her time reading on the ship though, with no interest in tours. She hadn't gone on even one.

No wonder we hadn't met her yet!

I didn't find any of this strange, however. Ellen was reading to self-soothe, and that made perfect sense.

Next, a heavy-set woman with thick, wavy, short hair was introduced to us. Her name was Lissa, and she was a nurse practitioner, traveling alone. She had her own cabin.

I noticed that she had a fancy manicure. It looked like a French manicure, except that instead of white tips on her nails, she had purple tips.

"I like purple, too," I told her with a smile. "Sometimes, I use an organic purple hair dye that only my white hairs pick up. It washes out after a while, but it's fun to have purple streaks until it's gone."

Lissa smiled back.

She was single, and she was taking a break from work to pamper herself. "It's working," she added.

Aunt Eloise smiled at her. "Good!" she said.

Lissa and the Callahans had become friends, and she and Ellen were having a great time reading together and sharing books. The books were mysteries and thrillers, and they happened to like the same genres. Having something in common always helps to form a friendship.

We arranged to find them at lunchtime and chat some more.

Meanwhile, I still wanted to walk around and look out the windows. Melissa smiled and waved me on, giving me a second, friendly glance as I hurried over to the side with a view of a huge building that housed the engineers and the mechanisms that controlled the locks. I was having a great time!

Once we were through all of the locks, it was smooth sailing, so to speak, and there was less reason to stare out the windows at the overcast shores.

Then it was lunchtime.

Lunch was an unhurried, casual meal as we had no tour to rush off to this time. We enjoyed a leisurely visit with the Callahans over an array of gourmet comfort food.

I don't know how else to characterize that lunch.

It started with pumpkin soup, which included roasted pumpkin seeds. It was delicious.

The soup was followed by a warm salad that included goat cheese – chevre, en français – and bacon crumbled on top, and a pasta dish with pesto and fresh, soft, green beans with finely grated cheese over it.

That wasn't all: there were huge shrimps on slices of French bread, resting on a dollop of melted Brie sauce.

As we sat there, chatting with Melissa and Matthew, I wondered what to ask them. I liked them a lot right away, but we were booked on different tours from each other for the entire trip. What should we talk about?

Politics was out. They were apolitical.

The idea of being apolitical left me nonplussed. How could one not care about politics? It affected everyone's whole life, whether you thought about that much or not.

I cast about for another topic. Then I decided to ask Matthew to tell me the story of his life. Asking people for that usually pleases them, and Matthew seemed glad enough to get this question.

"Well, let's see…I went to college in the Boston area, and then went to work in the family business for about twenty-five years."

"Oh, what college? What did you major in?" I asked.

Aunt Eloise turned to hear the answer.

"It was Emerson College, and I majored in partying," Matthew said in his thick Boston accent. "So, after about a year, I flunked out. That was when I went into the family business."

"Oh," I said, laughing at myself.

I wondered if I had asked the wrong question.

But Matthew just grinned, so I smiled, deciding not to worry. "Silly me – I always wonder what people studied, just because I like to do that."

He laughed. "That's okay!"

I grinned back and asked about the family business. It was a construction business. Matthew and his siblings (he had a couple of brothers) had sold it when he got divorced, and then met Melissa and joined her in the wine business.

And they had been happy doing that ever since.

We told them about our lives, and then dessert arrived: it was chocolate mousse with white-and-dark chocolate straws. It looked like a work of art in a preserves jar, and it tasted like one.

We really enjoyed sitting with Melissa and Matthew, and could easily imagine them laughing and having a good time wherever they went, whatever they did.

And I was always so serious, watching and studying.

That was how we operated in our wheelhouse – our element.

We found plenty to talk about, despite my initial worries about finding a topic, and had fun visiting with them.

Later on, all of the passengers were invited to go up to the wheelhouse in small groups to meet the captains and see everything, so we did, in small groups.

Aunt Eloise and I waited until an hour and a half after lunch, and then climbed the stairs to the upper deck.

The wheelhouse was a clever piece of engineering; it could be lowered with hydraulic gear so that only the windows were above the deck. The reason for this was to fit under low bridges.

The Hungarian captain talked to us a lot, and listened to my question about the river routes. He was very nice, and very blunt and to the point, which I liked. He was a large man, younger-looking than the French captain, with a spiky crew-cut of brown hair. He had a friendly smile.

The French captain was equally nice – he just couldn't talk to us in English. He was a tall, thin guy who smiled constantly. His hair was white and stubbly, and he had cat-like gray eyes. It was obviously that he loved this job; he just radiated contentment.

They showed us the wheelhouse, and I looked down at the gap between the deck and the door to it:

It looked like a comfortable place to sit and pilot the *Sif*. They showed us the controls, their seats, and the view ahead. Yes – it was definitely a fun job for a riverboat pilot – and it was a far cry from Mark Twain's experience on the Mississippi River, thanks to the technology that was at their command.

It wasn't surprising that the Hungarian captain spoke perfect English, as did the waitstaff, who hailed from the Greek islands of Samos and Mykonos, plus Bulgaria and Romania. What could they do with their native languages but stay home? And they did not want to stay home. They wanted jobs elsewhere. Perhaps they needed jobs elsewhere, with too few of them at home. One waiter worked as a waiter at home when he wasn't on the ship.

Aunt Eloise had a good question for this captain: "There are a lot of elderly people who book these tours. Do any ever get sick suddenly and have to be evacuated off of the ship?"

"Oh, all the time!" he said. "We have to pull the ship over to the shore wherever we are, put out the gangplank, and a helicopter takes them away."

"Wow. That must be dramatic."

"It gets less so the more we see it. Fortunately, it hasn't happened for the past couple of runs up and down this river."

Hmm…don't tempt fate, I thought!

We said thank you to the captains and went back to the lounge.

Desserts

Desserts

After the wheelhouse tour, there was a dessert party held on the upper deck, just past the lounge. Two long tables, covered with white clothes, were piled high with every French dessert we could dream of. Just over a railing in this front room was a staircase; the staff used it to bring food up from the galley to this level and to the dining room below.

It was a feast of tarts, mouses, and macarons in every flavor: raspberry, chocolate, pistachio, almond, and more. Coffee and tea were available, and it was a buffet, so we walked around it, loaded up small plates with the treats, and found tables to sit at.

The tables were small round ones.

We found Dionne and Isaac, and they sat with us for about twenty minutes, until they were finished with their macarons.

After that, a couple from the Naples Catholic Contingent sat with us. Their names were John and Jen.

We chatted about lots of topics.

At one point, Jen commented, "There ought to be a law against fake news! It had done so much damage, including in our church. People are barely waking up to reality from it. Florida has a lot of trouble with that."

John said to his wife, "Why are you commenting on the law? You're not a lawyer or a judge."

I couldn't let that slide.

It reminded me of a conversation I had once had with a couple who were both immigrants during law school. The wife had been a classmate of mine.

"She doesn't have to be either of those things. The law belongs to everybody. In fact, that's how lots of law have been written and later enacted. Someone would see something lacking in how society was run and say, 'There ought to be a law!' about it. And then legislators would write it and enact it."

Jen looked vindicated, as I had intended, and smiled triumphantly at her husband.

"I shall consider myself corrected...and by a lawyer, no less," he said with a smile. He smiled at his wife, too.

I hoped that it was sincere, and that he wasn't upset and planning to be a jerk over it later. You never know with some guys.

As this exchanged played out, I noticed the waiters' reactions. They were, of course, subtle, but people can't entirely conceal their own facial expressions. The waiters, who were from Romania and the Greek island of Rhodes, had had facial expressions that had gone from troubled to pleased when they heard me say that the law belongs to everybody.

Aunt Louise had a most unsubtle expression on her face. She openly grinned at me.

I grinned back.

Also that afternoon, the chef and the maître d' teamed up to show us how to make chocolate lava cake. They made a comedy act out of it, with the chef taking the lead, of course.

He explained, as he stirred melted chocolate in one bowl with a giant whisk and egg yolks in another, that we didn't want chocolate scrambled eggs, so it was the eggs that slowly got added to the chocolate, not the other way around.

Then it was time to add some Grand Marnier. The maître d' shoved the chef's arm a bit as he poured, thus increasing the alcohol content of the mixture!

It was all an act; the chef wasn't bothered by this at all.
He just laughed and whisked the booze into the mixture.
We all laughed.

George came and sat with us, having sought me out just for that purpose of discussing overpopulation, endless growth, and ecosystems collapse.

We talked on and on about the consequences of human overpopulation, the loss of other species' habitats to our own as we relentlessly reproduced and expanded in animal territory, and so on. And we discussed the ethical constraints of doing something or nothing about it all.

At one point, we were interrupted by a woman who was sitting across from my aunt.

"You sound so callous about this. It is all analysis with you, and no feeling for the lives such decisions would affect. What about the disappointments of people who want to have children but can't, for whatever reason? And you're suggesting that people should actually be prohibited from doing so! If I hadn't been able to have children, it would have devastated me for life!"

It did not escape my notice that her ire was mostly leveled at me.

I turned to her and smiled.

"I see that you directed most of your comments and glances at me, not at George," I responded.

The woman appeared taken aback for a moment, but quickly resumed her barrage of criticism. "Well, you are a woman, and yet you are going against God, talking of stopping people from reproducing."

I smiled again. "Well, aren't you sexist against your own gender!" I pointed out. "It's really about Nature – human nature. This is precisely the point. Letting Nature go unchecked, as our invasive species has been allowed to do, is what got us and our ecosystem into this mess."

"But what about God?!"

I smiled. I was doing a lot of that, but she amused me.

It was a rather deadpanned smile, though.

"I'm an atheist. Obviously, you are not."

"No, I am not. Did you know that there is a group of twenty-five of us from our Catholic church in Naples, Florida, with our priest? We brought him with us on this trip. We're going to use this dining room every afternoon for mass. The ship's staff has approved it."

"Yes, I know. That means that you have been missing the afternoon excursions," I remarked.

"Yes, we do that every day. Would you like to join us?" she asked.

"No, thank you."

"Why not?"

"I'm an Episcopalian atheist heretic who goes to church for the music. My father does that, too. He has perfect pitch and loves great music."

Aunt Louise sat next to me, and shook with laughter for a moment. Then she settled in to her meal again, composing herself.

"You are different – you aren't concerned about offending people with your honest answers."

"No. I figure that, as long as I express them politely, if people don't like my answers, that's their problem and not mine. As for the difference, I'm on the autism spectrum. The majority of our species is neurotypical. We should not all be the same. If we were, humans would never have discovered fire, let alone built the Large Hadron Collider."

My interrogator did a double-take, letting her mouth fall open briefly, but then closed it.

George looked as though he were about to burst out laughing. I was under no illusions – he was obviously neurotypical – but he did know what it meant to be on the spectrum.

190

Meanwhile, it bothered me that we hadn't introduced ourselves, so I had to ask, "What's your name? Mine is Arielle. We are chatting without having done that part of the conversation."

The woman did a double-take, smiled, and said, "My name is Christine."

Of course it was. I smiled back and said, "Nice to meet you."

She smiled again – a real smile.

"Which of these desserts did you like best?" I asked her, changing the subject to something that she couldn't possibly get upset over.

She looked at her plate, startled. She had finished what she had chosen, as had we all.

"I think I liked those little cakes best – the ones with vanilla and chocolate streaks on top."

"Those looked good. I liked the macarons – raspberry and hazelnut. And the chocolate and apricot cake."

That was something that everyone on the ship had in common: no matter who we were and no matter what we believed, we each enjoyed every delectable bite of the most wonderful desserts.

Intrigue On a Longship Cruise

A Provençal Feast

A Provençal Feast

For Provence Night, the entire dining room had been redone. Each table had a patterned cloth, and we all sensed a slightly different, festive air about the place.

The wait staff was walking around with their customary bottles of red and white French wine, but that was all. Tonight, dinner was being presented and served buffet style.

Each table, both for dining and for gathering individual courses of this meal, was a work of art.

We all paused to stare at it once we had chosen a table. It was tempting to just stop to stare the moment we walked into the dining room, but that would have caused a foot-traffic pile-up, so we moved out of the way and then stared.

We saw our new friends, Melissa and Matthew as we walked in, and I suddenly thought of another question for them: "What was the name of your wine shop?"

Melissa grinned and told me, "It was called 'Sous La Table'."

My aunt and I laughed when we heard the name, and Melissa was delighted to see that we got their joke. For readers who don't know French, here is the translation: "Under the Table".

They ended up at the table next to ours, and we sat with Carolyn and Amy, the mother and daughter whose aunt had taught at The MacDuffie School.

It would be nice to sit with them, I thought.

But, as it turned out, there wasn't much time for chatting.

The feast took up most of our attention due to the necessity of getting up over and over again to gather something for each course.

No one minded. It was all just too much fun, and so delectable, and such a special treat, that we were all too happy to focus on this.

Salad and cheese were first. Antique food packages decorated the tables, which had labels to tell us what we were offered. There was brie, there were crackers, and there were olives, to name a few items.

As I carried my first plate of hors d'oeuvres to our table – breads and crackers and dollops of sauces, spreads, and cheeses with various fruits – I noticed other people throughout the dining room doing the same thing.

Intrigue On a Longship Cruise

Among them were those two Russian scientists. Andrei put his plate on their table and left the room, heading for the rest room. Boris was at the table a moment later, carrying his own plate of goodies.

What I saw next seemed a little odd: Boris took a cracker with garlic spread off of Vasily's plate, ate it, and replaced it with one of his own. That cracker, from a distance of perhaps five feet away, looked a bit different in texture from the others that I had seen at the buffet table.

But it would have been strange to comment on it just then, so I merely observed this and continued on my way to our table, with my aunt following me as she chatted with Carolyn.

Still, I wondered why Boris would replace that cracker.

I decided then and there not to leave my food unattended for a moment. I would eat whatever I brought to the table, and make sure that my aunt did the same thing, finish with it, and then move on to the next item.

Maybe I was being paranoid, but I was determined to enjoy the entire week of touring, and not get sick. I had already worried that Max, the bankster, might give me his cold just by breathing near me, and then he had said that he had visited P4.

Between the MAGA guy and Boris, I didn't know which of them seemed riskier to be around, but I figured that if I just kept my distance, I would be fine.

I ate my cheese and olives with Aunt Eloise, picked up my camera again (yes, I brought it to every meal!), and headed out again.

In the very center of the room, where the omelet chef worked every morning, we found instead a very colorful array of fresh vegetables and every kind of salad we could dream of.

After the salad was eaten, we turned our attention to the small plates of smoked salmon and deviled eggs, each of which had a chive on top. I admit that I had two of each of these.

It seemed like an endless feast of delights; there were buffet tables laid out all around the room, with each array more beautiful and tempting than the last.

Next up: bouillabaisse. This is a Provençal fish stew from the city of Marseilles, which we had flown over on the southern coast as we arrived. I had been to that city with my MacDuffie School French class, but somehow, we hadn't gotten around to trying bouillabaisse then. I wondered why that hadn't been part of our tour.

This was the first time that I was having it made in France, and it was as velvety and thick with fish and shellfish as I had hoped.

Of course, no meal is complete without vegetables. The chef had left nothing to chance, and forgotten nothing. Chef Ronne had outdone himself, and I reminded myself that he had to keep up this performance week after week, and execute it with enthusiasm. As far as we could taste, smell, and see, he was doing that. He even had lavender sauce with these dishes!

This feast of the senses, and the retelling of it, is no doubt making anyone who reads this and sees the photographs I took of it hungry, just as my aunt has said that my books do. Oh well…!

We had the bouillabaisse, red wine, ratatouille, roasted potatoes with lavender sauce, a little more red wine, and a great evening.

As if that weren't enough, the cruise director and the excursion director dressed in Renaissance costumes and went smiling and joking around the room.

Dinner conversation with Carolyn and Amy fit in nicely once we had our bouillabaisse and vegetables. That took a while to eat, so we were able to sit and chat long enough for me to tell them the story of touring the Breakers mansion in Newport for the Christmas walk-through.

This started because Amy suddenly said to me, "You mentioned that you used to be a historic interpreter. You must love this trip!"

I laughed, "Yes, this is exactly the sort of trip that a museum junkie and history lover dreams of. Are you enjoying it?"

"Oh yes – it's far better than a filthy, giant, floating hotel of an ocean cruise ship with hundreds of people on it. At least everything is kept clean and you have a chance to get to know people and really see everything on the ship. And it's not bad coming and going from it. Those cruise ships put you on an enclosed boat to go to shore with uncycled air – awful!"

"You've been on one?" I asked.

"Yes," Amy said. "Never again."

We nodded.

"So," Amy continued. "Can you tell us a story about being a guide?"

I laughed. "Really? You want that now?"

"Yes!" she and her mother chorused.

Aunt Eloise and I exchanged glances.

"Tell her about the tours we took in Newport, and that guide you hit it off with so well – what was her name?"

"It was Noelle," I said. "She was our guide when my aunt invited me on a servants' quarters tour of The Elms, which was built by a family that made its fortune with coal. She was mischievous; she toyed with the tour group. I forget exactly what she did to play a guessing game of a joke on people, but I suddenly spoke to her when she did it: I said to her, 'That's terrific! I love it! I never dared do anything like that when I was a historic interpreter at the Mark Twain House, because I was in my twenties, and young people just get called obnoxious if they do anything impish. Maybe now, I might try it."

"Was she an older lady"? Carolyn asked.

"Yes," I said. "She had gray, chin-length hair and bangs. And she really knew every detail of information on life in that house behind the scenes, every chore, every historic artifact that was used to pamper that family and how it worked, you name it!"

Carolyn and Amy nodded, impressed.

"I want to go on that tour," Carolyn said.

"So do I," Amy chimed in. "What about the other part of the house? Did you see that, too?"

"Oh yes. But it was self-guided, with a player and an earpiece, much like the ones on this ship's tours, except that we hooked the player to our hips and were left on our own to wander through the owners' part of the house."

"Tell them what happened when we saw Noelle again," Aunt Eloise prodded me.

I grinned back, and said, "Okay...here's what happened. Aunt Eloise invited me twice last year, once in November to see The Elms, and again for the Christmas walk-through of The Breakers, which is the Vanderbilt's mansion."

"What is a Christmas walk-through? That sounds really nice," Amy said, looking like she wanted to sign up for one.

"It's where guides are stationed in every room, and we stay put in our assigned rooms to talk about just that room as people walk through the entire historic house museum on their own, having been told the rules, which are not to sit on, lean on, or touch anything. We're like guards and lecturers combined for those events."

"I take it you did that at the Mark Twain House," Carolyn said.

"Yes, but just once a year, and during the day. The Breakers probably does it a few evenings a year, in between Christmas and New Year's Eve. This was a beautiful evening, with musicians in the great hall by the grand staircase, and a tower of red poinsettias."

"Tell them what happened with the food," Aunt Eloise said.

"Okay. There is a loggia at the back of the house. It has mosaic tile inlaid from floor to ceiling, depicting dolphins, and in the summer, three openings with curved tops go right out onto the lawn. In the winter, wooden inserts seal it all off. Cider, petit fours, gingerbread, and cookies were served in there during this walk-through."

Carolyn said, "I think I know what's coming..." and she grinned.

"You guessed it! Aunt Eloise said that we should move on soon, because we had to finish the ground floor and go see the upstairs, so I said, 'Okay, but we should get rid of all of our food and drink before leaving this room.' Accordingly, my aunt immediately started finishing up. We threw our plates, cup, and napkins into the huge rubbish bins, and stepped into the morning room."

"And then..." Amy prodded me.

"We went in there just in time to come face-to-face with Noelle, and to watch her tell two people who thoughtlessly brought their cider and cookies in there to go back! Noelle saw me a second later, and we looked at each other like a pair of comrades-in-arms. It was great."

Aunt Eloise was grinning from ear to ear at this point, and shaking with laughter.

"You are a great story-teller," Carolyn said. "Too bad you aren't giving tours any longer – we would look for you!"

"Thank you very much! But it was exhausting to do it over and over again on the same day. I think that the guides we are meeting only do their routines once per day, which seems different. Maybe it's all tiring, though, I don't know…but they do get plenty of exercise from all of the walking involved. We Americans ought to do that, but we don't live in walkable cities. Well, most of us don't."

"I love Newport for that reason in particular," my aunt agreed.

After that, it was time to get our desserts.

To a dessert-lover and baker such as myself, my favorite part of the meal was the final course. I had some decisions to make…

Which desserts – yes, plural! – would I have? There were pear and peach tarts, and apple ones. There were more macarons, too, and this time, they were presented in beautiful antique boxes. Well, I had already had some of those, but one more raspberry macaron wouldn't hurt, along with a slice of pear tart and a slice of almond custard tart, which I noticed as I carefully perused it all. There! Decision made.

Perhaps when I got home, I could try to make that pear tart. It didn't look too difficult, I thought, just a matter of slicing everything and laying it out just so…and I could spoil Kavi with it.

Dance-Off!

Dance-Off!

After the Provençal feast, we needn't have worried about a lack of exercise.

The next activity that evening enabled us to burn off some of the calories we had just consumed, which felt really good.

I confess that I went back to the cabin to get rid of my camera once I found out what was in store, though.

It would have been impossible to enjoy dancing while worrying about that piece of equipment.

Now I really felt like I was relaxing, because I wasn't worrying about it!

It was great to have it for food and sightseeing, but not now.

I was free to move about the ship…well, the upstairs lounge.

The crew had moved the furniture away from the bar area to make a decently sized dance floor, and Denis was back at his piano.

He wasn't doing a sing-along tonight.

He was playing some fast-paced songs, old classics, and to top it all off, a disco-globe had been hung from the ceiling.

I thought that was hilarious.

That thought was premature; I should have held it until after I saw Jonathan and Guy.

The two of them appeared dressed for a night out on the town.

They wore snazzy suit jackets, and each one looked like a psychedelic painting. Jonathan's had a metallic theme to it, with small, symmetrical rows of sparkly squares in silver and muted blues and reds. Guy's was an explosion of fiery color splotches.

Guy also wore sunglasses that matched his jacket – colored!

They both grinned from ear to ear, stepped out onto the dance floor, faced forward, and started gyrating to the tune that Denis was playing *Dance All Night*.

We all burst out laughing at the sight of them, and they just grinned even more. They seemed to love it.

No cruise is complete without dinner and a show…or a party!

People joined them, and soon the dance floor was full.

Karen suddenly surprised me by grabbing me by the hands and pulling me up there with her and Max! It was fun. Aunt Eloise sat and watched, smiling at us.

After about half an hour, I had had enough, and we left.

Intrigue On a Longship Cruise

Sounds in the Hallway

Sounds in the Hallway

Late at night, Aunt Eloise and I thought we heard something strange. As our room was the last one on the port side of the water level of the ship, and as it was about half past one in the morning, we didn't quite wake up.

I sleepily heard the sounds, but because no alarm went off and no announcement came over the ship's public address system, I didn't worry. Neither did Aunt Eloise. She just kept sleeping.

That didn't surprise me; she had often told me the story about how she had slept through a middle-of-the-night fire drill at the Rhode Island School of Design, in the dormitory, during her first year there. Her roommate had sat her up, put her robe and slippers on her, put her flashlight into her hand, walked her outside, waited for the all-clear announcement, and then walked her back to bed and put everything away for her.

I had gotten up, opened our door, and looked out, but seen no one in the hallway, so I had closed the door again and locked it. Then I looked out the windows, but it was so dark that I hadn't seen much, so I had closed the curtains, go back into bed, and said "No."

What I had heard was a frantic shout from about halfway up the hallway, followed by rapid footsteps, then more voices, all in frantic tones. All of these sounds had seemed to come from the level above ours, though, so they weren't very loud.

Next came the sounds of more people in and out of a room halfway down the hall. Well, I heard that, and Aunt Eloise breathing the sounds of someone who had fallen back asleep.

But I couldn't just go back to sleep right away. I was curious enough to listen from the bed.

After a few more minutes, I heard people in the hallway again.

They were talking quietly and moving quickly.

During all this, I felt the longship moving down the river, but that was nothing unexpected. We were going toward Lyon. But then I felt something different: we seemed to shift direction slightly. We were moving toward the shore!

At this point, Aunt Eloise did roll over and say, "Arielle, does it feel as if the ship is moving a bit sideways?"

But she had no recollection of that the next morning.

Incredible, but not unexpected for my aunt...

Intrigue On a Longship Cruise

The next sounds I heard were those of a helicopter on the shore. Otherwise, the ship was quiet.

Having talked to the ship's second captain on our wheelhouse tour, I could pretty well guess what was happening, so I wasn't alarmed – just concerned about some unfortunate person not being well enough to stay aboard the *Sif*.

Then I decided to go back to sleep.

There was no way I was going out of the room to ask about that during whatever was happening. I could ask about it later rather than involve myself and thus add to the mix of activity.

There was nothing I could do to help anyway.

Curious people just get in the way.

I would find out all about it at breakfast, I decided, and fell asleep.

Double-Moored by the Presque-Ile

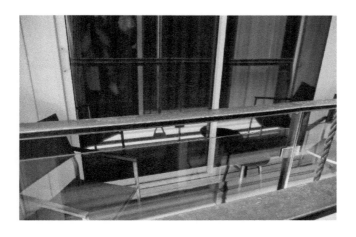

Double-Moored by the Presque-Ile

When we woke up the next morning, we had arrived in Lyon.

I looked out again and saw that we were double-moored, and realized that we were the inner ship, so people from the other one would be passing through ours to get to theirs.

The other ship was perhaps a foot away from ours, neatly aligned alongside the *Sif*, and its staterooms with verandas abutted our French balcony room. I knew this because I knew the design of the ships, and these river ones were all the same.

It made me glad that Aunt Eloise and I had opted for the less-expensive rooms without a little deck as I looked at the now-useless space with two chairs and a table. No view – just close up against us!

We were moored at a quai on the Rhône River, facing north, with something called the Presque-Ile to the ship's port side. The literal translation of "Presque-Ile" is "Almost-Island".

The reason for this name was that the northern end of this piece of land connected to the shore, and the Rhône River branched with the Saône River, which was on the other side of the Presque-Ile. At this point, the Rhône diverted toward Switzerland, while the Saone meandered north.

A bridge was just up ahead, and a cobblestone area stretched below it, just off the *Sif*'s gangplank.

We saw all that after we got dressed and went out to the dining room for breakfast, and found Melissa and Matthew. They were booked on the same tour as us, but not in our bus's group, we discovered.

We would all be seeing the same things today, though, in Vieux Lyon – the historic district. Tomorrow, they would be going on the Beaujolais winery tour, of course! We would not.

We had booked a different tour before we ever met them, and we promised to tell them about it when we returned from it.

Breakfast was ordered, and we settled in to eat and chat.

I had the Norwegian yogurt with raspberry topping, orange juice, coffee, fruit, and Pain Perdue – "Lost Bread". In America, we call that French Toast. I just wanted to see what it would be like here in France, and I was hungry. It was good.

French people, I knew, just have coffee and a croissant for breakfast, but we Americans and Canadians wanted to eat more than that, and the cruise company wasn't about to prevent it.

Malena was taking care of our table this morning, and I asked her about the sounds that we had heard in the night.

"Oh, yes, someone was sick and had to be taken off the ship," she told us.

"I could feel the movement of the ship toward the shore," I said. "It was definitely moving sideways a bit."

She nodded and smiled. "Yes, I felt it, too."

"Do you know anything about the emergency – as in, who it was?"

"No…well, I know it was an older man from the upper deck, but I don't know his name," she said.

We all looked at her, concerned, but weren't sure what to say next.

"Should we be worried?" Aunt Eloise said. "We just started traveling again after the pandemic."

"Oh!" Malena said. "No, it wasn't that kind of emergency, but I can ask more about it for you, and see if anyone will tell us more."

"Thank you," we said, and turned to look at our food, but without really seeing it for a moment, as we contemplated the implications of all this.

A couple of minutes later, Clotilde approached our table.

When I saw her, I smiled and said, "Bonjour Clotilde! We are having a wonderful time thanks to your efforts."

She smiled her businesslike smile and said, "Merci! I understand you were asking about the medical emergency that we had last night."

"Yes – we wondered if it were anything contagious, or perhaps something else, limited to just that person, and we wondered who it was and if they will be okay."

Clotilde nodded. "It is not contagious as far as we know, and we are keeping updated on that. If it changes, of course we will be informed, but we don't anticipate any lockdowns, so please don't worry."

"Well, that's good news," Aunt Eloise said. "Can you tell us who it was and if they are going to be okay?"

Clotilde looked a bit uncomfortable, but then decided to tell us a bit more. "It was one of the Russian gentlemen," she answered, "and we won't know how he is doing for a while."

We all nodded. "I see," Aunt Eloise said after a moment. "Well, thank you very much for telling us."

"You are welcome," Clotilde said. "Enjoy our tours today."

With that, she left.

I glanced around the room, looking at everyone, and then I saw him: Boris was at the buffet island, loading his plate.

He looked unconcerned.

Max and Karen came up alongside him, and Karen spoke to him.

I could hear them, though it was a bit faint from where I was sitting.

"I was so sorry to hear that your friend got sick during the night. Will he be okay?" she asked.

Boris looked up at her, and replied, "I hope so. Something he ate disagreed with him."

Max coughed and blew his nose.

Damn – he had a cold for sure! And something that Vasily ate was bothering him that much?!

Well…that was what Boris said.

I wasn't sure what to believe.

Nothing I had eaten on this ship had bothered me, nor had it bothered my aunt.

I was still keeping my distance from Max and Karen – physically, I mean – to avoid catching a cold, though after reading about how a virus could spread in the circulating air of any enclosed space, I had my doubts about that actually working.

I decided that worrying any further about that was pointless, finished my breakfast, and followed my aunt out of the dining room.

Intrigue On a Longship Cruise

Lyon Sites and Sights

Lyon Sites and Sights

Aurore, a tall, elegant, statuesque Lyonnaise woman with shoulder-length, curly red hair that she kept out of her face with a barrette, was our historic interpreter and guide for a whirlwind bus and walking tour of the city.

It was a gray, overcast, rainy day, so she wore a short, off-white raincoat and rainboots. She also wore a very sincerely friendly smile. Clearly, she enjoyed meeting new people from other places and showing them her beautiful city.

The city's famous Painted Houses were the first sights we saw, and they were amazing – detailed, colorful murals covered entire facades of buildings that might otherwise look like nothing special, transforming them into educational looks at famous people from various points in history.

It all started in 1978 when a group of students from Lyon's School of Fine Arts rebelled against the established way of thinking and presenting art because they wanted to bring art to everyone. So, they left and did this beautiful work all over the city. A complete catalogue of these fascinating murals can be viewed online at: https://www.offbeatfrance.com/lyon-murals.html, and it includes a murals map.

Aurore had the bus park along the street and let us out to see some.

We saw a tall building with people from various time periods depicted on balconies at every level. The paintings were expertly rendered, complete with shadows that gave the impression of three-dimensional structures jutting out from what was actually a flat surface.

The Lumière brothers, who invented the first motion picture camera, ambassadors from the 18th century, a Roman emperor, an astronomer, and many other people, were shown on this wall.

A detailed rendering of a bistro, complete with depictions of what looked like most of its menu items, graced another wall at street level:

The most exciting mural, to me, was the one of Paul Bocuse.

Master Chef Paul Bocuse died in January of 2018 at age 91. At 1 and 2 Rue de la Martinière, we saw a detailed painting of him at street level. I remembered learning about him in the 1990s, when my father and I took a tour of what is known as "The Other CIA" – the Culinary Institute of America, in Hyde Park, New York.

On that tour, we were told that Paul Bocuse, the "best master chef in the world," of which there were then only 50, chose to send his son to study cooking at the CIA. A master chef test cost, at that time, $11,000, and involved 4 days of cooking and baking, all watched and tasted by the examiners.

I knew what he looked like already, but this was something really special, plus it ingrained into my memory the fact that Chef Paul Bocuse was not only French, but also Lyonnais. Chef Bocuse worked in the nouvelle cuisine, focusing on presenting fewer calories and more fresh ingredients, all while making it the most delectable gastronomic experience. No wonder people loved him!

I must confess that I had some photography problems that are typical for tourists in that I could not always get the perfectly-angled image due to people walking by and limits of space. It just isn't always possible to back off and frame things just right in a short amount of time, and one can't ask people to get out of the way for the perfect shot all the time. I did my best, and got what I got.

When we had taken enough photographs of the murals, Aurore had us get back on the bus to move on to our next stop.

The Basilique de Notre-Dame de Fourvière presides over the historic district of the city from a hill. It was, of course, an impressive-looking edifice, and we could see it as we approached. I had to wait until we were walking up to its front gate to get a decent photograph of it, however, rain and gray skies notwithstanding.

Struggling with raindrops on my camera lens and a huge, red, umbrella perched awkwardly on my shoulder, I managed to get a few more, close-up photographs of it before going in.

A sign on the gate and the carvings over the wooden front doors were the first things I paused for, because I wanted to show the family at home, later, the general layout and smithcraft of the place. Once in a great while, something this beautiful is still created, but it's expensive. What used to be funded collectively, out of religious fervor and tithing, is now done mostly by billionaires, and usually, it is modern walls of glass, which, to me, isn't as special. This cathedral was built between 1872 and 1896.

On the way in, I noticed that the metal statues over the doorway were intact, and photographed this beautiful figure of an angel. The decapitation craze of the French Revolution had not been able to mess with this particular medium of art.

Once inside, the art show could begin. Art was how the church had communicated scripture to the illiterate masses. If a person can't read, they can always relate to pictures.

We saw plenty of pictures in paintings, murals, mosaics, sculptures, stained glass, and tapestries. It was all very beautiful.

Aurore led our group to the rows of wooden pews in the nave, near the entrance and far back from the altar, and proceeded to talk about the history of the cathedral. I wandered a bit away from her, half-listening, but mostly focusing on the exquisite artistry of the place, documenting it with my camera. I had read about such things many times, and what I really wanted were these images.

There were some beautiful Medieval frescos painted on either side of the nave.

One of the nice Catholic women from the Naples, Florida contingent, who knew that I was an atheist, approached with a sly smile as I clicked the shutter repeatedly. It was Christine. She said, "How do you like all this religion?" I gave her a devilish grin back and said, with enthusiasm, "It's art! And culture! And history!" She didn't push for more, and went back to her seat. I gathered more images in peace.

Later, I looked up the details about the organ, because, as I had told this woman previously with another diabolical grin, my father and I are heretics who only go to church for the music. The organ was installed in 1896, by the Lyonnaise firm of Michel-Merklin.

Aurore talked for a while, then led us outside to look at the view, and at a panorama model and round map of the city. She pointed out the modern financial district's skyscrapers in the distance, the shopping area in the middle distance, the political center, and more.

I asked her about the French equivalent of the CDC – the Center for Disease Control in Atlanta, Georgia. My reason for doing so was that I had read in a book – part of my research in writing the *Nae-Née* series – about this. Therefore, I knew that the 2 CDC authors of it had advised a French billionaire on how to get one for France.

That billionaire was Charles Mérieux, founder of Fondation Marcel-Mérieux was from Lyon, and he wanted it for his city. Already, Aurore had told us that Lyon aimed to rival Paris for every feature, though on a smaller scale. "P4!" she said, almost immediately. "Pathogen 4."

Here is the book that I had read:

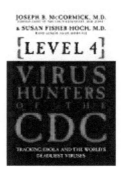

The facility is complete, and in a huge, modern complex south of the main city area. Aurore included this in her lecture when we were back on the bus, driving to our next stop. We did not go there; she was simply telling us about it, doing her job by giving a complete, detailed answer to any and every question that we asked. All of the guides that we met on this trip did that; it was very professional and impressive.

But before we left the cathedral…I lost track of my aunt! I went to the bus and looked. No Aunt Eloise. I ran back to the cathedral. No Aunt Eloise. I returned to bus, pausing to speak to Clotilde, who had shown up in her jeans and red jacket to check on our group. She hadn't seen her.

I waited on the bus anxiously, wondering if I ought to abandon the tour. Finally, my aunt appeared – last of all. She had gone down into the crypt with her phone and lost track of time, then come up and hurried back to the bus to join us. Crisis over. Here are the images she took with her phone:

"What happened?" I asked her.

"I didn't realize that you had gone outside with the guide when I went down to the crypt to see the artwork there," she told me.

"Oh." We laughed. It was all good; we were back together.

As the bus drove us off through the city again, the rain picked up, but I persevered with my camera, because everything was interesting, and I wasn't about to give up on getting images of things that caught my attention.

We drove past the Cour d'Assises in the Palais de Justice, on the opposite side of a footbridge that arched across the Saône River to meet at the front of its grand colonnade:

The Cour d'Assises handles criminal cases, I learned later on, when I looked it up. Notably, this is the only French court that has jury trials; most trials in France are by judge only, and appellate cases. This building is known not only as the Palais de Justice, but also as the Palace of the Twenty-Four Columns. It was built from 1835 to 1845. It is overlooked by the Basilique de Notre-Dame de Fourvière and by a miniature version of the Eiffel Tower.

As we drove along, the Catholics lamented the drizzly weather, and Christine suddenly said, "Father, is there anything you can do about this rain?"

I glanced across the aisle and down a bit, and noticed the priest sitting there in his windbreaker.

'Really?!' I thought to myself. 'All he can offer is impotent magic,' but I kept quiet, of course. Religion is what people who want something more when science has nothing more to offer – or when they don't like the data – turn to.

Of course, none of us liked the rain!

Father O'Shaughnessy responded by singing the secular song "You Are My Sunshine" as we drove along.

Aunt Eloise and I shook with silent laughter, unnoticed, as members of his flock joined in.

Intrigue On a Longship Cruise

A Traboule and a Romany Couple

A Traboule, a Romany Couple, and a Vial

Our agenda for the next phase of the morning's excursion was to take a walking tour of the historic area of the city, learn about that, and then walk around. There were perhaps twenty-five of us in our group, plus Aurore.

She led us down a street that seemed to be a dead-end, pointing out decapitated statues and plaques. The doors were beautiful, large, wooden ones with curved tops set into walls of pink stone and framed with mortared arches.

Near the end of this street, she paused to tell us that she would be taking us through the buildings to the other side, onto the opposite street, using a passageway called a traboule.

Traboules typically date from Renaissance times, and serve as a quick and convenient way across an area of town that was not laid out as a grid, and thus has many dead-end streets.

The entrance to the traboule, a beautiful wooden door with a curved top, which was on the Rue des Trois Maries, had a plaque next to it, and was accessed by ringing a bell.

Aurore told us that, originally, traboules were just a convenient solution to the problem of a lack of city planning. Street layouts had not been thought out in advance of building construction, so there were some places where one could not quickly and conveniently go from one block to another.

As a result, these traboules were made with passageways to enable pedestrians to walk straight through to the river. Silk workers used them to transport their wares through the city, and women doing their laundry benefitted, among others, because they could carry their things via a more direct route to the river.

We stood outside the doors, admiring them. They were beautiful, and it was intriguing to think of what lay behind them, even though, to the people who lived in the apartments of those buildings, it was something that they were thoroughly accustomed to – the backdrop of their lives.

Or maybe they loved knowing that they lived in a historic place.

I would!

Aurore rang the bell at this point, and I wondered whether or not it was with a prearranged signal of a ring. There was no time to ask, because she led us in and took off at a brisk pace.

We went in and found ourselves in a pretty, salmon-pink-stucco passageway lit with wall sconces. Halfway down the hall, we emerged into an atrium with winding staircases that led up to the apartments.

We looked up at an open sky with a rose-hued courtyard with winding stairways and balconies that led up to the apartments. After we had stared upwards and admired that, we returned our gazes to the cobblestoned area and listened to the history lesson.

Aurore went on to explain how helpful traboules had been for the French Resistance during World War II, when the Vichy government, which colluded with the Nazis, ran this part of France.

A resistance worker being followed by Nazis would ring the bell, and the people in the apartments would make sure it was an authorized entrant, with a special signal of ringing the bell, such as a tune, rhythm number of rings, etc. Once the correct signal was given, the apartment dweller would buzz them in, thus leaving the Nazis locked out. The Nazis would not be buzzed in, as they did not know what code to ring.

We listened to our guide until she led us out. As we stood there, I noticed a thin, dark-haired couple with cranky facial expressions standing off to the side. They had come in through the opposite door, and were now watching our guide deliver her lecture.

They were listening without much interest.

It was odd behavior.

Intrigue On a Longship Cruise

I looked at them, wondering why they wouldn't just go on their way, since they were obviously not tourists, and then it hit me: they were Romany, and they were scoping us all out, figuring out which of us to target for pick-pocketing and when to strike.

They were dressed in nondescript clothing that blended into the neighborhood, with jeans and jackets and comfortable shoes. It was their behavior and lack of a reason to be with our tour that gave them away.

I was very annoyed.

I wasn't concerned for myself, as I had put my passport and Euros in a money belt under my shirt, then covered that with a long, zipped-up, blue L.L. Bean rain jacket that went down to my knees. My hands were gripped around my camera, so I didn't see how I made an attractive target. Aunt Eloise had been just as careful.

But some of the men in our tour group had, against all advice, shoved their wallets into their pants pockets.

I decided to make a little scene and see if it helped.

"Do you want to go through?" I asked loudly.

The two of them glowered at me, irritated that I had called attention to them.

Undeterred, I looked at the rest of our group and said, "I think these people want to go through!" as if we were blocking their way, and perhaps they didn't want to interrupt our guide by walking past us.

More glares from the Romany couple.

All that this got me was a few odd glances from our traveling companions.

How clueless could they be, I wondered?!

There was just no signalling to some people, I decided.

Was it because I didn't know how to do it without being blatant and direct, I wondered? Was it an Aspie thing to neurotypicals that just didn't connect this way? Whatever it was, I had tried my best. I gave up and listened to Aurore, but I was still wary of the Romany people.

Aunt Eloise and I watched both them and our guide, and were a bit relieved when she finished speaking and led us out the opposite door, onto another beautiful, historic, cobblestoned street with wooden doors with curved tops and brightly-lit shops.

We stared into one of them at displays of long, thin, open boxes of macarons, and sweet loaves of bread speckled with pink praline, the signature candy of Lyon.

Francois Pralus
27 rue Saint-Jean
69005 LYON
Tél.: +33 (0) 4 78 62 74 09
France
https://www.chocolats-pralus.com/

We went into the shop, and immediately inhaled the most wonderful aroma of warmth, butter, sugar, and almonds, among other wonderful things.

French butter was different from American butter, and we hadn't smelled it for a long time. Perhaps it was because the French didn't use any additives or insecticides or hormones in their food, we guessed. Whatever it was, it just made everything they had to offer to eat or drink better.

Behind some glass in that shop were the bakers, hard at work producing more wonderful treats to eat:

We tasted some of the bread in the shop with our cafés au lait, which had pink-praline-encrusted almonds baked into it. That was a signature Lyonnais sweet. We loved every mouthful of it.

Aurore led us down the street, inviting us to disperse for the next half-hour or so to enjoy the shops. I asked her about the marionette museum and shop.

This is jumping ahead a bit, but I'm going to tell it at this point anyway:

When we returned to the ship, two of the men in our group did not have their wallets.

I hoped that they then understood why I had made that scene...

Intrigue On a Longship Cruise

Guignol, Madelon, and Café au Lait

Guignol, Madelon, and Café au Lait

We were looking for a uniquely Lyonnais experience, and because Lyon was an important city to the French silk industry, both in the Renaissance and in the 19th century (plus Guignol was a silk worker when he wasn't doing marionette shows!), we settled on the textiles museum.

Aurore led us on, down the cobblestoned street, toward Le Petit Musée de Guignol, which, despite its name, was actually a shop. It was stuffed absolutely full of the most beautiful marionettes of all sizes.

"The shop is sometimes closed even during the hours that are posted for it to be open," Aurore warned.

"Oh, no!" I said. "This will be my only chance at it, and I want to buy a puppet, or maybe even two!"

We walked farther down, and I tried to remain upbeat.

"Come on, Aunt Eloise – you who make puppets will love this!"

"Love what?" she asked, intrigued.

"We're going to see the Guignol museum and the marionette shop attached to it." I had researched the Guignol marionette before leaving on this trip, and Aunt Eloise had admired it.

"Oh yes – you showed me the puppet online. But who is he?" My aunt wanted his backstory.

"Guignol is France's version of Punch. Madelon, his wife/fiancée/girlfriend – they change the details to get more variety in the scripts – is the version of Judy. These puppets – er, marionettes – were created in 1808 by a Lyonnais dentist to amuse his patients after surgeries, while they were in pain. This, of course, was before there was ether, so they also had to endure the procedures and all that pain while fully awake."

Aunt Eloise looked horrified, so I went on, "Guignol is a silk worker. He represents the textile industry of France, and does social, economic, and political commentary. The other cast-member marionettes are, as I said, Madelon, plus a gendarme, a cobbler, and a burglar. That's who Guignol's stick is for – the burglar." I thought for a moment, then added, "I would imagine that the puppeteers have to be careful not to get too overzealous and damage the paint on the burglar marionette."

Aunt Eloise smiled thoughtfully and said, "No doubt."

"I'm surprised you hadn't heard of Guignol before," I said. "You went all over France in the 1960s with Grandma and Grandpa."

"It just didn't come up," my aunt said. "Your grandfather was so busy making educational films that we just focused on historic sites."

"Oh well." I thought a moment. "What was I trying to remember…oh! I saw Guignol and Madelon in an episode of *The Marvelous Mrs. Maisel*, when her mother went to Paris. That was a thrill, knowing what I was seeing, though I did wonder about it being there instead of in Lyon…"

"Well," my aunt said, "just because he's from here, that doesn't mean he can't travel around France; he's a puppet, after all."

We laughed.

"I don't want to own the entire cast of the show, but I do want a Madelon marionette as well as a Guignol one," I told her.

"Well then, lead on! I can't wait to see this – if the shop is actually open," my aunt said.

Aurore was listening to this. "You really have researched this," she said with a smile. Having moved a few paces down the street from us, she suddenly called back to us, "It's open – the lights are on!"

Hurray! We caught up with her, and with that, arrived at the front door of the shop.

We paused outside to admire the window display, and went in.

The first thing we saw was a tree of Guignol finger-puppets. They were not as artfully made as the larger ones, but I was impressed and intrigued by them nonetheless. They looked like tiny trinkets meant for tourists who wanted an inexpensive souvenir.

There was nothing wrong with that, but I had made my mind up before coming on this trip to get something more substantial, and I wasn't going to change my plan at this moment of truth.

We went farther in, and saw many more puppets, most of which were of a size suitable for a marionette show, and the entire cast of characters were represented.

In the center of the shop, there was a tall, triangular, mini wooden theater display, complete with a backdrop of red curtains. In each of the two sections that faced front were two of the puppets: Guignol with the Gendarme in one, and Guignol with the burglar in the other.

At this point, I was so excited to be there, and so focused on what I was seeing, that I forgot a few things other than using my camera. Unfortunately, I kept at it once we were inside the shop, in my delight at seeing this place!

"Pas de photographie, s'il vous plâit!" came a voice at the back of the shop.

Suddenly, I realized where I was – inside, not outside.

There she was, behind the counter – the woman who ran the shop, I presumed. She was middle-aged, bespectacled, and had long, auburn hair and a loose, comfortable blouse on.

I switched the camera off and put the lens cap on, apologizing and looking suitably shocked at myself. "Pardon!"

The woman just nodded. She seemed used to such incidents.

That shop was really quite spectacular, and Aunt Eloise was duly impressed by its offerings, which covered every inch of the place. I couldn't wait to get Madelon, so she let me go ahead and do that. After smiling and saying "Bonjour!" cheerfully and making a selection, I was soon in possession of a pair of beautiful puppets.

Guignol had a beautiful red bow tie, purple eyeshadow with a little green, and a lovely suit with brass buttons. Madelon was outfitted with a white ruffled cap and a floral gown, and had black hair, and huge, doe-like, black eyes.

I let the woman behind the counter put each one into its own brown paper tote bag, having realized that there was no point in wrapping the item, as TSA would have just disassembled the entire package, possibly damaging her. I would carry the bags folded over in my large, zipped, quilted tote bag on the plane.

Next, we visited the museum, where we had a wonderful time seeing marionettes that had been made over the past two centuries on display, and we read the short descriptions about them, having a fun time practicing our reading knowledge of French.

When we were finished with all of that, which included a brief show (in which Guignol attacked the burglar without damaging his paint job!), we headed out onto the street again.

Aurore had told us all to meet for a café au lait at the Rocambole Café, which was just around the corner from the historic street with the Guignol shop and museum.

We found it and used its rest room along with a long line of most of the people on our bus. Then we found a table by the windows. I noticed Karen and Max sitting with their friends at a table along to the wall to the right.

I took out the puppets, put my hands up into them with my fingers in the armholes, called over to her: "Karen!" and held them up.

She looked, smiled and nodded, and I smiled back. Then I put them away.

Aunt Eloise and I ordered one café au lait to share, because we knew we were able to return to the *Sif* and eat another wonderful lunch there. No sense in getting too full to enjoy it!

The café au lait arrived, and I noticed Boris standing by the counter, watching me. "Is he following us?!" I commented, annoyed.

"Oh, he's probably just enjoying the historic district like we are," my aunt said, turning around to glance at him.

I didn't pursue the subject, but I kept an eye on him.

We took out the bag of the signature Lyonnais candy that we had bought in the patisserie along the way to the marionette shop. It was pink praline over almonds, and it was delicious with our hot drinks. We had wanted some to take home with us after tasting that bread. We just ate a few, tying the bag shut again with its ribbon after that.

"It looks like it was never opened," my aunt remarked.

I smiled, stood up, and glanced up to see Boris still watching me.

"Hi Boris," I said. "We heard about Vasily. I hope he's okay."

Boris looked at me strangely. "Yes, everyone does."

That was all that he said about that.

He hadn't had any coffee, but instead had come out of the rest room to loiter in the street until it was time to board the bus.

He was out on the town, touring and still enjoying the trip, and his traveling companion was gone, and as far as anyone knew, very sick. What did he want?! He certainly didn't seem to be worried about Vasily at all.

I was annoyed, but determined not to draw attention to myself over this odd situation, so I didn't comment further. What could I say, anyway?

I led my aunt onto the bus and found seats for us in between Carolyn and Amy and Dionne and Isaac.

Boris looked as though he had been hoping to sit near us.

For some reason, I didn't want to sit anywhere near him.

I think I was angry with him at that point in time for looking so unconcerned about Vasily. Were they not friends?! They had been colleagues. Why wasn't he at the hospital checking on him instead, and trying to contact Vasily's family?!

I decided not to ask him any more about any of it, and chatted with my aunt and Amy as we rode back to the *Sif.*

The Abbey of Cluny

The Abbey of Cluny

The Abbey of Cluny is an hour north of Lyon, in Bourgogne – that's Burgundy. Nine of us made the trip in the light rain. The last bit of the trip was behind a student driver.

Our guide was a tall man in blue jeans with a long beard named Jacques. He worked as a historic interpreter in a museum in Lyon during the months when Longship River Cruises shut down (December through March). He was excellent. He had researched the abbey and monastic life in depth, and his lecture took us through the entire life of a particular monk, from childhood to old age, plus full details on what he could and could not do at all times, and why.

I had read about the Abbey of Cluny when I had been researching how Medieval people took care of their needs without all of the modern, pollution-heavy technology that we rely on today. I ended up learning about how wealthy monks and nuns did that more than anyone else, but it was still very useful information.

This place had fascinated me enough to sign us up for a tour because it had been, like other abbeys and convents, a self-contained and self-sufficient, cloistered community, in which everything needed to enable a comfortable life with food, clothing, and shelter – just the basics, but few other luxuries – was produced on-site.

Such things included wool from sheep, hay for the livestock to eat, wheat grown in the gardens, vegetables, you name it. There was almost

251

no need to get anything from elsewhere, which further enabled the monks here to live a cloistered, isolated life in the Middle Ages.

This is the book that it appeared in, in the chapter about monastic life:

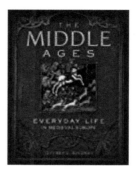

The bus pulled in to a large parking area just outside of town, and we all got out. Jacques announced that we would walk to the Abbey from here, and that, after the tour, we would have to walk back to meet the bus on our own, so to pay attention to the route we took. He would meet us at the bus.

We headed off down the nearest street, which had ivy-covered walls to our right:

A little farther down, we crossed a small bridge. After that, I looked back the way we had come to learn the route:

Jacques led us to the right, then to the left, and then straight ahead, and we found ourselves in a wide, cobblestoned courtyard with a few vehicles in it.

Up on our left was the entrance to the museum.

This is a map of the Abbey of Cluny, which we saw on a huge sign just outside the visitor center's entrance, showing both as it was before it fell to ruin (shadowed areas), and as it is today:

We walked up to the building and found huge glass doors, one of which was wide open, welcoming us in. It was great to see a historic building that had been kept as much as possible intact, with modern accoutrements added to convert it into a visitor center.

Perhaps that thought was premature...

Inside, we found ourselves in a gift shop. I looked around quickly, and decided to do my shopping in the brief space of free time that would come at the end of the tour.

Meanwhile, I noticed Jacques talking with the guy behind the counter, and Jacques didn't seem any too pleased. It turned out that the rest rooms were out of order – and the guy hadn't called our ship to say so!

Apparently, his boss had worried that we might not come to visit if we knew that. Jacques demanded that other arrangements be made, and we were soon told, after a phone call was made, that we would be allowed to use the facility in the café next door. Great – problem solved.

With that, Jacques got down to the business of conducting our tour of the Abbey of Cluny.

The abbey used to include a huge cathedral plus extensive grounds with living space for the monks, stables for their animals, storage rooms for their supplies, and wine-making and food preparation facilities. It was known throughout Europe as the place for aristocratic families to send one son each – their second sons.

I knew from my studies of history that the oldest sons inherited the family's property, and if there were more sons, they tended to have military careers. I could already see the population control scheme of aristocratic families; the idea was to keep the property undivided, so there was no motivation to encourage more marriages after the first son was married off, preferably to someone with political connections. Birth control might have helped!

Jacques told us that, most of the time, there were around 200 monks here, but at its peak, the Abbey was populated by over 400 of them. Then, at the time of the French Revolution, they lost the protection of the king (due to the guillotining of the king), plus the Vatican wanted more control over the monks. With no place to be, the abbey shut down, and the townspeople cannibalized the place for building materials for their homes, much as had happened with many an ancient Roman site.

And that is how it fell to ruin!

In the area just past the front desk and gift shop, where Jacques was telling us all this, was a table with a model of the abbey, made of wood and metal, showing the extent of the original complex, complete with the dormitories, stables, and farm areas, as it was hundreds of years ago: The metal parts are all that remain now.

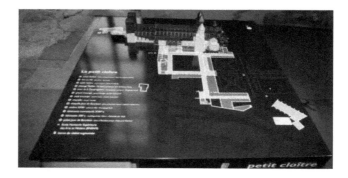

This other model, in wood, shows the entire cathedral section:

Here and there in this front space were some areas of the original stonework, covered by heavy plexiglass:

Jacques got right to work telling us all about the place and taking us around to see everything. He started with the history storyboards, but didn't spend much time lingering there, so I quickly shot photographs of them to look at when I was home and at my leisure to study them. This is just one of those boards:

Leading us through this area and to a doorway, Jacques continued to talk about the masonry, and to lay out the itinerary of the tour. He would show us pieces of carved stone that had been salvaged from rubble after much of the Abbey was demolished to build structures that now made up the surrounding town – pieces that were particularly beautiful, but not suitable for new buildings, and we sat in a hallway around a glassed-in courtyard to listen to him.

I looked back at the door that we had come through, and decided that it was worth documenting. It was a beautiful wooden door with intricate ironwork, lit with floodlights that were set into the floor:

The stones that we saw represented bits of column tops and wall decorations.

We spent about fifteen minutes sitting on the benches in this hallway, listening to Jacques describe the construction of the Abbey, the layout, and daily life – the secular aspects of it. It is always those basic aspects that keep a religious or academic place going, and enable the inhabitants to conduct said religious or academic life.

At this place, both pursuits went on; the monks had plenty of books, plus they copied many of them before the printing press was invented.

Jacques led us outside next, and we looked both up and back at the outside of the building before following him into the remains of the huge cathedral.

Once in there, Jacques walked us all around those remains. It was eerily empty and stripped off all ornament. The cathedral was just bare shapes, like a giant model of itself. I hadn't been inside the ruins of a cathedral before; usually, they are well-preserved houses of Medieval art, architecture, and music, complete with a functioning worship schedule. Now we were seeing one that had fallen victim to a massive regime change.

I guess it just amazed me that, in the heart of Catholic France, any such site could have been damaged at any time. But, religion was not wanted while the masses were angry at the excesses of the wealthy, and this place had presented a clear target to them, as a bastion of hoarded wealth and comfort.

Anyway…in we went, looking around and upward:

Jacques talked about life in this space when the cathedral had been intact, and some of us stayed close to him to listen, while others, myself included, wandered around to get a closer look at everything, half-listening and taking photographs.

Aunt Eloise listened more than I did, but I wasn't sorry. She hadn't read that book, and I wanted to walk around and look. Jacques wasn't moving as he lectured – he was in one spot, telling all that he knew, and I could hear him somewhat.

In fact, I could hear him just enough to tell that I wasn't missing anything that I absolutely had to hang onto every word of. I hoped he wouldn't mind, but he didn't seem to; he wasn't bothered at all as half of us walked all around this huge, empty space.

Jacques led us out of the cathedral and through a large, empty chamber that had been a chapel once. We saw a receptacle for holy water, which now stood empty.

Then he took us into the abbot's chamber. Only those who were highly literate were allowed in here, Jacques told us, because that would enable them to figure out the order in which to read the story that the 12 faces in the room told. The bearded ones were to be read first, and the last apostle to be read was the young-looking one, who had no beard.

The abbot's room had its own fireplace, plus another, smaller one in a little room off to the side that had no light in it. Apparently, these two rooms made up his apartment, with a sitting room and a bedroom as that inner one. I took out a small flashlight and tricked my camera into photographing its fireplace.

It must have been terribly cold here in the winter, I thought, looking at this space, for someone to need to be that close to a fireplace in order to read and sleep.

Next, Jacques showed us to a courtyard that was back out and through the cathedral we had seen earlier, where he concluded the tour by lecturing about the life cycle of one monk.

Giving him a face and a personality, complete with homesickness as a little boy, made it seem more real.

As established earlier in the lecture, the boy was the second son of an influential, wealthy, aristocratic family.

He was brought to the abbey as a child, perhaps six or seven years old, never to see his family again.

The boy was beaten – not too often – just enough to make him let go of the outside world.

He gradually rose to greater power and privilege with age, until he became an elderly, incontinent man.

At that point, he was banned from the cathedral, but nursed by the other monks, with every attention and plenty of books to read, so he was never bored, and never left with any physical need unmet.

That concluded the tour, and Jacques led us out.

He told us to enjoy the shop, and to meet at the bus in half an hour.

We thanked him and went into the café to use the rest rooms.

Aunt Eloise and I had not chatted with anyone on this tour. The people on it included some retired Canadian teachers who were traveling together as a couple, plus a few other older American couples.

Everyone had just wanted to listen quietly and look around, which was what we had done. It was relaxing and interesting that way.

Once we were comfortable and back in the shop, I got several postcards as souvenirs for myself, and a magnet with a photograph of the exterior of the abbey on (taken on a beautiful sunny day!) for Uncle Louis.

Outside, I paused for a photograph of the place in the rain.

The walk back was easy, and we soon found our bus.

On the bus ride back to Lyon, I noticed some things, and leaned forward from the front-most pair of seats to ask Jacques about them.

"I keep seeing white cows in the fields We don't have cows like that in the United States," I said.

Jacques grabbed the microphone to answer me and share his response with the entire bus.

"The cows you are seeing in the countryside are a breed called Charolais, and they are indigenous to this region of Europe, and valued for their beef. It is some of the best beef in the world, and it has a distinct taste."

"Hmm. Steak and frites on the right side of the *Sif*'s evening dinner menu..." I said to my aunt in a low voice.

Aunt Eloise laughed.

I thanked Jacques and didn't ask him any more questions as we rode along. I just enjoyed the ride along with everyone else.

News of the Weird

News of the Weird

When got back from our tour of the Abbey of Cluny, it was getting dark out. We tipped and thanked Jacques, and walked up the gangplank.

Chef Ronne greeted us with trays of large paper cups full of delicious, fragrant, spiced, red, mulled wine. It was the perfect drink after a day of walking around in the rain.

We came on board, turned in our I.D. cards, got our room key-cards, and went to our cabin.

I swapped out the camera battery again for its fully charged one and plugged in the other one with its charger, and we got ready for dinner.

But first, we had some time to ourselves, and I wanted to do some research on Google Maps.

"I'm going upstairs to the library to plot our route for tomorrow morning, back to the historic district of Lyon, so that we don't get lost and end up late for lunch and our afternoon tour."

"Oh, good idea!" my aunt said. She was a great planner, too — always flawlessly organized, and never late for anything. Actually, she tended to be a bit early for most things.

I had a plan: there was a lecture we would attend on the ship tomorrow morning, and then, after that, we would have about two hours of free time, which we hoped to spend taking another look at that fascinating part of the city that was called Vieux Lyon.

After stopping to see Ana, the concierge, at the front desk and getting a map of the city from her, I went upstairs. We had to go up there anyway, because there was a meeting every evening in the lounge before dinner.

One of the computers was free, so I settled in and got Google Maps going. These computers were programmed to search on Google in English, I had noticed, when I had first used them. Smart move on the part of the Longship Cruise company; even though I had studied French, it was better to look up directions in English if I was determined not to get lost, which I was!

I took out a blue pen and marked up the route for tomorrow morning, noting where the Guignol shop was, and where the café that we had visited was, plus a couple of other items that looked interesting, but that we hadn't yet decided to visit.

Aunt Eloise appeared next to me when I was almost done and said, "The morning lecture will help us to make up our minds about that."

I agreed.

With that, we went into the lounge for our evening spiced nuts and lecture, and sat around with Melissa and Matthew until people started to disperse for dinner.

They were going to visit the Château du Pierreclos tomorrow, and would be gone all day. It was the Beaujolais and Truffles tour. There would be a cheese-making demonstration, too.

"That sounds great!" Aunt Eloise said. "If we were ever to do this again, we would sign up for that, and some of the other art and wine tours."

I nodded and agreed with her. "Truffles and fine wine? Count me in – you can't go wrong with that. The trouble is, everything sounds good on this trip!"

"Well, that's France for you," my aunt replied.

Clotilde walked by just then, heard us, and smiled happily.

We got up and headed down the stairs, past the huge portrait of the Norse goddess Sif, and into the dining room.

Ellen and Lissa had already found a table for six and were seated with Alice and Declan, so Aunt Eloise and I had to find somewhere else to sit. We waved to Ellen and the others and wandered around until we found seats elsewhere, with Rhea, Erin, and Eric.

One seat remained empty...until Boris asked for it.

Damn! I was really starting to dread him.

"Hi Boris," I said. "You aren't going to bring out those rye crackers again, are you?"

He looked at me like he was annoyed at being preempted.

"Actually, I had some in my room, but I won't ask you again to eat any, since I can see that you really don't want them."

I breathed a sigh of relief, and secretly was pleased that his seat was all the way across the table from mine. "Okay – good!"

I paused a moment, then asked, "How's Vasily? I hope he's going to be okay!"

Boris looked at me. "He's been sleeping a lot since he got to the hospital, so I haven't had a chance to talk to him yet."

That didn't exactly ring true.

"Do they know what's wrong with him?"

"No."

Boris seemed oddly unconcerned, but I didn't see any point in pushing for more details, because I didn't actually believe I would get them.

Boris gave me the creeps at this point. He was coldly unfriendly, whereas Vasily had been a rather sweet, smiling, amiable guy.

We settled in to order our dinners.

Ivan appeared with the menus, and we perused the evening's fare:

Salade Niçoise; rainbow trout on carrot puree with small white potatoes; chocolate hazelnut mousse cake with raspberry sauce and more lingonberries.

Okay, I admit it: that wasn't all that was offered, but it was what we all ordered – every single one of us. No steak and frites here tonight for anyone at this table!

As usual, everything was a work of art and delectable.

The salad was light, which left us ready for more food.

The fish dinner looked like it was ready for a gourmet food magazine photographer to document it, but it would have to settle for me, the shutter-happy food tourist.

That's what Erin called me as I raised my camera to it, anyway.

"Yeah, that's me," I agreed. "I don't care if it seems silly to anyone else – this is the fun of it for me, and I want to show the meals to everyone at home along with the other images I have!"

"Nothing wrong with that," Rhea agreed. "I hadn't thought to keep my camera with me during meals, though; I thought it would get in my way too much. Now I'm wondering, as I watch you, so determined to get all these pictures; maybe I could have worked a few in."

"Well, we're not done yet," I said. "Maybe tomorrow…"

"Maybe," she said, and stuck her fork into her plate.

Dessert deserved the same attention. It was just so pretty, with its pink streaks of raspberry sauce under that mousse cake, and crumbs artfully scattered across a long plate that suggested the shape of a ship.

"This dessert dish looks like it was chosen on purpose, just to evoke thoughts of a river ship," Aunt Eloise remarked.

We all cracked up.

Aunt Eloise looked up at us, and then said, "I guess it doesn't take an artist to notice that."

We nodded, and ate our dessert.

A little while later, we went to the lounge upstairs.

We found Dionne and Isaac and sat with them, wondering what was next on the agenda.

We had been told to go up there for a game night.

Why not? We weren't there to sit in our cabins.

Joe was in there, across the room, sitting with some other people.

Intrigue On a Longship Cruise

Stacey was not there. I suspected that she wanted to relax and be on her own some more. Her job was, no doubt, strenuous, and she had given the impression of a woman who was seeking a rest.

We were to be divided into teams, based on the groups of chairs – four to a group – and play trivial pursuit, Clotilde announced.

Really! "What fun!" I said to Aunt Eloise. "Want to play?"

"Yes," she said, grinning, "but who knows how we'll do…"

"If they ask too much about sports, I won't know the answers," Dionne said.

"Neither will I," I replied, "but there are always other topics."

"This feels like a party cruise now," Isaac remarked.

Questions were from many topics, and we knew a few answers. It was fun!

When Joe's team scored big, he pumped the air with both fists, and cheered with a roar, like we were in a football stadium.

That, I felt, was embarrassing to be witnessed by the crew, the Canadians, and anyone else on this ship. There was something about aggressive American cheering that seemed rude, overly loud, and crass.

The crew, of course, reacted as if nothing unusual or remotely impolite had occurred.

Well, yeah…and I kept my facial expressions neutral, too, as did my aunt and our teammates.

My aunt, however, quietly poked me when that happened, and I turned to look at her.

"What would you call that?" she asked. "I know there's a word for that kind of behavior."

"He's got a galloping case of American exceptionalism – the belief that we are somehow superior, even though we're just another group of people on this planet."

"Oh…great word!" she said quietly.

I don't think anyone other than Dionne and Isaac heard us but they were nodding when I looked away from my aunt at them.

This was an interesting experience in every way. So many different kinds of people were here, and we could observe them all. It was quite a change from life at home, on my own, with my books and computer.

I was glad to be here, seeing it all.

And I was getting sleepy, thanks to being up for so long and eating great food and drinking French wine that had no insecticides.

So was Aunt Eloise.

After our team won a round, to which we reacted with a few happy but quiet smiles, we said good-night to Dionne and Isaac and went back to our cabin.

I took a shower and got ready for bed.

Aunt Eloise liked to take her shower in the morning, so she had already tuned the television to *CNN*. Jake Tapper was announcing something that immediately caught our attention:

"In France, a scientist who worked at Pathogen 4, the French version of the Center for Disease Control, is in the hospital with an unknown illness. Thus far, it has been determined that it is not a case of exposure to some virulent and contagious pathogen, which has left doctors puzzled as to a diagnosis."

I looked at my aunt. "That's not Vasily, obviously. I wonder what's wrong with that scientist..."

Fortunately, Tapper wasn't through with his report:

"The scientist, Jean-Claude Babineaux, apparently fell ill after a day off, during which he visited with people outside of his workplace in a park. He didn't feel ill until hours later, at which point, in the middle of the night, he went to a hospital in Lyon with convulsions. He has since been having hallucinations, and is experiencing – which is horrifying – dry gangrene. Doctors are worried that he may lose a foot and a finger."

Aunt Eloise and I looked at each other.

"I think that's who Max said he visited in Lyon before meeting Karen and heading for Avignon to meet this ship!" I said.

Aunt Eloise looked back at the TV screen. "Well, let's hope it's not contagious, and that this scientist recovers soon...with his foot and finger intact."

"Yeah..." Something about this story nagged at me, but I couldn't remember what.

Tapper moved on to some other story.

After a few minutes, we switched to *BBC News*. Might as well hear another take on current events, and one from a place that was much closer to our current location!

The journalist on that channel repeated the same awful story about Dr. Babineaux. "In related news, she said, "there is another case of unexplained hallucinations and convulsions in a hospital in Montagny,

France – the Hôpital Givors. The patient who is sick is also a scientist, but he is retired, and did not know the other man. He is Russian, and was traveling on a Longship River Cruise when he took ill and had to be evacuated from his ship in the middle of the night."

Aunt Eloise and I looked at each other.

"It's Vasily!" We said, both at the same time, then turned back to hear whatever else the reporter had to add.

"We shall watch both cases as this story develops to see if there actually are enough similarities to determine whether or not this is the same illness. Meanwhile, the public should not be concerned, as doctors suspect food poisoning rather than any pathogen."

"Damn that Boris," I said. "I liked Vasily, and Boris doesn't even seem to care about him."

"Well, at least it's not a pathogen that we can catch," my aunt said. "I'm going to go to sleep now."

"Okay, good-night," I said, and shut off the lights and television, setting my travel alarm clock again.

As I dozed off, that feeling that this illness was something I had come across before nagged at me again.

Where was it?

Not in a scientific journal article; the memory that nagged at me, just out of reach, wasn't work-related.

Still wondering where I had encountered it before, I fell asleep.

Intrigue On a Longship Cruise

A Lecture, Silk, and a Shadow

A Lecture, Silk, and a Shadow

The second morning that the *Sif* was in Lyon, Aunt Eloise and I stayed aboard for a lecture by a magician of an artist. His name was Vincent Jeannerot. He was a middle-aged man with short, graying hair and glasses, plainly dressed, and he soon had us staring with longing at his creations.

Monsieur Jeannerot was a scarf maker, but that hardly does justice to his work. He had the ability to both create and transfer the most gorgeous botanical patterns illustrations onto silk scarves.

The artist's shop, Aquarelles Botanique, was located in the historic district of Lyon, and I made a note of its address, folding the corner of the page in *Le Magazine du Vieux Lyon: Patrimoine Mondial de l'UNESCO*.

He brought several examples of his work to show us, and the first one was amazing. It looked like the artist had taken a spray of fuschia blossoms, dropped them onto a black canvas, arranged them with flawless symmetry, and painted them in living detail and vivid color. It was the most gorgeous thing I had ever seen in a scarf, and I have admired the designs of Tiffany & Co. of their fabulous irises in stained glass.

After we had all stared – no, gazed at in admiration and longing – the first of his exhibits, the show continued. Piece after piece of silk with wearable artwork on it was trotted out and held before our eyes.

The scarves were either huge squares or long rectangles, all in silk. They came in blues, pinks, ivory, black, and other colors. All had the most wonderful floral images I had ever seen on any scarf, and I had seen quite a few, because that is what impresses me aesthetically.

There was one with a border of pink, a background of whisper-pink, and inside, periwinkle blue hydrangea, sapphire-blue clematis, pink roses, and huge raspberry-pink peonies splashed across it. I had thought that each scarf was even more beautiful than the previous one...until I saw that one.

That wasn't all.

Monsieur Jeannerot also made torchons en lin, which are linen dishcloths. Each one had a different floral or fruit print, such as purple wisteria, pink rose, peonies, figs, truffle mushrooms, olives, artichokes, beets, and aubergines (also known as eggplants).

But I wouldn't buy one of those.

I could never bring myself to dry a dish with it!

I could, however, wear one of those gorgeous scarves.

Hermès had nothing on this guy. Nothing!

I couldn't stop admiring it all:

Roses, wisteria, begonias, irises…they all appeared on those silk expanses in vibrant, vivid, fabulous detail, as if leaping off, inviting us to inhale their delicious scents.

The art was just that good – that true to life.

We decided then and there that we would spend the rest of our free morning going back to the historic district of Lyon on foot, to find that shop and buy some scarves.

Exploring on our own would be fun!

Plus. we were now thoroughly armed with knowledge of how to manage, out and about in Lyon, thanks to Clotilde's lectures.

At this point, I will pause to mention what we learned during those lectures, before telling the tale of our independent excursion.

I want to do this because there was just so much to do and see, all in the space of a week's time, and we could not do it all. We had to choose. That was why I had left one morning open, and in the city of Lyon, rather than book up every single time-slot.

Aunt Eloise had consulted with me as we had planned this trip, but we still found ourselves wishing that we could attend everything – well, almost everything. But, some things had had to fall by the wayside while we went out to see whatever we had signed up for. The problem was that different fascinating options ran at the same time.

Somehow, the Excursions Director, Clotilde, managed to visit us all at each one, just to check on us. I swear I caught a glimpse of her on every tour! She was amazing; she was married, and would go every other week to see her husband, and return to work on the ship.

Clotilde gave lectures on many topics, including one on how to pronounce French words and to interact with French people in shops (don't pronounce the "s" on plural words, and say "Bonjour!" to shop people and others before starting to talk with them about ANYTHING else).

I made sure to do that anyway, except in that shop for the Guignol puppets, when I was foolishly awestruck, but I don't think that the woman in there was offended; I think she realized that I was just so impressed by what I was seeing!

One lecture was about Provence, and in it, she told us about French lavender and about its curative properties. When that slide appeared on the screen in the lounge, I recognized it immediately from a jigsaw puzzle that I had at home: it was the famous Sénanque Abbey, with its lavender fields in full bloom.

Her story was about a hike with her family during the summer. Her nephew had been bitten by mosquitos, and was itchy, scratching at the spots.

"Come here," she had said to him. "I have a remedy for you!"

She put lavender oil on the spots, and he felt better right away.

We were intrigued; we had not heard of lavender as a remedy for that before. It did keep scorpions away, I recalled, thinking of the little trays of dried lavender on the windowsills of the mansion in *A Good Year.*

This was fun, learning new things every day!

Another lecture was on the region of Provence. It focused on geography, agriculture, and products that the region is known for. Avignon and Arles are in Provence.

Just to be thorough about explaining our trip, however, I will add that the other cities we visited were in other regions of France, including <u>Auvergne-Rhône-Alpes</u>. When we were driven to the Abbey of Cluny, we had gone an hour north of Lyon into Bourgogne – that's Burgundy, in English.

By the time our week was drawing to a close, Clotilde had shared general knowledge of Provence cuisine, lavender, truffle mushrooms, wineries, the sycamore trees that lined the streets all over the South of France, and the artists Paul Cézanne and Vincent van Gogh.

Sometimes, it was relaxing to just sit and listen and look at her slides after a day of traipsing around a Medieval city, visiting the historic sites. Some of the things in Clotilde's lectures were repeats of what the guides had just told us, but hearing again was a good review, a way of reminding us of what we had learned.

I didn't want to forget anything.

We left the ship at approximately 10:15 a.m., after I had checked the route on Google Maps.

"I hope I don't forget anything," I said. "I have to remember our entire route, and match it with the map that Ana gave me."

The concierge had a huge map, in color, of every city. She printed them up for passengers as a standard service, to keep us from getting lost. We didn't all track our movements with phones!

"You never forget anything anyway," my aunt said with a laugh.

"Well…I hope not." I said, and we got ready to go out again.

I took the map and folded it carefully, keeping it readily accessible in the pocket of my jacket, which I soon slung over my shoulder, as the pace of walking heated me up a bit too much to wear it.

My aunt was carrying her rain jacket instead of wearing it, too, and we were in luck; the sky was gray and overcast, but it wasn't raining.

"This is going to be fun," I said. "It reminds me of the high-speed walking I did all over London when I had a term there in college. I walked really fast everywhere, and it felt great, being outside and seeing a city in detail."

"I love it too. Lead on!" my aunt said, with enthusiasm.

I took her to a footbridge that led us across the Saône River this time, straight up to the beautiful, white marbled edifice that housed the criminal court, both the trial level (on the right, called the Cour d''Assises), and the appellate level (left, called the Cour d'Appelles). "Having a lawyer lead me on a walking tour comes with some things I would not otherwise have noticed," my aunt commented, admiring its 24 Corinthian columns.

We arrived on the Quai Roman Rolland and paused to admire the building, then turned north, walked around the side of it on the Rue du Palais de Justice, and found ourselves at last on the Rue Saint Jean. The shop was just a few more blocks north, which was good, because my aunt was getting a bit tired of walking.

Soon, we walked around the corner and found the shop:

Vincent Jeannerot
Aquarelles Botaniques
GALERIE PERMANENTE
4 rue de la Loge
69005 LYON - FRANCE
+33 (0)6 11 07 90 16
contact@vincentjeannerot.fr
https://www.vincent-jeannerot.fr/

Aquarelles Botaniques was a tiny, hole-in-the-wall of a space, but inside, all that we saw was beauty. The place was simply decorated, with clean white paint and a few display tables, on which the scarves were arrayed, folded neatly.

"It's exactly as I saw it on Google Maps when I dragged the little stick person here," I told my aunt, walking in and pausing to say "Bonjour!" to the woman behind the counter. She smiled, said "Bonjour" back, and let us look.

I already knew what I wanted, and part of the game of touring was efficiency; we couldn't afford to dawdle for too long, because we would miss lunch and our next tour if we did that.

I therefore immediately took a scarf just like the one that I had been so entranced by to the counter and bought it.

Aunt Eloise had a general rule of not acquiring more things at this point in her life, but she broke down and bought a beautiful scarf to wear. It was the black one with red-and-pink fuschia blossoms.

"We're so bad," I joked. "But we'll wear them."

"We're NOT bad," Aunt Eloise said. "You will wear yours to parties and author events, and I will wear mine to art exhibits and out with friends."

Aunt Eloise said, "And to think that I almost didn't buy anything, but as an artist, I am just so impressed by the skill involved in this. I can show it to people at home when I wear it, and tell them all about it." She understood the process of creating these scarves down to the last detail.

"Well, of course! That's the point of buying them – to share the art with admirers who couldn't come here and see this in person as well as to enjoy it ourselves," I agreed.

When we came out of the shop, we were on a narrow street. No one was nearby, but I didn't want to worry about a pickpocket.

I reminded myself that we had each put our passports and money into money-belts under our shirts again, so as long as we didn't go into a crowd and push up against people, we should be okay.

However, I also wanted us out of this alley.

Therefore, I hustled my aunt back out into the square around the corner from the Café Rocambole, on the Rue Saint Jean, and relaxed a bit once we were out in a more open space.

I had the odd feeling of being shadowed somehow, and I had no intention of being cornered anywhere, especially after that experience in the traboule.

"Is anything wrong?" Aunt Eloise asked.

"No…" I said, looking around.

Just then, I noticed the guy from our ship walking down the street, toward us. It was Boris. He was glancing around, seeming to be looking for something.

"Hello," I said to him, not intending to have any more of an interaction with him than absolutely necessary. "You liked this area, too?" I smiled politely.

He looked surprised to see us for a moment, then recovered and gave us a slight smile and a nod. "Yes, I thought I would check out the bakeries some more," he replied.

He wasn't carrying any bags, though.

Perhaps he hadn't yet found what he wanted, I thought to myself.

"We did our shopping already," I said.

He glanced at our bags, and nodded.

"What happened?" I asked him. "You couldn't find that patisserie again? It's back that way, down Rue Saint Jean," I said, pointing down the alley and then left, where it connected with that street.

"What?" the man asked, startled. "Oh. Right. No, I changed my mind. I don't want to have to carry a whole loaf of bread with me." With that, he fumbled in his pocket and glanced toward the river.

"Oh," I said. "Yeah…we don't want to have too much to carry home with us, either. Only what we planned on carrying in advance, and lightweight, flat stuff," I added, thinking of my Guignol and Madelon marionettes, and indicating our scarf packages, which were flat. "We're going back to the ship now."

"Well, we're about ready to go back," I said. "See you later, on the ship!" With that, my aunt and I smiled again, and turned to leave.

He nodded, said "See you there," and didn't move.

We glanced at each other and started walking toward the river. About twenty feet away from there, we looked back, and he was still standing there, watching us.

I just wanted to get away from him.

Why was he so set on sticking with us?!

Granted, I noticed everything around me, and was difficult to corner or to induce to do anything that I didn't want to do, but anyone who was still undeterred from following my movements was worth keeping track of.

"May I come with you?" he asked.

My aunt and I exchanged glances.

"Okay," I said. We were, after all, passengers on the same ship.

We started walking back the way we had come. I was determined to keep to wide streets all the way, and my aunt kept looking at me, clearly hoping I was taking a direct and open route. I looked back at her, unable to communicate this intention, but that was my exact plan.

Boris asked once if we wanted to go down a side street to see something in a shop there, but I said, "No, if we pause to do anything else, we'll miss lunch or our next tour…or have to rush so fast that we won't enjoy it, or forget something important."

He looked a bit frustrated, but just nodded and followed us back.

I tried to make conversation about the tour for the rest of the walk, but it was difficult. This was very odd, considering the fact that he had come on many excursions throughout the trip. How could he not have taken in any of the historical data that the guides had shared?

"Are you worried about your friend?" I asked, wondering if he might actually be distracted for that reason.

"Oh, no," Boris said. "Vasily is sedated, and there's nothing I can do for him for a few days, so I decided to finish out the tour."

Very odd, indeed. He seemed more interested in watching everyone else than in traveling, and was shockingly unconcerned about Vasily, considering the fact that his diagnosis was as yet undetermined.

We had to walk across the width of the Presque-Ile, and we made good time, keeping up a brisk pace.

Boris had no choice but to keep up with us, and he made no more requests to stop in any out-of-the-way shops.

We crossed through the Place Bellecour, which had a red-gravel area and a huge statue of Le Roi-Soleil, Louis XIV, mounted on his horse.

From there, we continued to a spot near the bridge of the Presque-Ile, pausing to admire a huge, multi-colored, metal sculpture of a bouquet of flowers: It was made of stainless steel, and we looked at the information on the park fence about it, which said that a Korean artist had made it in 2003. It was called the Flower Tree.

We turned around before crossing the bridge to see some swans in the Rhône River, and a huge Olympic swimming pool across the way. It is heated year-round, Aurore had told us the day before, and was built when Lyon was competing with other cities to host the Olympics. It didn't win, but the city enjoys the pool anyway.

Boris left us at this point, and we didn't miss him.

We moved along, with one more pause for a photograph of the ubiquitous roosters that graced the city. They decorated the posts on the bridge, which was called the Pont de l' Université, due to being located across from the campus of the Université Jean Moulin:

With our shopping over, the *Sif* in sight, and the realization that we had been quick enough that we would have twenty extra minutes to spare, we were no longer worried about missing anything on our schedule.

I even paused to photograph one of the beautiful university buildings, Université Jean Moulin Lyon 2, which teaches arts and humanities, as we neared the quai:

Jean Moulin was a hero of the French Resistance, who was tortured to death by the Gestapo monster Klaus Barbie in 1943. The law school is part of this university, too; how fitting, considering the university's namesake, to celebrate someone who fought for the rule of law against fascism.

The quai was called Quai Claude Bernard, I now knew, having checked out our route so thoroughly before we had left. I was just that determined not to get lost or run late.

Aunt Eloise appreciated that!

We got back to the ship, put our scarf packages into our suitcases, flat and on the bottoms (which would be the upright sides once they were packed), and freshened up in time for lunch.

We found Carolyn and Amy and sat with them, because they were going on the next tour with us later.

All of us ordered a shrimp salad.

During the meal, Aunt Eloise proceeded to expound on the details of our little outing and the lecture that had motivated it for a few minutes, until we realized that I was the only one who was listening with real attention and interest.

We quickly turned our attention to Carolyn and Amy. They had been patiently listening, adding nothing, waiting for us to finish enjoying the scarf topic.

"Sorry!" I said. "We were having way too much fun."

They laughed, understanding how much in her element my aunt had just been, and Amy said, "That's okay. We're all here to have fun."

"Tell us what you did this morning," I said. The two of them had gone out into the city as well, enjoying some time on their own before the afternoon tour that we had all signed up for.

It turned out that they had gone to a department store called Printemps, which means "Spring".

She showed us an image of its entrance on her phone:

"They don't allow photography inside, of course," she added. "And using the rest rooms was quite a production: we had to pay with 2 Euro coins to access the toilets, which are sealed off in individual rooms, but the sinks, soap, and hand-dryers are all free."

"Wow," I said. "That is very inconvenient. The store is paying for its rest rooms, though, even if people don't buy anything."

Carolyn said, "We did buy things, though! We bought some perfume, because we missed Fragonard in Avignon."

We nodded.

"That's not all that we saw," Amy told us.

She showed us another image on her phone:

"This was a fountain that we saw on the way to and from the Printemps store. It is the Place de la République. The whole thing is like a flat, shallow infinity pool!" Amy said.

Despite the fact that it commemorated the French Revolution of 1789, was a modern monument.

"I wonder if people use it as a wading pool during the heat of the summer," Carolyn said.

Amy looked it up on her phone: this open space has a métro line running underneath, so a previous monument, with a sculpture, was removed and the fountain replaced it.

"Well, that makes sense," we remarked, and finished our last bites of dessert: banana pudding with the now-ubiquitous lingonberries.

It was comfort food, and very good. It even came with vanilla bean ice cream. We enjoyed every bite.

"Well, that was very nice. Let's go!" Aunt Eloise said.

With that, we all got up and headed out to the lobby to wait to be called for our next bus tour.

Intrigue On a Longship Cruise

Wry Rye

Wry Rye

We turned on the news – *BBC News* this time – in time to find out more about the stories we were following in the few minutes between lunch and the bus ride for our next tour.

The story about Dr. Vasily Legasov and Dr. Jean-Claude Babineaux was on again.

They weren't doing any better. In fact, they were worse: Dr. Babineaux's entire left hand was turning black, and so were both of his feet. Vasily's left foot had started to do that, too. The hospitals still hadn't figured out what was causing this.

Something started to come together in my mind, but it wasn't there just yet. Damn it – whatever it was, it was important!

"You have such a wry expression on your face right now," my aunt commented, glancing at me.

I looked at her, nonplussed, and then I stared at her, stunned.

"That's it – rye!"

"What do you mean? You don't look wry now!" Aunt Eloise just looked confused.

I explained. "Not wry spelled 'W-R-Y' – rye spelled 'R-Y-E' – it's all about rye, the food!"

She stared at me. "What's about rye? You don't like rye. You wouldn't even drink the rye whiskey."

Another series of thoughts flashed through my mine – none of them good.

"Oh no…" I said, with an icy, sick feeling spreading through me.

"What? What's wrong?" my aunt asked, turning to look at me.

"It's a hit job, and a red herring of a distraction against the main agenda," I said, still staring at the TV screen.

"What do you mean?" she asked, appalled.

"Yes, yes, I don't like it, and it's a damned good thing that I don't, because if I did, I might be in the hospital now, too. It's also a damned good thing that you have been – I don't know, either following my lead at eating only what's served by the *Sif*'s chef and crew on this trip, or deciding not to eat food that lacks good explanations for where it's been, but you've been careful, too. Much to the disappointment of a certain purveyor of rye crackers."

"Remember this magazine that I bought in the airport on the way here?" I said, holding the issue of *National Geographic History*.

"Yes…"

"Well, in it, there is an article about ergot poisoning. All of the symptoms described in the news reports about that P4 scientist, and for the ones about Vasily, match it."

My aunt stared from me to the magazine, the color draining from her face.

I opened it up to the story and showed her the photograph of a stalk of rye with ergot fungi growing on it, out of the ear.

"The ergot fungus, a black growth that can infest rye, is also called Claviceps purpurea. If that rye is harvested with the ergot unnoticed, ground into flour, baked into bread, and ingested, it produces toxic alkaloids that cut off the blood supply to the body's extremities – this means arms and legs. It feels like fire, and can even leads to the loss of limbs. It also causes convulsions and hallucinations."

"So, not all of the people who ate ergot-infested rye ended up dead?"

"No. Sometimes the monks took in sufferers and fed them wine and bread made out of wheat, and some recovered, but many were crippled for life.

She looked from the photograph to the one across it, which depicted cripples in the Middle Ages, who had lost their lower legs. They had wooden pegs to rest on as they begged for food.

"Medieval Europeans called it St. Anthony's Fire," I added. "Poor people tended to eat rye, because it cost less, and they were so hungry, and had so few food options, that they used it regardless of the condition, which they couldn't always understand anyway, while the wealthy ate wheat, which didn't carry this risk, so they didn't get sick."

"And you think that Vasily and this French scientist, Jean-Claude Babineaux, have ergot poisoning?! They're going to lose their lower legs, and possibly their hands?!"

"Yes, that's exactly what I think," I said, glaring back at the TV.

"Why is this happening?!" my aunt wailed in disgust.

"I have a theory: unemployment and frustration at having skills that aren't being used and paid for anymore, and anger at a loss of empire. There are lots of biopreparat scientists with no jobs, and they present a threat to the world. The threat is that they will market their skills to any buyer, no matter what the danger to whomever may be concerned, or that they will steal or breed microbes and release them to make some extremist statement…about whatever their agenda is."

"Steal or breed microbes...?"

"Yes. They could use their access to stored stockpiles, or just breed some, such as anthrax, in their own kitchen. They know how."

Aunt Eloise looked horrified.

"Remember," I went on, "bioweapons are the cheapest of the three big threats, others being chemical and nuclear weapons. Some disaffected biopreparat scientist could just do this independently, and if they breed the microbes, do it on their own, with no one any the wiser until they pull the trigger on their homemade stockpile."

"Do you think that's what's going on?"

"Yes, I think that that is exactly what is going on," I replied. "Whatever you do, eat and drink ALL of whatever you have while you are at the table – leave nothing unattended to be touched by anyone else. Otherwise, abandon it. Don't accept ANY food from Boris or anyone else who isn't a chef or a wait staff person while we're here."

"He had rye crackers. Do you think that he is the one?"

"Maybe. But what if he's not acting alone? He's not the only one with ties to P4. Max visited Dr. Babineaux before the trip."

"So, either one of them could get their hands on a microbe..."

"Well...that's what we don't know. Did whoever it is steal them? Stealing could be done by someone who knows the procedures of a biopreparat facility, and a politically connected person could find that out from a tour, which Max has had access to, and which Boris has worked with. But neither of them was anything other than a guest at P4, so Dr. Babineaux could have been the 'in' for that...I don't know. There are too many variables that I just don't know."

"But what about the bioweapons? Where and what are they?"

"Like I said, I don't know. But I think that someone near us has them. I don't know how they got them, how they are keeping them...in a safe or a fridge, perhaps, disguised somehow, maybe...but I think that the ergot thing is really just about getting people out of someone's way."

"So...we've got a murderer among us."

"It seems that way."

"So, what do we do?" Can you explain this to, I don't know, the cruise director?"

I paused to think that over. "That aspiring comedian? Well...maybe...he would have to take something like this as a serious thing and not as a joke...or maybe the excursions director..."

"Why her?"

"I think I may have an opportunity to talk with her in the course of the day rather than by deliberately seeking her out. At least, I would hope so. I can't just walk up to the desk and tell her about it with any random passenger hearing it. That could cause a panic. And there is another problem with trying to warn about it."

"What's that?"

"Credibility. I'm not a biopreparat scientist, nor even a scientist. I'm just someone who studies about such threats. I've never worked in a security organization, nor in a spy or surveillance agency. I'm just me, an intellectual on the autism spectrum. I mean, look at what happened with the Romany pickpockets in the traboule: two guys on our tour lost their wallets, but while we were there with those Romany pickpockets, and I tried to make a scene to warn everyone, all I got for my trouble were condescending, uncomprehending stares."

"But they understand what you were trying to do now," Aunt Eloise said.

"Well, yeah, now that it's too late to do them any good!" I replied, disgusted. "I guarantee you, right now, those two guys are probably out trying to get replacement passports, new credit cards, and whatever else they need just to get home, and they're missing whatever excursions they planned to go on. But oh no – don't pay any attention to that odd woman, they thought!"

"Sigh…" That was my aunt's favorite expression of disgust.

"Yes, 'sigh' indeed, but meanwhile, we can't afford to wait until it's too late for this problem. The consequences of letting a microbe loose are far worse and much farther-reaching than those of a pickpocket. It's bad enough that the rye crackers, if that's what did this, got deployed."

'So…what do we do now?" Aunt Eloise asked.

"We go out on our next tour as usual, and behave as if nothing is wrong, and I will look for my next chance to talk to Clotilde. I think that's our best option right now."

"Will she listen to you, though?" my aunt worried.

"We'll see. I may just have to ask her to help me contact P4 and Interpol. Its headquarters is in Lyon, on the north part of the Presque-Ile, which would turn out to be convenient if she listens to me," I said.

"Let's hope we find her then, and that she does," my aunt replied.

I picked up my camera, we took our earpieces, and we headed out.

Intrigue On a Longship Cruise

Too bad that those ear-pieces only worked one-way...it would have been nice to use them to call for help, if necessary.

Intrigue On a Longship Cruise

Escaping to a Château

Escaping to a Château

The Château de Fléchères was north of the city of Lyon, in Fareins. It even had its own street: the Allée de Fléchères.

It was just off the main route, and we saw the small but majestic building through the trees as we came alongside the property, before turning off onto that street.

The bus pulled to a stop near the front gate.

When we left the *Sif*, it had been cloudy, as it had been all morning, so of course we had each taken a red cane umbrella with us, but now, as we arrived, the sun came out, shining brightly.

I remembered reading that anthrax didn't do well in sunlight.

But I didn't know what microbe we were being threatened with.

We all got off the bus, and I looked around again at our group.

Clotilde was nowhere to be seen.

I tried not to focus on biopreparat problems for now, but I couldn't help it.

I was looking around at our group, noting who was here and who was not. And just who was here?

Only women, as it turned out.

It seemed that historic preservation and historic restoration didn't capture the fancy and interest of the men on the trip. Their wives were here without them.

Of course, there were plenty of women who were traveling without husbands, including myself, my aunt, Carolyn, and Amy, but I couldn't help noting that Karen was here, and even Stacey.

"Hey Karen," I said. "No Max? And you're out on an afternoon tour?"

She smiled. "I asked Father O'Shaughnessy if it would be all right to come on this one, and he said yes – I can always do my prayers when we get back. He's going to wait for me, and do them with me."

"Oh. Sounds like a plan," I said.

"Max told me to go ahead and have fun; I've always wanted to see a real château," Karen added.

He did, did he? I thought to myself. All I said was, "It looks like lots of women have always wanted to see one. Look at our group: it's all women."

Karen did a double-take at that. "Oh yeah...isn't that nice"!

I didn't bother to ask if Max was in the dining hall as we toured, attending mass.

What difference would that make, if he was indeed the one we needed to worry about?! Whoever it was, they could – and probably would – wait until more people were aboard, so as to inflict maximum damage. At this point, I thought it was Boris. Was Max in on it?

This was pointless, this obsessing and worrying.

I wasn't going to let them win by spoiling my fun on this tour, while I could do nothing else but take the tour. It would make no difference to the outcome anyway, whether I enjoyed this excursion or spent it in a state of anxiety...and I needed to stay calm and ready to take Clotilde aside as soon as I saw her and convince her of the danger.

I turned my attention to the historic building beyond the fence.

Aunt Eloise had been particularly excited to take this tour because at home, she had been watching something on PBS called *Escape to the Château*. If I called her on a Saturday evening, I had to make sure it was not during this show, because she really liked it.

I had watched an episode or two before it finished for the season; it was like *This Old House*, but in France, and with British buyers doing the restorations. They wanted the châteaux as wedding and other events venues.

After checking carefully – after booking us for this particular tour and before embarking on this trip – I had confirmed that this particular château was not on that show.

Now that we were on the tour, it was going to be spoiled with anxiety over the possibility of danger waiting for us, back at the ship.

Perfect. Just perfect, I thought.

I was angry, and felt like I couldn't do anything about it beyond fully understand and appreciate the danger.

I hated that.

And I had to act like a happy tourist for now.

For me, that meant continuing to take photographs and to listen to our guide, because the people on our group were used to that level of detail-absorption from me. If I suddenly stopped doing what I usually did, it would only draw unwanted attention, and I needed to keep any extra focus off of myself while I looked for a chance to do something...

I took a breath and looked at our guide, Simone.

She was a woman in her forties, I guessed, with chin-length brown hair. She wore casual pants, a blouse, and a plain jacket, and, of course, comfortable shoes. She smiled at us, happy to be here, and led us through the gate.

We were on a long driveway that moved up from the main gate, over a short bridge, and to the stone wall that surrounded the château.

We looked down on either side of the bridge as we crossed it. This château even had a moat! It seemed to be just for show; it was shallow, and the water in it was clean. This led us up to an open drawbridge.

A drawbridge? This wasn't a Medieval castle. It was built during the Renaissance...

"The builders of this place must have wanted to hang on to the security design of the Medieval Age, even though it was the Renaissance by then," I commented to Aunt Eloise. "Maybe it made them feel safer, out in the countryside."

She looked at me. "Maybe. Makes sense."

She was being rather quieter than usual.

I must have scared the hell out of her back in our cabin...

...but I couldn't take it back, and I didn't want to.

At least she would take my warnings seriously.

Simone brought us to the front gate, and began to tell us about the place. It was originally built in the 1600s. Its moat, which is now mostly empty, contains benign items such as clear water, frogs, and lily pads.

Simone was deliberately keeping us outside for a little while, because there was a lot about the exterior to point out and discuss.

She told us that the château was usually closed on Tuesdays, but that it had been opened just for us. With that, she led us through the drawbridge…and into the courtyard for a magnificent sight:

As we had all expected and hoped, the château was beautiful – just like something right out of a French fairy tale.

Once again, I reveled in the lovely weather after a week of rain, enjoying how clear and sunny it was for this tour, because the grounds were part of the attraction, and I would get some great photographs.

It remained to be seen whether or not there would be a 'later' in which to enjoy them, but I intended to live each moment as if there would be one, and continued to enjoy the tour.

"Huguenots – French Calvinists – built this place," Simone told us.

She also told us that a group of historic preservation enthusiasts – 3 French men – had bought it, and were in the long process of restoring it. And…they also had another château! As for this one, they had been working on it for years, and it would never be finished, but that was the fun of it for them.

One of them came into the courtyard to visit with us for that part of the tour, and to show us some things.

Simone directed our gaze upwards, and pointed out some details that were intricate, beautiful, and functional all at once. None of us had seen anything like it before, and we all stared, fascinated, as she explained them.

There was a stone plaque over the door that had lost some of its inscription over time, and sundial clock that was divided into 2 parts, one on either wing of the château. The sundial had not been affected by the ravages of time and acid rain. It was fine, and once you knew how to read it, it was still possible to tell time by it on a sunny day.

Simone showed us how the roofing tiles were being restored, with a beautiful shade of dark blue paint. It was a slow, expensive process:

The side sections were done, and the middle still remained to be done. The side sections looked gorgeous, and we could imagine how good it would look when the entire roof was newly re-blued.

One of the first things that we found out was that the owners were French, not British. The chateau owner who joined us in the courtyard had a great time watching Simone explain it all; he added a few things from time to time in French, which she then translated for us, happy to add it all to her tour's lecture.

"That explains why this chateau hasn't been on *Escape to the Château*, then," Aunt Eloise said to me.

I nodded and smiled.

Maybe we could stay calm and keep up appearances long enough...

We went inside, and were told that flash photography was allowed – just don't ask who is in the artwork, because most of it is not original to the house. It was assembled by the current owners. Everything is a period piece, but originals cannot be had due to the chaos of the French Revolution.

Inside, we saw two hallways, one straight ahead, and another to the right. We went forward, into the one with the red curtains.

We went into the drawing room, which was to the left.

Simone told us that the owners lived in a tiny portion of the château, which had a modern kitchen and bathroom, in what seemed like a "backstage" area that visitors would never see. Seeing it would ruin the mystique of this experience anyway, they thought, and we agreed with them.

As far as we were concerned, what mattered to us was that we were actually inside a château! We were thrilled to hear all about the restoration efforts, and a little bit about what it was like to live in it.

Simone led us into the main drawing room, and told us that the furnishings and paintings were not original to the house, as those had been lost around the time of the French Revolution. Nevertheless, the owners had gone to a lot of trouble to acquire furnishings and paintings from the 17th and 18th centuries.

It looked as though they had done a pretty good job of it!

We were told we could sit anywhere but on the center sofa, as it was a fragile antique. We didn't sit down though; we would do that later in the tour, when we returned to this room for a treat to eat, Simone announced.

Really? We all perked up at that, looking forward to whatever it would be. Meanwhile, we paced around looking at everything. There were lots of things to see: game pieces on a side table, a stained-glass chandelier, art on the walls, and more.

There were many rooms to see. The dining room had a secret door in the corner, for servants to bring in the food. It didn't look that secret; it just blended into the wallpaper, with the outline of it showing clearly.

Simone told us that the owners ate in here every day. "But they bring in their own food," she added.

We looked out the back windows, and continued on to the next rooms.

Simone led us into the hall and over to the staircase, which clearly was a long way from full restoration. It looked solid enough, and safe, but the wall decorations were faded. Despite their ancient condition, though, beautiful scenes could still be seen along the stairwell walls.

Upstairs we saw a restored bedroom for the lord and lady, and her boudoir, which meant the room where she had her lovers visit her.

That was not unusual in a time of arranged marriages, often with a much-older husband whom she did not choose. A political alliance is not romantic.

We all turned to look at Simone when she said the word "boudoir".

She had to have been expecting that!

"Marriages were political, and they were blessed by a high-ranking church official…along with the marriage bed," she added. The marriage bed was elaborately outfitted, as one might expect, and ensconced between a huge set of curtains.

Winters were cold in France. The curtains trapped at least some heat around the bed.

Simone continued, "Lovers would be received in another room, even though it was the next room."

She led us over to the boudoir and showed it to us.

"Today it's just a dressing room, not such a racy thing!" she added.

I imagined the lady of the château, forced to live with a man who had been chosen for her, and daring to enjoy trysts with men that she had chosen herself whenever she could manage it.

If this were a home for an aristocratic family post-Revolution – and there were a few who had come back in the 19th century and bought their châteaux back and restored them – it could actually be just a dressing room. No need to arrange them for political advantage without a monarchy…

The next room we saw was full of frescos and one huge portrait, of the Huguenot King Henri IV. "Henri IV actually switched back and forth between Protestantism and Catholicism as it suited him, depending on the political advantage he was seeking," Simone said.

That figured. Kings did that. It was interesting to hear of one besides Henry VIII of England who did it, though.

The frescos were quite a sight. They wrapped all around the bedroom's walls, showing courtiers prancing, dancing, and playing musical instruments.

And then there was the bed. In a concession to safety, the entire château had been electrified, and the light fixtures on either side of it had bulbs that mimicked candle flames without the danger of actual candles. No one was sorry about this bit of inauthenticity.

We left the Henri IV bedroom for an adjoining room, which was set up as a dining room.

We continued on into a large upstairs drawing room.

It was impressively furnished and decorated, and well lit by the sunny day. It even had a fabulous tapestry hanging on one wall:

Next, we saw another bedroom, which had more frescos and the most beautiful blues for its bed and chairs. There were many more photographs in my camera by the time we had looked at everything, but the point of this narrative is not to put every last one here, so a few shall suffice.

The last room that we saw upstairs was an office. It had ashes in the fireplace, frescoes of colonnades that gave the room the optical illusion of a large, three-dimensional setting, and a beautiful embroidered chair. It made us wonder what the original furniture had been like. These were all aesthetic guesses, after all — stunningly beautiful guesses, but guesses, nonetheless.

After we had seen all this, it was time to go back downstairs to the first drawing room we had seen, where the owner of the château waited for us. He was all set to serve a traditional Lyonnais tart with pink almond praline on top, plus champagne, or orange juice, or mimosas.

The tart was delicious! It was soft, and the almonds were easy to eat. The pink sugar made a pretty presentation. I had orange juice with my slice, as did Aunt Eloise. Some people opted for champagne, and several for mimosas.

At this point, Simone informed us, with a sidelong smile at our host, that he had originally been unwilling to offer mimosas, as they are not a traditional French offering with anything, particularly this Lyonnais tart. "But," she concluded triumphantly, "we are catering to tourists, and making them happy is what counts!"

He knew what story she was telling, and he nodded and laughed about it. It was good that he had a sense of humor, since he had chosen a project that meant dealing with strangers. These tours helped to cover expenses.

We continued our question-and-answer session with him, translated by Simone, and were told that, for a full history of this place, we could visit its website: https://chateaudeflecheres.com/en/the-chateau

After that, we were invited to see the grounds, out back. Orange trees in huge pots graced the curved double staircase that ran down to the garden.

The garden was an impressive sight somehow, despite its rather small size. I was probably comparing it with Versailles, which was rather silly. This garden's shrubs were flawlessly sculpted and trimmed, it had a pool of water in the middle, and I could imagine a period movie being shot here someday.

Perhaps that would actually happen, once the roof was fully repainted, I thought, as I took some more photographs of it.

"We have to go down there and look around," Aunt Eloise said, and she went down the staircase, using the stone wall as a railing.

I followed her, doing the same thing, as did at least half of the women in our group. They fanned out around the part of the lawn that was closest to the building for a few minutes, and then we all turned back.

The drinks we had just consumed were getting to us.

We all walked straight through the chateau and out into the courtyard, where we found and used the rest rooms, which were in the stables. They were to the left as we faced the drawbridge, and quite comfortable, with modern fixtures and amenities.

Okay, I know it's not historically accurate, but it's reassuring to know that up-to-date plumbing is available, accessible, clean, and otherwise part of the experience. Well...Aunt Eloise can abide and enjoy camping, but not me!

And...there were no horses, of course; as the owners had cars.

Once we were comfortable again, we had one more thing to see. Down in front was the cuisine – the kitchen. It was under the château, through a long tunnel! Seeing it was worth going down there.

The servants who worked in this cuisine had lived down there.

There were two rooms to see, one of which had an enormous fireplace outfitted with a kettle, a small over for bread, a huge paddle for taking loaves out and putting them in, and other equipment. The other room had a washing and mending area for linens and dishes. It looked well-researched, although we were seeing it without Simone.

The chateau owners had taken great pains with this part of the restoration project, and the result was impressive, with copper cookware, kitchen tools that included a scale (European recipes use weights rather than volume for their measurements), and lots of squashes. Squashes keep, so they make ideal food props!

We had to hurry back up to the courtyard when we realized that it was getting late, so we did. Looking north, we saw the small tunnel that led to the drawbridge, and the stables, bathed in bright sunshine.

With that, we realized that we had just finished our final tour of the trip. We had loved it!

To add to the upbeat feeling of it all, there was Clotilde at the end of the bridge, waiting for us.

Great – I might actually be able to take her aside and talk to her.

Another Use for a Cane Umbrella

Another Use for a Cane Umbrella

Clotilde looked at me differently than she had all week.

It wasn't exactly the look that I had expected, which would have been a dismissive one, but it wasn't a look that told me she was convinced of what I was telling her, either.

We were standing a bit away from the bus, hopefully out of earshot, while people got back on.

I had made up my mind that Boris was the suspect to focus on.

Aunt Eloise was standing off to the side, watching me talk with Clotilde, and doing her best to keep other people from interrupting us.

"You want me to call Interpol and P4?" Clotilde said.

She looked incredulous. Incredulous that I was asking for something so specific, and a little bit scared.

Good.

This was scary.

"Tell me again why."

Obviously, I had my work cut out for me to convince her of the danger that we were dealing with. And, I needed her help, fluent in French and with the culture of how to ask for that help. I could only stammer along slowly in French, and this was an emergency.

"Okay...you know those Russian guys who are traveling on the Sif, Boris and Vasily, who got sick and had to be medevaced off?"

"Medevac? What is that?"

"Evacuated due to a medical emergency."

"Oh – yes! What about them?"

"Have you been following the news reports about Vasily, and did you know what the two of them did for a career?"

"No. Tell me." She looked like someone who wished that an annoying and peculiar conversation would end.

I took a deep breath, and said, "Okay – get ready for a long data-dump of an answer. I'll pause and go back over whatever is necessary. If you've heard of this stuff before, I'll be surprised."

"Tell me."

"They worked in a field called biopreparat. Sorry to throw yet another English word at you, but it's important. It means preparation against the possibility of a bioweapons attack. They worked with the most dangerous, virulent microbes, developed vaccines against them, and probably, since that's what the Russians did up until Glastnost, stockpiled germs for use as bioweapons. Much of that stockpile, but not all, was allegedly destroyed. Some is still kept, though."

Clotilde listened to me without a word, staring at me steadily.

Then she spoke. "And you think that Vasily's illness is related to this? How? And how does P4 fit into it?"

"P4, as you should know, handles those highly virulent pathogens, and under very tight security. It is very likely that Boris and Vasily visited scientists there before joining our tour."

She stared at me, worried. "They visited other bio…what is it?"

"Biopreparat scientists, or at least one of them. And I think that it is the one who has also been in the news, because he is sick now, sick with what sounds like the same thing that Vasily is sick with."

Clotilde recoiled a bit. "Is it contagious?"

"I don't think so, but I do think that I know what it is, and that Boris caused it to get these two men out of his way."

Clotilde turned to make sure that her face was not visible to the people on the bus, because she was looking scared.

"Yeah," I said. "That's how I felt this afternoon, just before we left the ship, when I heard one more news report and finally put it all together. I was afraid to just walk up to the front desk and ask for help with this problem in case Boris heard me. He already knows that I know what the word 'biopreparat' means, and he didn't like that. In fact, all week, he has been following me around, and more than once, he tried to get me to try some of what I think caused this illness."

"What is this illness?"

"It's something called by two names: St. Anthony's Fire, and ergotism. It causes convulsions, hallucinations, miscarriages in women – though that's not an issue for the sick patients, because they're both men – and, most horrifying of all, dry gangrene. That means that feet and hands turn black and die. It feels like fire running through the feet and hands as they die and rot off."

"And the doctors in the hospital have said all this, that the patients have this, this St. Anthony's Fire?"

"No. They haven't figured it out yet, so they only see the symptoms. It was common during Medieval times, but it is almost unheard of now. I think that's why they don't have the diagnosis yet. And Vasily and this P4 scientist, a Dr. Jean-Claude Babineaux, are in two different hospitals, so the connection hasn't yet been made."

"But how do you know that this is what is wrong with them? What causes it?"

"It's caused by a fungus in rye. I don't like rye, and Boris has rye crackers that he made himself. He eats them, he says. He showed me some, twice. The first time, the crackers were one color, which was all beige, like one would expect of rye. The second time, they were speckled with black. That's what ergot looks like."

Clotilde stared at me. "Why would someone do this?!"

"That's the part about why I want you to call P4. If I'm right, and I hate to think that I might be, we will need them to take away whatever Boris has. I'm worried that he had brought some horrible pathogen on board, perhaps in a disguised container, and kept it in the refrigerator in his cabin. I don't know what he's got, but if he's got something, it's going to be very, very dangerous – probably lethal, and in a slow, horrific way to experience."

She seemed at a temporary loss for words, but found her voice again after a moment and asked, "But, why do this?!"

"Why? Lots of biopreparat scientists from Russia have been cut from their jobs and have no income. Some are angry; they don't like the comfortable, democratic, developed western world, they don't like our cultures, they find us smug, and that's why they would want to hurt us. France has the most beautiful ecosystem and culture of Europe, while the Russians have a freezing cold, inhospitable part of the planet, with no warm coastlines for shipping – only the icy Arctic ones. Envy, anger, disenfranchisement, what more do you need to have a recipe for risk?" I said, hoping that I was getting through to her.

"So, you think that they would set something off here…"

"Yes, I do. The two choices are: one, sell biopreparat skills to a nation that is not a friend of the western ones, or two, make a big statement with an act of terrorism – bioterrorism. It's inexpensive, too."

"And you want my help in calling Interpol and P4?"

"Yes, I do."

"You speak French, I noticed. Why ask me, and tell me all this?"

I gave a short laugh. "Have you heard me speak French? It is slow, halting, and grossly inadequate for an emergency of this sort. Also, I come across like an excited intellectual. I need another person to help me, one who speaks French rapidly, and a native speaker like you will be able to do that. Also, I am a lawyer, and one of the first things that they teach you is not to speak for yourself if you need an advocate, but to get some help. So, I'm getting some help."

And I looked at her, appealing to her to actually help me, and fast.

Clotilde leaned back and thought about this.

Just then, my aunt walked up to us, looking very intense.

"Clotilde, are you going to help? It seems that we need to act quickly, and to at least get word to the doctors who are taking care of those two sick men that it might be ergot poisoning."

Clotilde looked at her, then nodded. "Yes, you are right. I will call from here, and then we can go back to the ship and see what can be done, and if anything needs to be done."

She looked at me.

"I hope that this is a false alarm," I said. "I really do. But I have a sickening feeling that it's not."

She nodded, took out her phone, and looked some things up on it, scrolling through a couple of items. Then she made a call.

I hoped it wasn't some stupid call to have me removed. That's always the worry when someone tries to do the right thing…but I did hear her use the French word "ergotisme" and then go on to say a lot more, which I was able to follow somewhat, so I decided to stay hopeful.

A moment later, she put me on the phone. It was on speaker mode.

"Hello?" I said, hoping that she had indeed called for the right kind of help.

"Hello. Is this Arielle Desrosiers?"

"Yes. Who am I speaking to?" I asked.

A man with a slight French accent spoke to me. "This is Jean-Pierre Valland. I'm with Interpol. I understand that you suspect that two sick scientists have been poisoned with ergot, and that you suspect that a pathogen might be released."

"Yes. That's right," I said.

"Can you tell me why you suspect this?"

I went through the long and detailed explanation that I had just taken Clotilde through. The agent listened, stopping me now and then to check some details.

"Are you, by any chance, looking these things up on a computer as I am telling you about them?" I asked.

"Yes, as a matter of fact, I am," he replied.

"And? Does that help?"

"Yes, it does."

"Don't you need the names of both Russian scientists, particularly the one who is not sick, and who has those rye crackers? It's Boris Volkov," I added. "Maybe you can find some scientific journal articles that he has authored somewhere, like the PubMed database. That might help."

Silence for a moment, and then, "Yes...I see some here. I'm not a scientist, but he has written a few. Who is the other one, who got sick?"

"Vasily Legasov. But he's incapacitated now, and he seemed so nice. I'm sure that Boris just wanted him out of his way, and he is in fact now out of his way."

"Yes...he is..." said Agent Valland. "I'm just scrolling through the names of the scientists who have published together, and...yes! Found him, with Volkov. So that proves that they know each other from work as well as on your tour."

"Okay, so what happens next?" I asked.

Agent Valland said, "I would like to meet you at your ship and talk with you. I'll bring some people with me, and we'll try to approach as if nothing odd is going on for now. We can't make it obvious that we are who we are, or we won't catch anyone or stop anything – if, in fact, there is anyone to catch or anything to be stopped."

"So, we should go back now and look for you?"

"Yes, please go back, and I'll find you."

"How will we know it's you?" I asked.

Clotilde looked interested in this answer, and reached for her phone.

"I am wearing dark blue pants, sneakers, and a blue buttoned shirt. I have straight, short, light-brown hair and no glasses. And I will look for you. Tell me: what do you look like?" Agent Valland asked.

I leaned over to speak into Clotilde's phone. "I have dark brown hair that is starting to go gray, with traces of purple in it, brown eyes, and I'm five feet, four-and-a-half inches tall. I'm wearing black pants, black shoes, and a bright pink shirt with a black sweater, and carrying a bright blue rain jacket. I also have a Nikon camera with a large lens."

"I see. All right. Go back to your ship, and I'll meet you there. Please put your cruise organizer back on the phone for a moment."

I hoped that this was for real, and that they weren't plotting to cart me away to the nearest obliging loony bin the moment we got back for my trouble, only to have everyone else get exposed to some pathogen.

But it sounded, from the French conversation I heard, as though Clotilde was only giving Agent Valland directions to the *Sif*, so that he could go right to it.

After she ended the call, we all got back onto the bus.

Aunt Eloise sat in our seats, and Clotilde sat up front, alone. She seemed to be avoiding conversation with the driver, who gave her an odd look, but then pulled out onto the highway.

It wasn't a long ride back, but for us, it was a tense one.

I hoped that the other passengers on the bus were able to just talk amongst themselves and ride in blissful ignorance.

And I hoped that when we got back to the Sif, things would work out okay for all of us...except for Boris.

If he was even on board.

I knew that biopreparat scientists were vaccinated against any pathogen that they handled. Could he have set something off and fled to watch the chaos from a distance and get away?!

This worrying did no good.

I checked my camera, looked out the windows, and rode in silence with my aunt.

It felt like a very long ride, even though it was only 45 minutes.

Maybe 45 minutes was a long time.

But any length of time seems long when you dread the end of it.

We did arrive, and, oddly, the sun was still shining, and the quai and our ship didn't look any different.

But, why should it?

Only we knew that something wasn't right.

We all got off the bus, and I glanced around, looking for a man with a blue buttoned shirt and dark blue pants.

I hoped he wasn't waiting in some obvious spot so as to tip Boris off as I scanned the quai and the ship's gangplank for him.

"I think that might be him," my aunt said, looking past the gangplank and to the left of it. We had gotten off the bus, walked down the steps to the quai below the parking area, and across the cobblestones.

Clotilde spoke to me. She was on her phone.

"I'm on the phone with Agent Valland," she told me.

Sure enough, the man we had noticed was using his phone, too.

"He says to board the ship, and he'll follow."

"Okay," I said, and I started to walk over to the gangplank, with Aunt Eloise close behind me.

Agent Valland and Clotilde walked up behind us.

I went a few paces up, and then I saw him.

Boris was just inside the *Sif*, in the lobby, and he was holding a large cannister…and reaching for the lid.

Boris had his back to us, and was holding his sealed cannister out in front of him.

Just then, Max and Karen came into view. They were walking down the last steps of the main staircase. Their cabin, like that of the Russians', was upstairs.

Max saw what Boris was holding, and his mouth dropped open in absolute horror. He froze, grabbed Karen's hand, and pulled her away – not that that would make any difference if Boris got the cap off of that thing.

Karen just looked confused.

I knew that was because Max had taken a tour of P4, and she hadn't, so she didn't understand the danger posed by that cannister.

I also knew, now that this was happening, that Max had turned out to be the red herring of this whole scenario. The look on his face gave that away. He was in a panic, powerless, surprised, and he didn't know what to do.

So…just a MAGA guy without a plan.

Meanwhile, Boris wasn't saying a word.

He clearly had a plan, and it was a terrifying one.

He was going to just open this container, it seemed, and let the damage it would cause do all of the talking, as chaos ensued.

It looked obvious enough:

He would twist that thing apart and release the pathogen, infecting everyone on this ship. From there, the germ would go viral – the kind of literal, off-the-grid viral that would immediately kill people. Lots of people. Once a pathogen is out of the bottle, it's too late.

But…simply dropping it on the floor would not make it smash open. Those things were not made of anything so easily breached as glass. Oh no – only plexiglass, or metal, or something else that was reliably durable, would be used as a container for such a deadly virus.

Boris would have to get that lid off, and it looked like it would take a few more seconds of strenuous twisting.

As we approached, my aunt caught sight of him and gripped my arm as if to tell me not to go any closer.

Instead, I took my camera strap off of my neck, put it over her head, and whispered, "Hold this."

We were carrying the red cane umbrellas that we had taken when we thought it would be a rainy afternoon. They were still neatly closed.

I took my aunt's umbrella and moved quickly and quietly the rest of the way up the gangplank, being careful to use the metal foot-grips and to tread lightly, thus not shaking the structure.

There had been very few times in my life when I had felt so gloriously, rapidly, and fortuitously sure of something, but this was easily one of them, if not the most memorable time I would ever have of such a thing.

As Aunt Eloise watched, horrified, I took advantage of the fact that Boris's attention was far too focused on the people in the longship – the staff plus the passengers who were walking around the lobby, milling about after returning from their tours – to notice me.

They were all scattered here and there around the front desk, the shop, the staircase, and near the cushy chairs and tables on either side of the staircase.

I recognized the faces of the other passengers and the staff of our longship after spending several days among them. They looked confused.

I was terrified, but I was also angry. I had come on a fantasy vacation to France to enjoy great sights, sounds, smells, tastes, and whatever else – not to get killed, and not by some damned virus!

There was no time to think about the odds of success or failure.

I moved off of the gangplank and onto the outer deck, and then gripped one of the two 3-foot-long, dark-red Longship Cruises cane umbrellas in each hand, hoping that no one would turn to look straight at me until I had done what I was about to do.

Ignoring the confused expression on my aunt's face, and glad that Agent Valland was still a few paces behind her, I rapidly tossed both umbrellas slightly upwards, catching the closed umbrellas halfway down and gripping them tightly.

Then I advanced on Boris just as he reached for the lid of the cannister.

Intrigue On a Longship Cruise

His hand hovered just above the twist-off cap, and I knelt behind him, stretching out with the hooks of the cane umbrellas toward his ankles.

This was happening so fast that, even though the other people in the atrium saw me, and even though some realized what I was doing, they did not have enough time to react.

I positioned the canes around his ankles and tugged as hard as I could just as his finger began to grip the top of the lid, hoping it was hard enough.

It was!

Boris toppled over and dropped the cannister, which went skittering away from us, under the staircase, and down to the lower deck.

I fell to my knees, hard, as I succeeded in knocking him over, but I didn't care.

If I was going to die, I had decided, at least it would be passive.

With that, chaos ensued, but it was a chaos inspired by relief, not of terror. The Interpol agent jumped Boris and handcuffed him.

I rolled out of the way, dropping the umbrellas.

Suddenly, four people in white biohazard suits - the P4 scientists I had hoped for! – dashed down the stairs to get the cannister.

For a moment, I refused to savor the victory, wondering if there were any more bad guys around to deal with, and wondering whether or not my actions had definitively dealt with the threat.

But they had.

"Ça va!" we heard a woman yell from below. It was a P4 scientist. She had the cannister, and it was still sealed! What a relief.

Her colleague had brought a vacuum-sealable biohazard lock-box as he followed her, and we all heard them putting the cannister inside and clicking it shut.

What a satisfying sound – a deeply satisfying sound!

We still didn't even know what it was.

It could have been smallpox. We would have been disfigured horridly and then possibly died. No, wait…we were of a generation that had been vaccinated against that one as children.

Bubonic plague? The Russians had a big supply of that one.

Anthrax? Boris could have made that on his own and brought it.

Marburg virus? That one was worse than Ebola…

But did he steal this pathogen rather than transport it here?

That would mean that he only had to get it from P4. Was it one of their containers? Quite likely.

Regardless, if that cannister had been opened, we would all – every one of us on this ship, plus anyone within at least a hundred feet of it – have been violently and contagiously ill with an untreatable disease in seconds.

There would have likely been no cure and no hope for any us while one was desperately searched for in the southern part of the city. It would have been too late to save any of us, so my seemingly wild risk in leaping at this terrorist was totally worth it.

And it had paid off.

A rather shocked-looking British cruise director, Jonathan, helped me to my feet. I had crawled backwards into him.

"All right, darlin'!" he said, grinning from ear to ear. "You got him!" He didn't let go of me, as I was suddenly teetering a bit, out of breath and still amazed that my gamble had worked.

I stood up and backed away, looking for a wall or a doorframe or a wall to pull myself up against.

A moment later, the adrenaline rush wore off, and I staggered over to the long, soft, cushy bench that spanned the length of the lobby on the shop side of it. People saw me heading for it, even though I didn't have the energy to focus on them just then, and made room for me.

Aunt Eloise appeared with my camera, looking as shocked as I felt. She didn't try to hand it back to me, and I was glad, because I wasn't ready to hold the heavy device just yet.

Someone got off the bench and gave her their spot on it so she could sit next to me.

Everything still looked strange to me. I felt like I was simultaneously high and disoriented as I watched the people around me dealing with Boris the Genocidal Maniac and his container of viral death.

"Take a deep breath – you stopped him!" my aunt said.

I looked at her.

Somehow, that brought me back to my senses, and I grinned.

I was starting to feel like myself again, and pretty good.

The P4 scientists stood out like sore thumbs, as they wore biohazard suits that were wired for communication. If anyone survived this attack, it would be them. The rest of us would not.

There were at least four of them.

Intrigue On a Longship Cruise

The Interpol agents...the only reason I assumed that they were Interpol agents was that they were people I had not seen before, they were physically fit, dressed in nondescript clothing, and wore serious and deadpan facial expressions while looking ready to spring.

I looked around some more.

Our shipmates – fellow tourists – were staring at me.

I looked away, then back at them.

I felt uncomfortable being stared at.

Usually, it was because I was the odd woman out, the different one.

This time, it was because of what I had just done, and it hit me: this was a good reason to be stared at.

I looked back at them happily.

I didn't smile, though. It was more like...relief. Relief and satisfaction that we were all going to be okay.

Chef Ronne came over to me with one of his creations. Today's drink was a mix of fresh-squeezed orange juice and vermouth. It tasted and felt great, and it steadied me.

We watched as the terrorist was marched past us, perp-walked down the gang-plank, and put into a police vehicle that had appeared while we were looking the other way. We could see it from the bench.

"How did you know that that would work?" Aunt Eloise wanted to know. She wasn't the only one. The maître d', the concierge, the excursions director, the chef, the cruise director, and several passengers who were weakly looking around them for the bench, the few cushy chairs by the stairs, and some other people – possibly more Interpol agents – all looked at me, waiting for me to answer.

I thought about that as I took another sip of the delicious drink.

I also took several deep breaths, determined to feel calm and like my usual self as quickly as possible, near-death experience or no near-death experience.

I stared at the floor, wide-eyed, and answered, "I could see that he would have to twist that lid off to infect us all, that he was going to do it, and that the only way to survive was to hurry up and take advantage of the fact that he was spending an awful lot of time talking about what he was going to do. Bad guys tend to do that, and if you don't spend time on emotion yourself, and wait until the problem is dealt with, that usually gives you enough time to do something about it."

They thought about that for a moment.

Then Jonathan said, "Well, yeah, but how did you decide that the umbrellas were the answer?"

With a wry grin, I looked up at him. "They were available, and those hooks just looked so well-suited to the purpose of knocking him over. I figured that if he lost his balance, he wouldn't be able to unscrew that cap. And he wouldn't expect anyone to be anything but too terrified to act. He didn't count on the fact that anyone might be too terrified NOT to act, as I was."

I took another gulp of my drink, and said to the chef, "This is delicious. Do you have any more of these?"

Chef Ronne smiled and said, "I'll make you some more."

We weren't allowed to leave the lobby just yet, however.

P4 scientists converged around us all, dressed in hazmat suits.

I decided not to panic.

Since I hadn't immediately collapsed from exposure to who knew what, writhing in agony, it didn't seem worth it. Someone shifted on the long bench in front of the shop to make room for me and my aunt.

I took the camera back at last.

The P4 scientists came up to each person in turn, swabbed our throats with a long cotton swab, made slides, and inspected the contents under portable microscopes.

I noticed the woman who had chased down the cannister watching me.

I looked up at her, wondering if I would see my own doom in her eyes, and then wondered if I would be able to read such a thing in her face anyway.

She made it easy for me: she smiled warmly at me.

Surprised and pleased, I smiled back.

"So, we are going to live?" I asked her.

"Oui," she said. "Yes. They are not finding any sign that any pathogen was released."

Smiles all around at that!

Well, except for the bad guy, of course. But he was out in a patrol car, cuffed, on the quai. Gone!

The P4 scientists, satisfied by what they saw under their portable microscopes, released the hood clasps on their biohazard suits and began to pack up their equipment.

The smiling woman had chin-length, wavy hair that somehow arced around her face gracefully without getting her eyes. Anyone who looked that thin and chic while being coiffed in such a way as to not be inconvenienced by style choices had to be French, I thought.

Sure enough, when she spoke, her accent prettily confirmed this.

"Bonjour," she said. "I am Dr. Claire Etienne. Nice to meet you!"

I smiled back and said, "Bonjour! I am Arielle Desrosiers, an American lawyer, and this is my aunt, Eloise Desrosiers, an artist. Nice to meet you, too! Very nice…" And I gave a little laugh. I think I was working off some unvented anxiety with it.

"Thank you for averting a disaster," Dr. Etienne said. "How can we stay in touch with you? We will have more questions."

I took out one of my business cards and gave it to her. "My e-mail, website, and other information is on that card, on the front. E-mail is the best way to get my attention once I am at home. My books are on the back of that, and you can view my curriculum vitae if you look around a bit on my website. My husband is a scientist, so that helped me to see what trouble was brewing here."

She flipped the card over, scanning everything, then looked up at me, and nodded. "So that's how you knew."

"Well…it's a long story, how I knew, but one would expect that."

"Yes," she agreed. "One would."

The chic French scientist smiled, and her three male colleagues gave a shout of joy. I looked at them. One was Indian, a handsome guy who looked like he could star in a Bollywood production. Another was the blond Danish guy, and the other was likely from France.

But I was so happy that I had another thought a nanosecond later.

"The vacation is back on!" I said loudly to the room in general.

The staff and the other passengers all cheered.

Intrigue On a Longship Cruise

Gendarmes and Statements

Gendarmes and Statements

Before anyone could stop me, I walked down the gangplank and up to the police car.

With the sun out at last, both literally and figuratively, we could see a beautiful view of the Basilique de Notre-Dame de Fourvière over the historic district as we looked up from the quai.

Everything felt much better now – everything.

The danger was over, and the future was bright again…for now.

Until the next threat in life came along, I supposed.

Hopefully, I wouldn't be so physically close to it then!

This was a bit more excitement than I had ever expected to have.

Boris the Terrorist and Genocidal Maniac, as I now thought of him, was in the back seat, cuffed. He wasn't going anywhere.

"I want to ask him something," I said to the Interpol cops.

They looked at each other, nonplussed, but opened the car door, keeping wary eyes on us both.

The prisoner looked up at me, furious but also puzzled. "What do you want?!" Boris demanded to know.

"I want to know what the point of the ergot poisoning was. It doesn't seem related to your plans to unleash a stolen bioweapon on the city of Lyon."

He looked surprised, but answered me as the cops, who also looked interested in his reply, watched.

"That was practice."

"Practice?! What for?!"

"For killing. I had never done it before. I also needed to get Vasily and Dr. Babineaux out of my way. They would have seen what I was planning and stopped me. Besides," he added, "the deaths that people died in the Middle Ages were varied and horrific. Death has gotten entirely too neat. People die surrounded by palliative care that enables them to ease into death rather than fully appreciate and feel it."

The cops and I exchanged glances.

"And you know what it's like to die just from studying it?!" I said, not asking a question but mocking him instead.

"Well, genocide can be accomplished in a variety of ways, and likely would have to be, because any one method won't do the job. No plague ever wipes out more than millions, and the Earth has billions of humans on it."

"I see. So...you are a mix of Hitler and Dr. Josef Mengele. We're all very happy to disappoint you in that genocide won't be the way that we reduce our species' numbers. 8 billion will just have to be reduced to under a billion and a half – or less than that – without a crime. It may be inconvenient and it not be nasty enough to suit you, but we don't care. We'll find a humane way."

"You won't. You waste your life writing books and merely discussing the idea of doing something about overpopulation. I actually took action."

I laughed at him. "I have readers and am known around the planet for my ideas, and I exchange them with others. I research feasible ways of changing global policy and share them with others. I can change minds, and have educated many people about overpopulation and its dire consequences. You simply seek to erase a few, so now you are identified as someone who is crazy. All you have accomplished is to get captured, and now you can't do anything else about anything."

Boris turned red and raged at me, writhing in his handcuffs.

"You were a nuisance from the start! You wouldn't eat any rye, because you are a spoiled, fussy, pampered American! I tried to find a high place to push you off of several times, but that was impossible, too! You probably don't like heights, either. You are too careful!"

I burst out laughing again, and a bit harder this time, then said, "I am 'too' careful, huh?! More like careful enough, and the gastronomic fussiness saved my life. Thank you for telling me what a difficult person to knock off I proved to be!"

Boris spluttered and raged incoherently in a mix of Russian and English.

I turned to the cops. "I'm done talking with him. I hope you made a note of his confession for the prosecution's benefit."

They looked at me again, nonplussed, then recovered and nodded as they shut the police cruiser door.

I went back up the gangplank and onto the ship to join my aunt, whereupon she and I were escorted up to the terrace, given seats, and told that we would be interviewed shortly by Interpol. We looked at each other, slumping in our chairs.

"Traveling with you has turned into an adventure in more ways than one," she remarked.

"I'm glad to see you're recovering from it so rapidly," I said.

"Well, considering the fact that we would all be dead or worse if you hadn't done something crazy, I have nothing to complain about."

The chef was back with another drink, which I finished in another three lovely gulps. He stood there, not surprised in the least, watching me. I guess he had expected the drink to disappear almost immediately. I had, after all, just had a rapid and shocking experience.

"Would you like another?" he inquired.

I looked up at him and thought about that for a moment.

Aunt Eloise and I had not eaten anything while we were out, and it was the middle of the afternoon. "We had been saving our appetites for another one of your lovely dinners," I said, but some hot coffee with milk might be nice, come to think of it," I said. Dinner, after all, wouldn't be served for another two and a half hours.

The chef smiled and said he would send us a pot of coffee and something to eat with it.

Meanwhile, the Interpol agents came in.

They were two French men, impeccably dressed in casual clothing, looking eminently capable of blending into the population of Lyonnais people who calmly walked around the city. They were thin, somber, and looked like they were in their thirties and forties.

They looked a bit awed and amazed at me for a moment, and then one of them spoke. "Je suis Jean-Claude Arouet, et ceci est Jean-Luc Rousseau," he said to us. "Nous sommes agents d'Interpol."

We nodded and said, "Enchanté a vous connaître."

Then I realized I should say something. "Je m'appelle Arielle Desrosiers, and c'est ma tante, Eloise Desrosiers," I replied.

Agent Rousseau spoke up. "We can conduct this interview in English, if you prefer." He gave his partner a look that I wasn't sure how to interpret, but that was nothing new. Let the neurotypicals figure such things out.

"I think I'll take you up on that. I'm still calming down after all that excitement. Aren't you, Aunt Eloise?" I asked her.

She smiled. "Oui. I mean, yes," she said, agreeing to converse in our native language.

These guys had been among the agents who had appeared behind us as we returned to our ship, I suddenly realized, recognizing them. Now I understood what they were doing: they were trying to blend in and see who else might be involved in this, and to find out, they had

had to let everyone move about, unaware that anything was wrong until it happened.

It must have been part of their job not to act, and to risk letting more members of the public get too close for comfort, but only those who had inadvertently wandered inside of the perimeter as their colleagues were establishing it, before it was apparent to all.

That meant that some people were too close to protect.

That had included us. Maybe I wanted more booze after all…

Too late. A waiter – it was Ivan – came up to us with a tray containing a coffee pot, some macarons, chocolat gateau, and a small pitcher of milk. The table, as expected with the excellent service on this ship, was set for a mini-meal, so he brought mugs, too.

The agents waited while Ivan laid it out and poured the coffee.

"Merci, Andre," I said to him.

He smiled, put some raspberry macarons on my plate, and left.

"Isn't he from Romania?" Aunt Eloise asked.

"Yes," I said. "I guess it's silly to thank people on this ship in French." I said ruefully. By now, I had gotten to know most of the waitstaff, and was used to everyone here.

I looked at Agent Rousseau. "Where's that nice agent who met us here – Agent Valland? Did he leave to lock up Boris?"

The Interpol agents seemed very patient, or had until now.

Now they wanted us to tell them everything that had happened.

Agent Rousseau nodded. "Oui. Yes. Please tell us everything that happened, including everything that made you think that Boris was a threat, from the beginning."

"Okay…" I thought for a moment. "I should probably start with the day that I met Boris and Vasily." So, I did that, and recounted the tale of the entire week, focusing on every encounter with Boris involved, beginning with the offer of rye crackers with odd black specks at the onset of the cruise, going through every peculiar encounter that we had had throughout our trip, and ending with the events of this afternoon.

They recorded it all on their phones.

I still had some of my business cards left, so I gave them each one.

Aunt Eloise told them her name, address, and other contact information.

"We are traveling without our digital data," I warned them, "so we can't log into our social media, e-mail, or anything else until we get home. We just brought our passports, our money, and our tickets. And the cruise documents."

With that, we produced our passports and let them take photographs with their iPhones.

The agents seemed satisfied with all that.

"Can we go home as scheduled tomorrow?" I wanted to know.

Aunt Eloise looked at them, wondering what they would say.

"Yes, it looks as though you can," Agent Arouet said. "If we really need anything else from you, agents in the United States can contact you. A P4 scientist will interview you shortly, but they don't seem worried that anything has happened to you. They just need to know everything that you told us, to completely ensure that the public is protected from whatever was in that cannister."

They paused for a moment and looked as if there were something else on their minds.

"Do you have another question for us?" I asked, curious.

"Oui…yes," Agent Arouet said. "Why did you do it?"

"Why did I do something about the guy with the vial? Why did I pounce on him and make an effort to stop him from opening that thing and killing us all?" I asked, just to clarify.

"Yes. Why did you do that? Most people who found themselves staring death in the face like that would have just…frozen."

I gave them a slight smile. "I am not 'most people', and I have no interest in dying just now, and certainly not that way. I was really quite angry when I tripped Boris with those umbrellas. I came on this trip to eat delectable food, see France, and meet interesting people, not get infected by a terrorist with some horrifying disease."

"But how did you get the idea to trip him as you did?" Agent Arouet wanted to know.

"It was a last-second idea I had, and I realized that it was a now-or-never one, so I did it before he could do what he was obviously about to do, namely, open that cannister. Death now and that way was a sure thing unless I at least tried to stop it, so I tried."

"I see." Agent Arouet seemed amazed but satisfied…and delighted by this answer.

So did his partner. I realized that I had saved their lives, too.

Agent Rousseau paused, and then said, "Our president will want to award you with the Ordre National de la Légion d'Honneur for this."

I stared at him, shocked, and then said, "Oh no…too much attention! And Kavi will miss it…" and trailed off, wondering how the logistics of that would be worked out. "I always react like this when something unplanned and unscheduled happens in life," I said to them.

Aunt Eloise laughed quietly. "Yes, you do!" she agreed.

"Don't worry," Agent Arouet said, "you can come back soon for that, and bring Kavi and your aunt to the ceremony. It would be in Paris anyway."

I gaped at them both for a moment, then looked at my aunt.

She nodded. "Don't worry – we'll come with you, and it will be planned."

I took a deep breath, and then nodded. "Okay, fine. Thank you!" I said to her, and to the agents.

They had no more questions, but they wanted to shake my hand, so I let them, and smiled.

"Would you like to work for Interpol?" Agent Rousseau asked, smiling. He couldn't be serious!

I smiled. "No thank you, I'm happy being a writer and researcher," I said, and laughed.

With that, they nodded, smiled, and took their leave, and we settled in to enjoy our coffee and macarons.

I ate a raspberry, a hazelnut, and a lavender one to celebrate. Aunt Eloise hadn't had a lavender macaron before. Then she found pistachio ones, so we tried that flavor, too. We were recovering nicely.

Still, as I sat there, I found myself thinking about this erstwhile terrorist and his methods. "What a stupid terrorist," I said out loud. "He wants to kill off huge percentages of the human population, but not everyone can be induced to eat what he wants them to eat."

My aunt looked at me. "Didn't you say that he was new at this?" she asked.

"Yes. He was raving, and that was one of the things that he blurted. I hope he was informed of any right to remain silent and then stupidly chose to talk, so that they can use all that against him in court."

"Me too. I wonder why he thought rye crackers were such a great choice for getting rid of people who might be on to him…"

"Well, he knew that food well, so it was familiar to him. It was the food that the poor of Europe ate, for the most part, in Medieval times. The wealthy ate wheat and barley flour. To stop the rot and death of limbs and try to save lives, Catholic hospitals, run by priests and nuns, would give their patients other food. The result was maimed, poor people who had to beg for a living."

I thought for a moment.

Then I said, "If he hates the rich enough to do a lot of them in, he should have targeted foods that only the rich can access. Poison the fois gras, for example. But again, not everyone is willing to eat duck liver pâté, so that method isn't guaranteed, either. Hence the theft of the pathogen."

"But that didn't work, either," my aunt remarked.

"No. He talked too much. Bad guys want attention, so they talk."

"Well, what's the point of committing a crime if no one knows why?" she asked.

"Indeed," I agreed. "That, at least, leaves us some hope of stopping them."

With that, we drank our café au laits, and lapsed into silence.

There are always next criminals, and there was never a way to know when or where they would strike. In our overpopulated world of strained resources, this threat would reappear again and again.

But...there had always been murderers.

So, there would be detectives, police officers, counter-terrorism experts, and bioweapons scientists to stop them.

I decided to enjoy what remained of our vacation.

But first, Dr. Etienne appeared, and introduced Dr. Thorsen.

"Bonjour!" we said to them, as they settled into the seats across from us.

Ivan appeared with fresh cups and saucers and more coffee, which they accepted.

"So," I said. "The Interpol agents told me you would need me to recount the entire tale all over again for your pathogen investigation."

"Oui – I mean, yes, we need you to do that, please."

"Okay," I said. "I will. Have the other P4 scientists taken that horrifying container back to your lab already? Is it gone from here?"

I knew that P4 was south of here, but later on, I checked it:

P4 Jean Mérieux-Inserm Laboratory
21 Avenue Tony Garnier
69000 Lyon
France

https://www.fondation-merieux.org/en/what-we-do/enhancing-research-capabilities/research-laboratories/jean-merieux-inserm-p4-laboratory/

"Yes," Dr. Thorsen said. "Drs. Arondekar and Sartre have it."

I was feeling pretty good now. Safe.

"What was it?" I had to ask.

The two P4 scientists exchanged glances. "This can't get out yet."

"So, you can't tell me? Do you know what it is yet?"

"Oh yes," said Dr. Thorsen. "Boris stole it last week, and we didn't want to cause a public panic by announcing that it was missing. Agents have been looking for it. It was hoped that announcing that a P4 scientist was sick in hospital would help us to get some leads. And did it ever!"

I stared at them.

"So…what horrifying pathogen was it?"

They exchanged glances, nodded, and then Dr. Etienne took a deep breath before speaking. I realized that she must be the senior scientist, because she was taking responsibility for telling me.

"It was bubonic plague."

For a moment, I couldn't breathe.

Then I said, "There's no cure for that one, right?"

They nodded. "Right."

I sat there for a moment, stunned by the thought of a new release of that microbe. Europe had already endured this, and no plague mask had ever helped with anything other than dulling the stench of rot.

Well…it was still sealed in its container.

I finally said, "Boris was willing to kill himself, then, along with anyone else he could kill. It was a kamikaze mission."

"Yes," said Dr. Claire Etienne.

My aunt just sat in her chair next to me, staring wide-eyed into her lap. She was done eating for now.

So much for calming down after an adrenaline rush.

Perhaps more talking would help to calm down.

It was needed anyway…

I settled in to tell them the entire tale, in great and full detail.

It took another twenty minutes.

They recorded it all, too.

This time, I remembered one more detail: the article that I had read in *National Geographic History* magazine.

The two scientists exchanged amazed glances when I got to that.

"It's quite a tale, I realize," I said.

Aunt Eloise shook her head. "Amazing, is what it is."

"Yes," Dr. Etienne said. "It certainly is, how you put all that together, and in time. Thank you very much! Thank you on behalf of France, too."

"But how did you put it all together?" Dr. Arondekar asked.

"I suppose that it is thanks to knowing Kavi Ravendra, my husband, who is a scientist. Through him, I have met scientists from all over the world: Americans, Indians, Japanese, Iranians, Romanians, Ukrainians, Nigerians, French, British, Swedish, Norwegian, Dutch, Belgian, and even a Russian or two before all this happened."

"Meeting them can't be all there is to it," he said, pressing for more.

I continued: "I have edited their journal articles and his, and edited their curriculum vitae. That means that I have interacted with them quite a bit, both in person and via e-mail. And that means that I have gotten to know them somewhat. Kavi gives them to me, and I have to contact them sometimes with questions to make sure that I am not messing with the scientific details when I polish their writing. A lot of scientists don't know how to write, and that matters, because if what they write isn't comprehensible to others, the effort to communicate it is useless. I edit for grammar, punctuation, spelling, and flow. Flow is more important than a lot of them seem to realize, until they get their articles back."

The P4 scientists burst out laughing. "Yes, it is!" they agreed.

"What else enabled you to spot this issue in time," Dr. Etienne pressed. "There must be something else."

I laughed. "Well, I do read a lot, and I read a book on biopreparat by three journalists from *The New York Times*. Boris would have really freaked out if I had told him that," I added. "But...I had decided to let the matter drop when he looked so annoyed at Vasily just for telling me that they had worked in that field."

"What book was that?" Dr. Arondekar asked.

"You're going to look it up, no doubt," I said with a grin. "It was *Germs – Biological Weapons and America's Secret War* by Judith Miller, Stephen Engelberg, and William Broad."

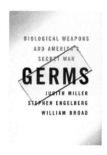

He looked it up on his phone then and there…and ordered himself a copy, which came as no surprise to any of us.

"I shall borrow that book from you when you have read it!" said Dr. Etienne.

My aunt smiled at me.

I looked at them. "Your names sound familiar to me. When I get home, I'm going to check the articles that I have edited for your names, and for Dr. Babineaux's name. I may have edited one or two by some of you. How is he doing?"

They looked sober – no, somber.

Uh-oh…

We looked back at them.

"Tell us. It's bad, isn't it?"

"Yes. He has died, after losing his feet and part of a hand."

"Oh no," we said. But I had expected this once I understood what had been done.

"He loved to try new foods," Dr. Etienne said, nodding sadly. "And it killed him. He was too trusting."

We looked at her, taking in this upsetting news, and then I said, "Is something being done to check on Vasily's condition at that other hospital? Boris fed him those ergot crackers, too. Vasily was a nice guy; he didn't deserve this."

"Yes, we have already contacted the doctors there. Vasily has lost a finger, and a foot, but the spread of ergotism has stopped. He will live."

I breathed a sigh of relief on his behalf. So did my aunt.

"Good. And bad, of course, about losing body parts. But at least it's stopped."

"Yes – and you stopped it!" the scientist said to me.

"Oh wow…I just wanted us all to not be poisoned, infected, or otherwise killed," I said. I never handled great praise easily. It made me feel a bit awkward. "I'm just happy that this is over."

"Well, it is over. Thank you very much, and it was great to meet you. And…we may see you again, in Paris!"

"Oh! Yeah…" I realized that they knew about the medal plans for me. "Okay…" I smiled awkwardly.

They gave me big smiles back.

With that, they stood up, grabbed their gear, and left.

Intrigue On a Longship Cruise

Pears and Paroles

Pears and Paroles

In French, a *parole* is a speech.

There would be many of those this evening.

But first, we went back to our cabin for about a half-hour's rest, and so that I could call Kavi and tell him what had happened.

"Watch the news, Kavi," I said into my phone. "I'll tell you the rest when I get home, in full detail," I promised.

"I'm counting on it," he said. "I had the sense that something crazy was happening while it was happening, by the way. Must be the effects of that link that Ileandra left us with, so I'm glad you called and told me. I was starting to get really nervous."

"I figured as much," I said. "It's okay now, and I can come home as planned. Don't worry; we'll see you tomorrow night at Bradley Airport. And…get ready to plan your experiments around leaving them for a trip back to France with me and Aunt Eloise soon. I don't know when, but I do know why, and you'll soon know full details about it – perhaps some even before I get a chance to fill you in completely."

There was a brief pause as he took that in.

Then he said, "Okay…I should pause work and do something else, and with you anyway, so great! See you tomorrow. I love you!"

"I love you too."

With that, we said our good-byes and ended the call.

We watched the crazy, pasty-faced, grayish lunatic on *CNN* and on *BBC News*, yelling as he was led away.

"You are just postponing the inevitable!" he shouted at the news cameras. The reporters made sure to record and broadcast every word. This was the big story of the moment, and I was actually glad to see him milking it for all it was worth. I wasn't glad for the notoriety he was getting, and I didn't think that he was doing it for that reason.

He was doing it to warn us all.

"You certainly don't need any warning," my aunt told me, sitting back against her pillow. "You have tried to warn people with your dystopian fiction novels. That's a much better way to warn people, because it doesn't hurt anyone."

"Thanks, Aunt Eloise," I said ruefully, "but no one – or, almost no one – actually reads those books, so far too few people are even noticing the warning."

"They will," she said. "Just wait. They will get tired of hearing news reports, and retreat into fiction. And then they will find yours."

I grinned. "One can always hope."

"I'm glad you are a calm harbinger of doom, instead of a terrorist brand of harbinger," she said, with an ironic grin and an equally wry tone in her voice.

"Yeah, well…you read my books and blog. You know that I don't approve of taking people's lives away from them, of removing all reason to hope, and giving up on people having the slightest willingness to change their behavior or think about the effect of their habits and practices on those who come after them, and who have to live in this world when they're done living in it."

Aunt Eloise said, "Recycling isn't going to be enough. I know it."

"Indeed. Reproducing, perpetuating one's DNA to gain a false or illusory sense of immortality, is what he is screaming about."

Indeed, he was. The cops were having a slow time of it, walking him from the patrol car to the courthouse – the very one that we had seen on our tour – which was giving him plenty of time to shout.

"There will soon be 8 billion humans. We are running out of potable water! We only have forty years of fertile growing soil left, and it's not going to be enough to grow fruits and vegetables and grains for us all – not even with greenhouses on city rooftops!"

A cop nudged him along, but he kept pausing as he moved up the steps of the Lyon courthouse. He shouted out again at the crowd. "We all want just a little more time, and we don't have it!"

The faces looking back at him seemed to be listening to him, but I doubted that his words would linger in their thoughts long enough to make any real difference in our collective fates.

"That's a magnificent edifice, so I hope no one interrupts this tirade and shoots him before he finishes," I commented.

Aunt Eloise turned to look at me. "You think that might happen?"

"It could. And after writing about this issue, I have come to appreciate the usefulness of bad guys. This is a classic bad guy. They always share their agenda and reasons. It's what gives them a sense of validation. And this bad guy has a message that we all need to hear and take seriously."

"Arielle, that is the most hilarious way to say 'Don't shoot the messenger' that I have every heard!" my aunt said, settling back against her pillows again.

I gave her a big grin. "I mean it, too."

Apparently, we weren't the only ones contemplating another person trying to take the law into their own hands. As we watched, the guy was surrounded by gendarmes, marched the rest of the way up the steps, and into his hearing.

No one shot him. At least, not yet.

He had had his say about something that mattered, and nothing else had happened to take the focus off of that.

I went into the bathroom and washed my face – makeup, cream, all of it came off, along with the sweat and anxiety from the day's adventures. Then I redid it all.

"Sorry for the long bathroom use," I said to my aunt.

"That's okay," she said. "I went in there and washed my face while you were talking to Kavi. We needed that!"

I laughed, and we put on our fancy new Botanique scarves before going to the upstairs lounge for our final evening lectures by Clotilde.

Clotilde and the rest of the crew were waiting for us with instructions on how to wind up our business for the end of our trip. This meant giving tips in envelopes, which were provided by the staff at the front desk, packing our bags and leaving them outside our rooms with the provided red tags, all filled out, in the morning before breakfast, and so on.

The senior members of the crew were all assembled at the front of the lecture area, with a microphone to pass around, to say a few words each. We enjoyed that, and we all clapped after each one of them spoke.

There was an awkward moment with the *Sif*'s French captain, though, because he didn't speak any English, and he seemed frozen at first, unable to get any words out.

And what did I do?!

I forgot that I wanted to keep a low profile, sitting a few rows back, in a cushy chair in front of the bar, and I called out, "Ça va bien – disez tout en français!" with a big grin.

Oops…

I had figured that Clotilde could just help him by translating.

No…he was determined! He smiled at me, and then tried again. It was impressive; he forced out a short remark in English, and we all understood him. We all clapped and cheered and thanked him.

And then…

We were left to mingle and chat amongst ourselves for a few minutes.

Clotilde asked me to describe what had happened with the Interpol agents and the P4 people.

I wasn't sure about this, but I acquiesced.

"Well…I can see that an off-the-grid transfer of the story has spread around with greater speed than a fiber-optic internet connection," I began, and people in the immediate vicinity roared with laughter.

Jonathan, the cruise director who was an aspiring comedian, looked like I had really gotten him.

Not that I wanted a second career as a stand-up comedienne…

I explained quickly what had happened, recapping in what I hoped was a shorter form than I might otherwise express myself, how I had figured out what the threat was and what had tipped me off.

That meant defining the term "biopreparat" for everyone, and mentioned that *National Geographic History* magazine article yet again.

Astonished looks all around, and I caught a glimpse of the priest…crossing himself. A few members of his flock did that, too.

Prayer wasn't going to save us, but I wasn't about to rub their noses in it. They knew that action and being a data junkie was what did it. I didn't have to tell them.

And they didn't have to tell me that they were just venting their shock and horror at this near-miss of a pathogenic horror.

Karen surprised me by hugging me, and I returned the hug.

Then I looked at her. She seemed uneasy.

"What's the matter? We're safe now," I said. Whatever was bothering her, it was likely unrelated.

"Can we go sit in the library chairs and talk?"

"Sure," I said, intrigued. Perhaps I would find out more about Max…I had wondered about him all week, even though I was now certain that he was just the red herring of the foiled biopreparat plot.

Aunt Eloise waved to me and said she'd find me in the dining room.

Intrigue On a Longship Cruise

We went out of the lounge, across the balcony, and sat down in the lovely wood-paneled space. People were walking past us, glancing at us, but when they saw that we were leaning in close to chat, they left us alone.

She took a deep breath, then told me, "Max is being sought out for questioning by the Justice Department about January 6th."

"Oh…" I said, understanding. "I can't say that I'm surprised. He was there…" I thought for a moment, then went ahead and asked her about it. "Do you know any details about it beyond that?"

She definitely looked anxious. "I know that when he met me at the hotel, he kept texting on his phone, and went into a conference room with some friends who had worked with him when he worked for President Trump on the pandemic response. They stayed there talking and making phone calls for hours."

I looked at her. "Did you go in there and hear their ends of those phone conversations, and hear anything specific that would explain why you now seem so anxious about it?"

She looked at me, scared. "Yes…not that I fully understood it."

I gave her an ironic smile. "Well, there's no need to completely panic as yet. You have a few things on your side, including one of the legally protected conduits of privileged communication, namely the marital one. You have the right to refuse to disclose whatever Max tells you to anyone else. Also, you don't as yet know that he is being accused of any criminal or treasonous behavior. It's all circumstantial and merely suspected at this point."

She brightened up at this information. "I don't have to tell…?"

"No, you don't. Of course, we do still live in a nation that operates according to the rule of law, so Max will have to be found to have done nothing that rises to the level of actually taking action that might possibly destroy our democracy."

Karen looked nervous again.

"Look, you are obviously freaking out over possibilities rather than confirmed legal charges, facts, or anything else. Just breathe normally and take it one step at a time. I'm not a practicing attorney, and I am a liberal Democrat, so I can't do much more for you than tell you not to totally lose it and panic just yet. You may yet be able to go back to your comfortable retirement with Max."

Karen gave me a weak smile. "I wondered if you had suspected Max of being involved in this plot with Boris at one point today."

"Only today?" I said, laughing. "Well...he did know Dr. Babineaux of P4 and see him on the same day that Boris did, but he saw him before that, and separately. Also, Max doesn't have the scientific expertise to commit that sort of crime. He only recognized the cannister for what it was thanks to touring P4 and the CDC, as far as I can see."

Now Karen really seemed to calm down. "Oh...that makes sense."

I nodded. "Go enjoy our last gourmet meal on the Longship *Sif*," I said. "I certainly will. And I'll bet that the chef has some sort of showcase of a dessert planned for it, too!"

Karen did a double-take, then she laughed along with me, and we went downstairs.

At dinner, everyone, including us, had our own say about the foiled bioweapons plot. The discussion was about little else.

"What a lunatic!" said one woman. "How could he possibly think it could be okay to kill so many people?!"

"Or any people..." muttered the woman next to her.

"Yes – any murder is unacceptable," the priest remarked.

Many eyes turned toward me, and to the professor I had spent much of the week talking with about human overpopulation – Isaac.

"What do you think of his plan to reduce our numbers?" This question came at us throughout the evening.

We were all against that, of course.

But our dinner companions wanted more than that.

I was happy to oblige.

"If he had actually managed to release that toxin, it would not necessarily have solved the problem he sought to deal with. It might instead have made an entire city a source of contamination, driven it into a state of quarantine that lasted much longer than 40 days (that is the literal meaning of the word!), and caused a panic as people attempted to flee before being swept up in it. Some people would have gotten out and spread the plague, too."

"How many would he have killed?" asked Max, who was sitting at the next table, leaning around in his chair to participate in the discussion.

He and Karen seemed calm now.

She must have had a chance to hear a few reassuring words from him.

He seemed merely interested in the data, and in a theoretical way, not a salacious or disappointed way. He was just curious, like everyone else. I decided at last that he was just a MAGA moron who had a sorely lacking appreciation for democracy, not a useful idiot in a genocidal plot. Good about that, and bad about the politics for our country.

The carrot purée soup arrived. Several of us had ordered it, and we paused to admire it before digging into it. I pulled out my camera.

Melissa laughed. "You're amazing. You helped nab the bad guy, and now you're back to photographing your food!"

"Damned right! I'm not going to let him ruin my good time," I said.

Isaac and Matthew clapped.

But back to Max's question.

I said, "Well, Lyon has a population of over half a million, plus tourists and business visitors. Killing off even that many would not achieve much in this guy's grand scheme of destruction. It would have been just a drop in the bucket of human statistics when you remember that, as a species, we are 8 billion. It would make quite a statement, but not the kind that would induce any positive policy changes."

Silence all around for a moment.

"That's really what it's all about, isn't it?" Aunt Eloise asked. "I mean, if we are actually going to save ourselves from our own impulses, we must have a public policy, as you say, and worldwide, as you keep telling us, that counteracts those impulses."

"Yes. We need an unpopular population policy, or that population will consume itself in its frenzy to survive once we have passed the point of no return in using and abusing our planet's ecosystems. And then, after horrid resource wars, we will be fewer, but at what cost? What will remain of our planet that will still be enjoyable, let alone livable?"

Karen was not satisfied. "We cannot tell anyone not to reproduce. We cannot disappoint prospective parents. We cannot go against God, or Nature, as you call it in your discussions. It's the same thing, I believe."

I looked at her, amused. "Religion will guarantee resource wars. It's all Nature – the impulse to reproduce, the impulse to kill for access to more resources, the impulse to judge and to see that one's side, one's point of view, is the only correct one. These all conflict with one another, and therein lies the fallacy that a secular legal system could assist with. It would mean coldly, dispassionately pushing impulses aside. We will need that."

"People will never agree to that," Father O'Shaughnessy said.

"No, they won't," I said. "At least, not in enough numbers to make a difference. Resource war will come as we crash ecosystems with too many humans for the Earth to realistically support. Just look at all the sewage that ocean-going cruise ships used to spew into the water, along with trash. Only recently have they started saving it to get rid of when they return to port. So much damage has already been done."

I turned and looked at my soup. My no-doubt insecticide-free, French-grown, carrot purée soup.

Sober faces looked at me.

"Do you see any hope for us?" Dionne asked.

I looked up at her.

"Well, some. I have neighbors, professors who lecture in the medical, law, and public health schools of the University of Connecticut and write peer reviewed articles together on the impact of climate change. They just wrote one on reparations due from developed nations to nations like Nauru, that are sinking out of existence due to sea level rise. So, there is hope as long as stuff like that keeps happening, but then I think, too few of us make choices that will make a dent in human overpopulation or ecosystems collapse, so…"

I trailed off at this point.

"So, not enough hope, then?" Isaac said. "That's not good…"

"No, not enough. As Koko, the gorilla who knew sign language said, our species is stupid about caring for the Earth. We're just not doing that enough."

The priest looked very unhappy, like he was about to add something, but then he surprised us all by letting the matter drop.

The entrée arrived: Frenched rack of lamb, which means that the fat is trimmed to perfection around each rib, leaving an easy to cut and eat, gristle-less morsel of lamb. That's not all: it was rubbed with salt and fresh herbs, including rosemary, and there was a sauce and some mushrooms and peas with it. It was laid over a bed of potatoes.

I hardly ever ate meat, but every once in a while, I would eat lamb. This was, after all, gourmet French food being prepared in France by a French chef, and I wasn't going to skip it. Besides, I was determined to enjoy the specials menu right up to the end of our trip.

"No one will sell anyone on any idea. This cruise is not only historical, archaeological, and gastronomic tourism; it is also intellectual and political tourism. We see what people care about by meeting them and sharing lovely meals with them, because that is when we talk with each other. And then we go back to our own groups, left to think about it all."

With that, everyone smiled ruefully, and turned to look at the beautiful, tall, upright pears poached in spiced red wine sauce that had just been placed in front of us.

"That looks amazing," Melissa commented.

It was the final dessert of our trip, and it was a tantalizing showpiece of food art.

It was delectable, too.

The spoon cut through it like soft butter, and the sauce had a wonderful, intense-but-subtle flavor.

"Wow," I said, "This IS amazing. I made poached pears once at home, for the winter solstice, and it was delicious, but it was a different recipe entirely. I poached the pears with chopped apricots and walnuts, and poured a chocolate sauce over them."

Aunt Eloise was staring at me. "I think I remember that, even though it was only in pictures!"

"It was memorable, that's for sure. But I only made it once."

"Do you photograph all of your creations at home?" Karen asked.

"Yes," my aunt answered for me. "She does. She also shares them on Facebook and Instagram, and makes everyone hungry and envious!"

I cracked up. "That's true. It's part of the fun of it."

Chauffeured to the Lyon–Saint-Exupéry Airport

Chauffeured to the
Lyon–Saint-Exupéry Airport

We had one more wonderful breakfast aboard the *Sif*, and then we had to get ready to leave the ship for good.

The light seemed dim, because we were eating before the sun rose.

We had said our good-byes to everyone, exchanged e-mails, gotten permission to seek them out on social media, and otherwise forged whatever connections we might possibly make before our departure.

The evening before, we had said good-bye to most of the staff, thanked them for their deluxe service that had spoiled us so well for an entire week, and tipped them.

We had found our maid at last, by coming back to our cabin at the right moment. Or, perhaps she was there by design, to see if she could collect any tips. She certainly deserved them!

"What is your name?" I asked her.

"Penelope," she told me, smiling sweetly. She looked like she was about twenty years old, if that. Her honey-hued hair was in a long braid, high on her head and hanging straight down her back. She had a sweet, friendly expression on her face.

"Where are you from?" Aunt Eloise wanted to know.

"I'm from Crete," she said.

"Oh…" I said, "Do you live anywhere near the ruins of Knossos?"

Big smile! "Yes, I do," she replied. "My sister gives tours of it."

"Wow." I paused. "It's lovely to meet you. So – you are the magician who makes our room look like no one has slept in the bed or used the bathroom every morning and every evening. I love how you folded the towels, like swans. Thank you very much for all that!"

"You are welcome," she said, smiling happily as we gave her tips in envelopes. Paper money tips – larger than a measly one or two Euros – were the standard, and we each gave her a ten-Euro note for this. She deserved it.

We had given five Euros to the concierge and to Clotilde.

I wondered if we had gotten it right, but we were new at this.

I also wondered if or when I would go on another cruise like this.

Perhaps Kavi would agree to come with me next time.

It would be great to see the Monet gardens at Givenchy with him.

And to not meet another genocidal maniac next time.

We found, as promised, that our bags, which we had tagged with Longship ones, were already gone. We had been told to prepare them before breakfast and to leave them outside our cabin, side by side, in the hall.

This was part of the amazing, ruthless efficiency that had made our lively flow so conveniently and seamlessly for the duration of our trip. We would have to do everything ourselves again in a few hours, when we made our connecting flight on our way home…

…but meanwhile, we were escorted to a small van in the early morning darkness.

This was the first time that we had left the ship before daylight.

Another pair of people was already inside, a couple from Colorado. We had seen them on the ship, but hadn't gotten to know them.

There just hadn't been time to meet everyone.

They knew us, though.

They saw who was climbing into the other empty seats and gave me a big smile and a "Thank you" for saving the trip.

I felt a bit awkward, still not used to the attention, but I replied, "You're welcome. I'm just glad the trip ended on a safe and positive note!"

They nodded enthusiastically.

The van took off into the darkness, and we were soon passing under the bridge that took us out of Lyon.

It felt odd to be traveling on land for some reason.

No problem, I thought to myself, soon we'll be in the air.

But not yet; we pulled up to the airport, and two women, a mother and her adult daughter, stood there waiting for us in Longship jackets and jeans and sneakers.

Antoine de Saint-Exupéry was himself a pilot as well as an author of the famous children's book, *Le Petit Prince*, so this airport was named as it ought to be.

I had read that story in high school French class.

So had my aunt.

It was a large, round, modern building, and we glanced up at its façade, briefly impressed by it. Then we followed the women inside.

They guided the four of us all the way to the ticket counter and watched us get settled, sticking around until we were through the gates and into the duty-free shop area.

We tipped them a Euro each, said "Merci!" and waved good-bye to them.

And that was it; we were on our own, wandering around the shops.

The couple from Colorado took off in another direction, looking at something at the opposite end of the concourse.

We saw what we wanted and headed for it: Valrhôna chocolate bars. We bought some of those, plus some small boxes of Valrhôna truffles, and waited to be called for our flight home.

"Well, Arielle, you've hosted an alien visitor, and you've foiled a genocidal maniac. What's next?"

I laughed. "I have no idea. Whatever comes along next in life, I guess. You never know what it will be until it does."

Aunt Eloise nodded. "True."

Intrigue On a Longship Cruise

Acknowledgements

There are many people I would like to thank for their help in preparing this book.

One is my mother, Carole B.C. Fox, who took me on a wonderful cruise up the Rhone River in October of 2018. I want to thank her for that, and for reading and editing the manuscript for this book and giving me great feedback on the plot. Her insights helped to improve it, and she enjoyed reliving the trip through this story.

Others are the officers and crew of the Viking ship *Heimdal*, who organized a wonderful trip, prepared and served delectable gourmet meals and beverages, and kept us in perfect comfort like magicians.

Still others are the wonderfully knowledgeable, friendly, and welcoming guides who showed us their beautiful cities and historic sites, with architecture, crafts, and fascinating stories and details.

And, just because I want to, I shall thank my cats, the Phantom Menace and Ms. Chief Cherie, for keeping me company while I wrote this story.

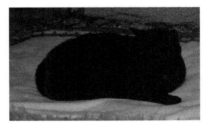

The photographs that appear in this book were taken by me (most of them!) and my mother (the others) on that trip.

The events in this story are, of course, made up.

About the Author

Stephanie C. Fox, J.D. is a historian, author, and editor. She is a graduate of William Smith College and of the University of Connecticut School of Law.

She is a book publisher, and she runs an editing service called *QueenBeeEdit*, which caters to politicians, scientists, and others. Its website is https://www.queenbeeedit.com.

Stephanie lives in Connecticut, and has written books about a variety of topics, including Asperger's, the global financial meltdown, honeybee colony collapse disorder, travelogues of a trips to Kuwait and Hawai'i, the effects of human overpopulation on the environment, and cats.

Lightning Source UK Ltd.
Milton Keynes UK
UKHW021519100223
416667UK00011B/405